'You can leav[e]
They have go[ne]

For a long moment he looked at her, his eyes raking her
up and down, taking in every curve and contour beneath
the robe and nightgown, clearly imagining what he could
not see. Emma felt her cheeks glow warm and moved
away from the window. 'Go away!' she insisted.

'You are very tempting when you are angry,' Ben said
softly. And, reaching out, he pulled her towards him and
kissed her. She stood quite still as his mouth moved over
hers, gently persuasive, his tongue teasing her lips apart
and probing her mouth. A tingling shiver snaked through
her, crystallising into a warm, liquid sensation as his hand
moved slowly down over her shoulder, brushing aside the
robe and lingering over her breast, burning through the
flimsy nightgown.

With a gasp, she tore her mouth free and abruptly
thrust him away, her cheeks flaming and her whole body
shaking. 'If you seek to seduce me, sir,' she whispered
hoarsely, 'and add me to your list of conquests, you will
be sorely disappointed!'

'I wonder.' With a slow smile, he let his gaze slide down
over her. 'It would be interesting to prove you wrong...'

REBEL BY MOONLIGHT

Elaine Reeve

*First published in Great Britain 1991
by Mills & Boon Limited*

© Elaine Reeve 1991

*Australian copyright 1991
Philippine copyright 1991
This edition 1991*

ISBN 0 263 77278 0

*Masquerade is a trademark published by
Mills & Boon Limited, Eton House,
18-24 Paradise Road, Richmond, Surrey, TW9 1SR*

*Set in Times Roman 10 on 11 pt.
04-9106-81623 C*

Made and printed in Great Britain

CHAPTER ONE

'WHAT in God's name do you think you are doing?'

Emma started and looked up guiltily, caught in the act of thrusting her best green silk gown into an old canvas bag. Seeing that it was only Kit, however, she relaxed. 'Come in and shut the door, for heaven's sake!'

Her whole future depended on him, the youngest of her four older brothers. Pray God she had not misjudged him. 'I am not going to marry Carlisle tomorrow!' she declared, a cloud of rose-pink following the green into the impossible space with the same grim determination that hardened her voice. 'I am coming to Boston with you.'

A shout of laughter greeted this proposal. 'Don't be ridiculous!'

The offhand dismissal earned a fiery glare from her hazel eyes. Many sleepless nights spent heart-searching had preceded this decision and she was not going to be thwarted now. 'I am perfectly serious!' She turned to pick up a leather pouch containing what remained of her mother's jewellery, her face set in the purposeful expression he knew so well. 'Cousin Maybelle will surely assist me to find some sort of employment.'

Suddenly filled with compassion, he sighed heavily. 'I know how you feel about this, Em, but——'

'Then help me!' She looked at him, her eyes sparkling. 'You must! You were the only one who spoke out for me. You cannot tell me now you truly wish to see me wed to that despicable old lecher!'

He gave an unhappy gesture. 'Of course not! But I do not have a family to support as James and Nick do.

And Bran is afraid Caroline will not find him such an attractive proposition if he is penniless.'

Fury flared in her eyes. 'And I am to be sacrificed to save them all?'

'James has worked hard to save this business, Emma. You cannot blame him.'

'I do blame him. He knows what Carlisle is and he does not care. He only cares for Wyatt Shipping. Well, as far as I am concerned Wyatt Shipping can go to the devil.'

'Emma!'

'Oh, don't pretend to be shocked!' she admonished him crossly. 'I have made my feelings plain enough these past weeks, surely!'

Six weeks, in fact. For six weeks she had battled with her brother James over his plans to marry her to the wealthy William Carlisle and, inevitably, she had lost. After their father's death a year ago, James had taken control of a shipping business heading for financial disaster. He had struggled valiantly, she had to concede that, but against a powerful tide, and when William Carlisle—who had long had his eye on her—came to offer a considerable sum of money in return for a small interest in the business and Emma's hand in marriage James could not refuse. It had not occurred to him that *she* would refuse. The arguments had been long and bitter, harsh things being said on both sides, things that would never be forgiven.

She was of age and in theory could do as she pleased, but with no income of her own she was dependent on James for support. It was more than time she was wed, he threw at her finally, and there was no one else for she spurned all suitors. Did she wish to end up a spinster? Did she want to see them all ruined? He was certainly not prepared to support her any longer if she refused Carlisle—it was a better match than she might have expected and she should be grateful!

Grateful! To be bartered like a piece of the cargo? But the alternatives were certainly not attractive and she felt herself being slowly worn down, inexorably steered into a marriage abhorrent to her.

She knew that if she simply refused to marry him James would indeed turn her out. And, although she had no doubt that she could make her own way in the world and turn her hand to whatever employment was offered, it would be impossible to remain in Plymouth, seeing them lose the business and bearing their unforgiving condemnation for her selfishness. Yet where could she go? Their only other relative was in Scotland and she would be unsympathetic. In Judith's eyes Emma's duty would be clear.

And then Kit announced that he had finalised his cargo for Boston, and a glimmer of hope flared in her breast and gave her courage. So she appeared to give in, to agree to wed the man she feared and despised, and while the banns were read and arrangements made she tried to think of a way to smuggle herself aboard the *Emma Louise* without Kit's knowledge. Right up until the moment he came into her room, she had been hoping to find some way to avoid involving him. But it was impossible. She needed his help.

'Kit, please!' A sudden burst of raucous laughter from somewhere below made her grimace. The three of them were downstairs celebrating their salvation. Tomorrow they and their ships would be saved and it was all they cared about. It did not matter to them that their sister would be going like a lamb to the slaughter. She moved swiftly round the bed and took both his hands in hers. 'Please! I have it all thought out, but I need your help. You must get me on board the *Emma Louise* tonight and I will hide in the hold until you sail.'

'In the hold?' he echoed. 'Are you mad? It could be days! If you "disappear" God knows when I will sail!'

Vehemently she shook her head. 'James will not permit you to jeopardise this contract by further delay when there are three of them to deal with my disappearance. It was only on my insistence that he permitted you to delay sailing to attend the wedding.' She searched his face for a long moment. 'Look, probably they will think I have gone to Cousin Judith, and waste several days on a wild-goose chase to Scotland. By the time they realise their mistake, we will be out in the Atlantic.'

'And I will have a mutiny on my hands!' he protested, setting her at arm's length. 'You have always been addle-witted, but this is lunacy!'

'Would you rather think of me in Carlisle's bed?' she demanded hotly, shaking her arm free of his grasp. 'I have bruises still from his attentions at our last encounter!' A shudder ran through her at the memory of that meeting with Carlisle. His sweaty hands had pawed her, his loose lips drooling with anticipation as his eyes raked her body greedily. Even at dinner he had fondled her legs beneath the table, fumbling over her skirts to thrust his hand between her thighs. And tomorrow night she was supposed to lie in his bed and—— 'And half Plymouth whispers about his perversions!' she threw at him harshly.

'I know.' He turned away and walked to the window.

For a moment she stared silently at his back. 'Kit, I will *not* wed that man. Not for James, not for Wyatt Shipping, not for you! If you will not help me, I will find some other way. Only—only for God's sake say nothing tonight so that I may escape while there is still time. Please.' Turning sharply, she pulled the heavy canvas bag towards her, and as she dragged it off the bed he came up beside her and helped her stow it behind the door.

'Have you any idea what it is like in a hold?' he demanded, and put up a hand to stay her protest. 'Oh, certainly you have been down in many a ship's belly, but with light to see and air to breathe and two or three others for company. But can you imagine a darkness so thick that you cannot see your hand before your face? No lighter shades or darker corners—just blackness. And rats—they will brush by your hand or run across your feet, or jump into your hair without you ever being able to see them——'

'It would only be a matter of hours,' she said valiantly, suppressing an involuntary shudder. 'I will endure anything to avoid this marriage.'

'The crew are superstitious to a man—a woman on board is bad luck, you know that. I meant what I said about a mutiny.'

'Then talk to them.' She quashed her rising impatience. 'Most of them have sailed with you before and you can handle a crew better than any of the others.'

He pulled a sceptical face. 'You have more faith in my skill than I! You would be confined to my cabin most of the time—no strolling on deck unless you are with me. No fresh water to wash with, only collected rainwater like everyone else. It will be six weeks of unrelenting boredom—if you are lucky. If we encounter bad weather it will be a nightmare. And if you are sick, you'll tend yourself!'

'I'm never sick!'

'You have never been out of the Sound!' he pointed out scathingly.

She shook her head. 'There is something else. Are you afraid Cousin Maybelle would not help me?'

He shrugged. 'I doubt they would refuse to take you in. But it is nine months since I was there and—dammit, Emma!' He turned away and walked back to the window. 'The colonies are no place for you! And Boston...' He swung round to face her. 'There has been trouble there off and on for years. Do you remember the massacre in '70? A mob attacked some of the soldiers garrisoned there and half a dozen colonists were killed!'

'That was three years ago!'

'And little has changed! The Americans hate the British, the place is full of troublemakers and militants provoking unrest and fuelling dissent——'

'Oh, for heaven's sake!' Her patience snapped. 'Why do you not go and get drunk with the others?'

He looked at her angry, mutinous face and heaved a sigh. 'Because I am going to help you, even though I know I shall regret it to the end of my days. There is one thing more, however.' His tone stayed her cry of relief, and she looked at him enquiringly. 'I will be carrying a parcel of tea. Ten chests, to be precise.'

'Tea?' She regarded him blankly. What was he doing with tea on board? There had been no mention of it on any of the documents. Most of the trade in that commodity was done out of London, coming in from Amsterdam and—— Suddenly she caught her breath, her eyes widening. Nick had just returned from Holland. Her mind leapt ahead. 'Smuggling!' she exclaimed, staring at him incredulously. 'You are smuggling tea!'

'Yes,' he told her flatly. 'We need the money. You do not need to know any more. I mentioned it only because we will be relieved of it off the Massachusetts coast and that part of the voyage will be rather more hazardous. Especially if your disappearance involves further delay. The sailing dates were sent with Ned Barton last month and the Americans will not wait for ever.'

Already they were smuggling! What further lengths would James go to in order to save them from ruin once she had fled this marriage? She shut her mind to such thoughts. She must not care. Her chin went up resolutely. 'It makes no difference. I do not care about the risks. I'll take my chances with you and be safer than ever I would be as Carlisle's wife!'

After a moment, he gave a brief decisive nod, and spent the next few minutes arranging the details of their clandestine departure once everyone was asleep. Then he left her, and she sank on to the bed, silent tears falling into the pillow. Though whether from relief that he was going to help her, shame at her craven flight, or sorrow at the irreparable rift between herself and the brothers she might never see again she did not know. But it was some while before she slept, snatching a few hours before leaving the big old Wyatt house that had been her home all her life.

CHAPTER TWO

THE night was cool and dark. Wrapping her cloak tightly about her, Emma crept on to the deck and slipped, unseen, into the shadows behind the companionway. The figure at the bow moved slightly and a light flared briefly across the swaying black water. For a moment nothing happened. Then, from the shore, an answering flash— twice, in quick succession.

Kit turned away and nodded to the mate, who moved to the gaping hole in the deck and signalled to someone below. They began to bring up the chests of tea, almost silently. She held her breath, marvelling. Never had she known a ship so quiet with so much going on. There was scarcely any wind to stir the rigging and only the creaking of the ship's timbers made any real sound.

How could she have obeyed Kit's command to stay below out of sight and thus missed the only real excitement the six-week voyage had to offer? It was not in her nature.

As she watched, tense and breathless, Kit leaned over the side, peering into the darkness. A lantern flared briefly. Emma shrank back, crouching down as the light was quickly covered with an oilskin to reveal only an eerie glow that would be almost indistinguishable a yard away. A rope ladder was thrown over the side and after several minutes someone came aboard and stood talking with Kit only a few feet from her.

In the faint patch of light, he looked like a pirate. Black boots, and black breeches with the long hilt of a knife protruding above a wide belt, and a dark shirt open at the neck. Emma's heart missed a beat as her gaze travelled to the man's face. How handsome he was! He seemed older than Kit and several inches taller, with a crop of dark hair that was tied at the nape of his neck.

He handed Kit a small packet. 'Tonight was your last chance,' he said. 'They've been watching us for days.'

'We were delayed,' Kit said wryly. 'Circumstances at home. I'll tell you about it later.'

Emma's legs were cramped beneath her and the pain of crouching so long was becoming intolerable. The slight movement as she changed her position drew the eyes of the American. She could not make out his expression, but did she imagine that the hand thrust so casually into his belt moved slightly to rest on the knife? 'Who's that?' The voice had an edge of steel.

Kit turned and there was an angry glint in his eyes as Emma moved from her hiding place. 'My sister,' he ground through his teeth. 'She will probably be staying with the Winstons—for a while at least.'

'I trust she can keep her mouth shut, then.' His tone was uncompromising.

'Of course I can!' she hissed furiously. 'I am not a child.'

The man ignored her, directing a grim warning at her brother. 'It'll be your neck, Wyatt. Now, I have work to do and you'd best get out of here.'

The two men shook hands and the dark figure of the contrabander eased himself over the side once more. Emma slipped quietly below, avoiding Kit's glare of displeasure as he turned to order the deck swept. The *Emma Louise* was soon under way again, following the coast round to Boston Harbour, the American long gone to conceal his contraband and Emma unable to sleep in the cot in Kit's tiny cabin, contemplating the uncertain future now only a matter of hours away.

By the time the Customhouse officer was finally satisfied with his search of the ship and the answers to his endless questions, the chill grey October morning was already well advanced.

Emma stood on deck, hugging her cloak around her and watching the activity on the bustling quayside. There was little to see here that was new to her. Young men stacked crates and heaved chests, old men sat on barrels, women carried great baskets on their hips and cursed the boys pushing barrows and handcarts across their path. The quay was littered with discarded crates, coils of rope and piles of nets. Gulls screamed overhead, wheels clattered over cobbles and the air was pungent with all the familiar odours of salt and fish, hot pitch and rope burning in pulleys, and, drifting on the breeze from the alleys around the wharves, the more distasteful smells of stale ale, rotting vegetation and sewage.

She could only be relieved the voyage was over. It had been everything Kit had said it would be and she shuddered still at the memory of the terrifying night she had spent in the hold, crushing darkness and scuttling, squealing rats still pervading her dreams. The crew had been mutinous and it had taken all Kit's skill to subdue them, and, despite her own despair at the unrelieved boredom, it was perhaps fortunate that the voyage had been so uneventful.

She thrust the thoughts away. It was over and she was here, and there were now new fears to concern her. What she knew about this family from whom she was about to beg help was little enough. The relationship was somewhat vague, in truth, for it was her grandfather and Maybelle's father who had been cousins and only Wyatt Shipping's recent dealing across the Atlantic had renewed the family connection. Maybelle herself was a widow. John, her son, owned the family's timber business and had been on the point of marrying a girl called Ann when Kit was last in Boston. There were two daughters. Beth, also a widow since the untimely death of her husband in a riding accident, had one son and was in poor health. The youngest was Jaycinth, and she, according to Kit, was a 'dazzling beauty'!

Emma sighed. She was pinning a great deal on their charity, for she would be embarrassingly dependent on them until she could find some respectable employment. The handful of sovereigns she had stolen from James's safe would scarcely even clothe her decently. Now that she was here, she was not nearly so confident of her ability to adapt to the life she had pitched herself into. Was she really capable of settling for a life of subservience, as companion, or seamstress, or some such thing?

'Ready?'

She turned with a start and gave Kit a rueful smile. 'I'm afraid I shall not make a very good impression.' Her dress was fit only for burning, the stout leather shoes she had worn the whole voyage had salt stains and holes in them, and her hair hung about her shoulders in a sticky tangle which she could scarcely drag a comb through.

He hired a room at the inn on the quayside and ordered a hearty breakfast, and as she set herself to a somewhat unappetising plate of eggs and ham and a pot of tea she thought it the best meal she had seen for weeks.

With all the immediate formalities to see to, he left her there with the promise that before he returned he would pay a call on Maybelle Winston and gently broach the subject of his recalcitrant sister.

'I suppose you must tell her the truth,' she agreed reluctantly. 'It is rather a sorry tale and does none of us any credit.'

But he was adamant. 'I am not leaving you here with a parcel of lies and deceit to find you out! If she agrees to help you, she should know what she is taking on.'

She smiled at his taunt, knowing well enough that he would paint as rosy a picture of her as he dared! What she would do if they would not—or could not—help her she dared not think. What Kit had told her when he

finally rescued her from the ship's hold and plied her
with brandy made it quite clear that she could not easily
go back to Plymouth.

'Carlisle was apoplectic, and would have killed James
if he thought he had any hand in your disappearance,'
he had told her, seemingly shocked at the violence of
the man's anger. 'And what James had to say does not
bear repeating. You'll not be safe in Plymouth for many
a month—you have cut the anchor well and truly, my
girl, and you had better start praying you like America!'
There was a grim reality behind the words. She had
thwarted two ruthless and unforgiving men. Worse, it
would be public knowledge, and she had made them both
look like fools. Though she did not say as much to Kit,
she knew she would serve ale in a tavern or scrub floors
in a kitchen before she would go back to England.

When he had gone, she surveyed her reflection criti-
cally in the mirror above the fireplace and despaired.
The hazel eyes that looked back at her were dull and
tired; her skin, usually so smooth and clear, was dry and
blotchy, her lips red and chapped from constantly licking
the tang of salt from them. The long honey-coloured
hair had run riot and she could have wept for the glossy,
fashionable cascade of ringlets and curls that had been
her pride!

Casting her eyes around the sparsely furnished, faintly
shabby room, she doubted that the place would run to
providing her with such a thing as hot water. But, since
there was no harm in asking, she went downstairs to
find the landlord.

A half-open door on her left revealed a full and noisy
tap-room, and she would have turned away but for a
brief glimpse of a figure standing at the bar counter
talking with the barman. She paused. It was the man on
the *Emma Louise* last night, surely? He did not look
like a pirate now. Even at this distance, his manner and
bearing and the quality and cut of his clothes betrayed

him as a man of some means and not at all the sort she
would have expected to find in such a tavern or indeed,
smuggling tea in the dead of night!

Why she should find his presence there disturbing she
did not know. Her recall of last night's conversation
suggested that Kit might have arranged to meet him.
Suddenly she realised that he had turned and was looking
directly at her. Nonplussed, she drew back, and would
have continued her search for the landlord. But in a
moment the door was thrown wider and she found herself
looking up into a pair of piercingly blue eyes that swept
over her and finally came to rest on the unruly mass of
her hair.

'So it is you.' His gaze returned to her eyes. 'It is
dangerous to lurk in the shadows of a ship's deck, Miss
Wyatt,' he said very quietly, his voice faintly menacing.
'And if you have any wild notions about telling anyone
what or who you saw last night you should think very
carefully about it. I have an acute sense of self-
preservation and very few scruples.'

Flushing with annoyance at his arrogance, she stared
at him coldly. 'Had I wished to inform the authorities,
sir, I rather think I would have done so when they were
crawling all over the ship at dawn this morning. Neither
am I likely to put a hangman's noose around my own
brother's neck!'

His expression cleared suddenly and he smiled dis-
armingly. 'It is unlikely, I agree, but in my rather precarious position I have to be cautious. And I rarely trust
anyone—however attractive.'

This rather mocking compliment she ignored. 'I consider myself duly warned, sir! Now, if you will excuse
me——' As she turned her back on him, he caught her
arm and swung her round, and, before she knew what
had happened, he had planted a kiss firmly on her lips.
Then, with little more than a throaty chuckle, he turned
on his heel and returned to the tap-room.

She ought to have been outraged, but a little thrill of something that certainly was not anger snaked through her, and she turned to go back upstairs in some confusion, her quest for hot water forgotten.

When Kit returned later, he looked so cheerful that she momentarily forgot the unnerving encounter with his friend. 'Well?'

He threw himself down in a chair. 'Do you think you can look after a four-year-old boy?'

She shrugged her shoulders. 'I imagine I have just about enough schooling to teach one that young!' She narrowed her eyes at him. 'What have you done?'

'Told Cousin Maybelle you would be happy to play nursemaid to her grandson in return for adopting you into the family!'

'Her grandson?' She wrinkled her nose. 'Beth's child?'

He nodded. 'Beth died six months ago. John is the boy's guardian, since there is no family on the boy's father's side, but, according to Maybelle, John's wife, Ann, does not want the child and has persuaded John to allow Maybelle to keep him with her.'

Puzzled, Emma frowned. 'Maybelle does not live with John?'

He shook his head. 'They have just moved into a house they have had built overlooking the Charles River. Maybelle did not want to move with them, and I've not had time to find out the reasons. She's not in the best health herself, so it is even more curious.' He shrugged. 'However, John has agreed to let her keep Matthew with her only on the condition that she finds someone suitable to look after him.'

'He has not got a nurse, then?' Kit shook his head, and she was silent for a moment. It was more than she could have hoped for. 'So my arrival is well timed. Looking after a four-year-old cannot be beyond even my limited capabilities.'

'It is not settled yet,' he cautioned.

'I know. But I will behave perfectly and she is sure to like me! Can we go now? I fear I can do little more to improve my appearance——' She broke off, suddenly recalling her abortive search for hot water. 'I saw that man downstairs, Kit, the one on the ship last night. I went downstairs earlier to see if I could coax some hot water out of the place and he was in the tap-room. He recognised me.'

'Did you speak?'

'*He* spoke! He warned me against betraying him. Threatened me, indeed. He is arrogant, your free-trading friend!'

'Arrogant, perhaps. Ruthless certainly,' he warned. 'You are likely to encounter him a good deal if you stay with the Winstons. His name is Ben Sullivan. He is close to the family and a partner in the timber business. Be careful what you say—I have no idea how much they know.'

'I am not a fool, Kit!' she cried indignantly. 'I am aware he'll not be shouting all over town that he deals in contraband.'

'No,' he agreed with rueful regret in his voice. 'You are not a fool, though it might have been better for us if you were and you had married Carlisle as you were told!' He dodged the blow she aimed at him and offered her his arm, laughing. 'Come, then. Cousin Maybelle sent her carriage. We shall see what she makes of you!'

The carriage was drawn by a single horse, and as they rattled away from the warehouses and rigging sheds, chandleries and taverns around the harbour and the narrow streets gave way to wider thoroughfares she could see that it was a popular mode of transport. As they swept up King Street she could not help but admire the impressive State House which commanded the fine square in which it stood, and the reality of Boston was rather different from the dreary town of her imagination. For Boston had been said to have suffered from

the self-imposed ban on British goods a few years ago—
a protest against the duties levied on imports such as
glass, lead, paper, painters' colours and tea. Many
American women had refused the silks, satins and frip-
peries bought in from England and worn homespun instead. Looking about her, it seemed that with the repeal
of most of those duties such gestures had considerably
diminished, for although the citizens were not dressed
in the height of fashion, and a great many were indeed
soberly and plainly clad, there were colourful silks and
velvet cloaks and every appearance of modest prosperity.

Maybelle Winston proved to reside in a fine stone
house on Tremont Street, and only a short distance from
the wide open space of Boston Common. A maid
answered the door and showed them into a warm, in-
formal parlour.

Small and slender, with lightly powdered auburn hair
beginning to grey slightly, Cousin Maybelle came forward
to greet them with a swish of black satin skirts and an
air of restrained energy.

'My dear! How callous of Kit to leave you languishing
at an inn—and not a particularly respectable one at that!
You look dreadful!' The lively blue eyes swept over her.
'Have you eaten? You probably have not had a decent
meal for weeks. Hannah, tell Ellen to bring some food
and—will you have tea?'

'Oh, no!' Emma protested faintly, taking a moment
to recover from this onslaught. 'I am afraid I had far
too much breakfast—a reaction, I fear, to the weeks of
ship's fare. But tea would be lovely, thank you.'

As the maid left, she found herself subjected to a swift,
appraising scrutiny. 'And some warm water and a change
of clothes would not be unwelcome either, I fancy!'
Cousin Maybelle declared with a chuckle. 'But later.
Come and sit beside me. Kit has told me everything,
and, although I am sure I should not at all approve of
what you have done, the man sounds like an animal and

doubtless I should have done the same in your position! Kit assures me that a message left with a friend will by now have reached James to put his mind at rest at least about your safety, if not your whereabouts, so let us dwell on it no longer. You and I are going to get along famously.'

'You are very kind,' she murmured.

'Nonsense!' A delicate hand waved away the apology. 'I act from purely selfish motives. You are the answer to a prayer. And,' she added, 'you must call me "Cousin" as Kit already does. It may stretch a point, but it will satisfy all the niceties without being over-formal.'

'Where is Matthew?' Kit warmed his hands before the fire.

'Ben came not half an hour since and took him down to the harbour. The boy loves to watch the ships. You remember Ben Sullivan, Kit?'

'Of course,' he answered readily, and not so much as a flicker of his eyelids betrayed his illicit dealings with Mr Sullivan.

'He is wonderful with Matthew. I believe he had much to do with persuading John to leave the boy here with me.' She shook her head sadly. 'Poor child. Such a tender age to find oneself an orphan. He never really knew his father,' she explained, turning to Emma. 'He was only a year old when the accident happened. But Beth immersed herself in the boy and rarely gave him up to the nurse. So it came particularly hard to him when she died, and the nurse left almost immediately. Ben has been a great help.'

She smiled a little, and Emma thought an almost wistful look came into her eyes, though it was gone in a moment. 'He will join us for dinner tomorrow night, Kit, and you shall have an opportunity to renew your acquaintance.'

The door swung open, and a girl probably a year or two younger than Emma walked in. Flame-haired, green-eyed, tall and slender, she had to be Kit's 'dazzling beauty', and, to her annoyance, Emma was instantly conscious of a pang of envy.

'Kit!' She glided forward with both hands out-stretched. 'How nice to see you again! I am sorry I was not here when you arrived earlier. A headache has kept me in my room all morning. And you must be Emma.' The green eyes swept over her, taking in every shabby detail. 'Mama said you might be staying with us to take care of Matthew.'

'I hope so, Cousin Jaycinth,' she murmured, trying to digest the implications of everything Cousin Maybelle had said. 'I trust your headache is relieved?'

A tap on the door heralded the maid with the tea-tray, and when it was served Cousin Maybelle went on, 'What Matthew really needs is someone who is able to devote time to him. And energy,' she added with a smile. 'But please—you must not think of yourself as a nursemaid. Think of yourself as Matthew's sister. You can have Beth's old room and Jinny to attend you when Jaycinth does not need her——'

'Oh, but surely——' Jaycinth's protest was silenced by a look from her mother, but the green eyes gleamed and her mouth set in a grim line.

'Now, I am sure you have plenty to do at the harbour and the Customhouse.' The gentle voice was brisk as she directed her gaze to Kit. 'I will have a room ready for you and dinner will be at seven. That will allow you the early night which I am sure you need.'

When he had gone, she bade Jaycinth show Emma upstairs, while she had a word about the revised ar-rangements for dinner with Ellen. Jaycinth stood up and glanced at the kitbag at Emma's feet. 'Is that yours? Bring it with you, then. Jack can bring the rest later— or is it still on the ship?'

'That is all I have,' Emma confessed with a faint smile, refusing to allow this self-assured beauty make her feel ashamed of the fact. 'I left home in rather a hurry.'

The girl raised her eyebrows and looked her up and down with an expression of barely disguised scorn. But she led the way upstairs and along to a room at the far end of a short passageway. Pale green and gold hung at the windows and around the bed, and graced the upholstery of the chair beside the unlit fire. Autumn sunlight sparkled in and threw patterns on the polished floor. 'It's lovely!' she murmured appreciatively.

'Well . . .' Jaycinth walked across to the wardrobe and threw open the doors. 'As you have Beth's room, you may as well have what remains of her clothes—you certainly cannot go about like that!' There was a bitter snap in the previously silken voice that momentarily took Emma by surprise, until she realised that the younger girl would probably resent this sudden intrusion, understandably.

'I'm sorry about Beth,' she murmured. 'Were you— very close?'

'Yes.' A gown of pale lavender with a cream underskirt and modest hoops was thrown down on the bed. 'You are about the same size as Beth before—she became too ill. Mama has saved one or two of the things she never wore to have taken in for me. But this really is not my colour at all.'

Emma had to agree, and said with feeling, 'I should certainly like to consign what I have left to the fire.'

'A good idea!' Cousin Maybelle declared from the doorway. 'Jaycinth, fetch the new underclothes that were delivered this morning!'

Dismayed, Emma began to protest, but Jaycinth's petulant voice cut in. 'Mama, I have been waiting weeks——'

'Pray do not argue!' Cousin Maybelle said firmly. 'I do not care to imagine the state of your underthings after six weeks at sea, Emma. I am sure you will not wish to wear them a moment more! Jinny will make any slight alterations that may be necessary.'

Emma swallowed a chuckle. The truth was that there was very little left of the underclothes she had set out with. They had not been made for scanty washing in salty water and ineffectual drying, and she was wearing next to nothing beneath her dress—a fact she deemed better kept to herself.

'I shall send for the seamstress to attend us tomorrow,' Cousin Maybelle continued as Jaycinth went out. 'For now, I will send Jinny with lots of hot water.'

Left alone, Emma sank on to the bed, aware of an overwhelming tiredness and not a little apprehension. Her life had suddenly been taken out of her hands and was being well and truly organised. As her gaze swept the room, she had to be grateful, of course. This must be preferable to being a kitchen girl, or tavern wench, or any number of fates which might have befallen her— not that Kit would have been persuaded to leave her in Boston had it come to that. But the dull existence of lady's companion or seamstress had certainly been a possibility. And this was surely an unexpected reprieve. Yet it was an unenviable position. A poor relation, totally dependent on her cousin, yet apparently to be given equal status with the daughter of the house...

She gave a deep sigh, and wondered why she did not feel ecstatic at the way things seemed to be turning out.

A scratch on the door preceded the entrance of two girls, carrying a tin bath. The youngest, small and dark with an elfin prettiness, declared herself as Jinny, bobbed a curtsy and introduced the maid who had earlier admitted them and served tea as Hannah. They lit the fire and then made several journeys with steaming kettles to fill the tub while Jaycinth brought the tissue-wrapped underclothes and a fine lawn dressing robe.

She began to feel like a prodigal daughter. But once she was left alone to strip off her unsavoury gown and thank God that Cousin Maybelle was not one of those who believed total immersion in hot soapy water to be a sin, she relaxed. Nothing, she decided, had ever felt so wonderful.

It was half an hour before Jinny returned, and by that time she was wrapped in the robe and seated before the dressing-table mirror with brush and comb. 'I'll do that, Miss Emma. The mistress says I'm to be your maid too, now.'

'Only when your other duties permit,' she insisted. 'You must not get into trouble because of me, and I can manage by myself. Have you been with Mistress Winston long?'

'Three years, come Christmas, miss. Since I was just turned fourteen.' She eased the brush through the matted cloud of hair. 'Mr Sullivan built a house out near ours and he got me the position here when Miss Beth came home.'

'That would be after her husband was killed?'

Jinny's dark curls danced under the white cap as she nodded. 'She never recovered from having little Matthew, poor soul, and when her husband died she went into a real decline. Lovely, she was, like Miss Jaycinth to look at, only softer, if you know what I mean. But so particular about her curls! It was she who taught me to do the ringlets properly—Miss Jaycinth says I do it even better than Mistress Ann's maid, Daisy.'

Emma smiled. 'Are there many servants? There are only Mistress Winston and Miss Jaycinth here now, I believe?'

'That's right. No, there's not many of us. The others went to the big house—Cedars—with Master John. There's Ellen, she's the cook and housekeeper, and her husband, Jack. He is the driver and sees to all the heavy work and odd jobs. Me and Hannah see to the ladies and help out in the kitchen and wait at table—and mind Matthew in between.'

'Heavens!' Emma's appreciative exclamation earned her an immediate ally. 'Well, there is one less task for you, for I am here to take over the care of Master Matthew.'

Jinny nodded. 'The mistress told us. And we're all very glad of it. The little mite is forever under our feet and in places he shouldn't be!' If she found anything remarkable in being told to act as maid for a distant, penniless relation taken in as a nurse for Matthew, she gave no sign of it, and continued her rhythmic brush strokes. 'Shall I just catch it up in ribbons and combs for now? You have such lovely hair it will need only teasing to set it into ringlets tomorrow.'

So relieved was Emma to have it clean again that she did not greatly care what was done with it, and said as much. When she was dressed she allowed herself a faint smile at her reflection. Despite the regrettable dryness of her skin, she looked a different person from the disreputable creature who had stepped ashore this morning. A little of the sparkle had returned to her eyes and her lips had lost some of the red soreness thanks to an ointment made from comfrey leaves which, Jinny revealed, the apothecary made especially for Miss Jaycinth.

'Mistress Maybelle will be in the parlour,' the girl informed her. 'I'm to bring tea in there as soon as you are ready.'

As she went downstairs, the sound of voices reached her from behind the partially open parlour door. 'But it is absurd, Mama! To take her in like this, on a minute's acquaintance! Already she has Beth's room, my new underclothes and my maid! It really is too much. After all, what do we know about her? Only what Kit has told you—and it scarcely recommends her...'

Emma drew back swiftly—and turned straight into the arms of Ben Sullivan. The small, dark-haired boy at his side stared at her for a moment and then darted past. 'Oh!' she cried, startled, and found herself mesmerised by the startlingly blue eyes. 'I'm sorry,' she said finally. 'I did not see you.'

A twitch of amusement pulled at the corner of his mouth. 'Obviously. Eavesdropping is a habit of yours, apparently.'

'I was not eavesdropping!' she protested hotly.

'No?' He inclined his head. 'Then I apologise. Appearances are deceptive.' His gaze swept over her, and there was something like approval in his eyes when he met her infuriated glare. 'And the transformation, Miss Wyatt, is breathtaking.'

'Thank you,' she said with a snap, not totally sure why she was angry. 'Now, if you will excuse me, sir, I have to join my cousin.'

As she made to move past him, he raised an eyebrow. 'Then I am afraid you are going the wrong way.' He put his hands on her shoulders and firmly turned her around, as one might a straying child, his eyes twinkling with amusement. 'I believe Mistress Winston usually takes tea in there at this hour.'

Blushing furiously, and hating herself for the weakness, she shrugged off his hands and walked into the room before him.

Cousin Maybelle treated her to another appraising scrutiny and nodded approval, before turning to greet Mr Sullivan. She effected introductions, and he smiled and bowed over her hand with a faint quirk of his mouth. 'My pleasure, Miss Wyatt.'

Their eyes met briefly. 'Mr Sullivan.'

Jaycinth's startled gaze took in the change the last hour had wrought in her cousin and said suddenly, 'May I go to Cedars, Mama? I am sure Ann will be intrigued to hear about our guest, and I can deliver the invitation to dinner myself.' Maybelle murmured assent, and, when she had gone, signalled to Emma to sit beside her. 'Will you stay for tea, Ben?'

'Thank you.' He smiled. 'Though I do not have much time. I must show myself at the mill today, however briefly!'

Over tea, with Matthew sitting on a footstool munching ratafia biscuits, Emma watched Mr Sullivan covertly and did not revise her earlier impressions. He appeared to be about thirty, and there was strength in every line of his body as he leaned back in the chair and stretched out his legs. In the set of his jaw, the muscular length of his legs in the fawn breeches and black boots, and the broadness of his shoulders in the dark brown coat cut to fit the taut physique of the man perfectly. Every inch a gentleman.

'Tell me, Miss Wyatt,' he said in a deceptively lazy tone, 'do you often accompany your brother on such long voyages, or does Boston hold some particular attraction?'

Under the somewhat mocking directness of those eyes, she found herself unwilling to reveal the reason for her flight. 'I came in the hope of finding employment,' she said finally. 'Cousin Maybelle has very kindly offered me a home in return for taking over the care of Matthew.'

He raised his eyebrows. 'Indeed? Do you have any experience?' It was his tone, rather than the question itself, that made it so impertinent. He was, after all, merely a family friend, and it was none of his business.

'No, none at all,' she told him candidly, meeting the penetrating gaze steadily and daring him to pass adverse comment. 'But I am certain Matthew and I will deal very well together.' She smiled across at the boy. 'Though we have yet to meet properly.'

He looked faintly sceptical and cast a swift glance at Cousin Maybelle, who said with a smile, 'Emma's arrival is most timely, Ben, and I am greatly relieved to have her here.'

Something in her tone puzzled Emma. Was there some undercurrent here? Perhaps she imagined it; she was very tired.

Sullivan returned his gaze to her. 'No doubt you will be a great asset to the family, Miss Wyatt.' There was still a reserve behind the smooth words as he continued to assess her. 'But,' he added, getting to his feet, 'I must intrude no longer. Matthew, behave for Miss Wyatt!' He winked at the boy, who made a comic effort to wink back, and thanked Cousin Maybelle for the tea. 'I look forward to dinner tomorrow, Miss Wyatt, and renewed acquaintance with your brother.'

She smiled, her heart beating faster than necessary. 'I am sure my brother will be equally pleased, sir.' For a brief moment his eyes held hers, devilry dancing in the blue depths, sharing the guilty secret of the night before, and when he had gone she discovered that she was glad she would be seeing him again so soon.

The remainder of the afternoon she spent with Matthew, who looked suspiciously at her out of grave blue eyes, answered her questions with reluctant monosyllables and seemed unwilling to give even the pretence of a smile. Perhaps, she thought in despair, this particular four-year-old *is* beyond my capabilities! But she took over from Jinny the task of seeing him safely abed for the night, and as she turned down the lamp he said suddenly 'If you go away, will I have to go and live with my Uncle John?'

Wondering if her reply would determine his acceptance of her, she hesitated for a moment. 'I'm not sure,' she said finally, 'but I think it might be so, if no one else could be found. Your grandmother cannot manage on her own.'

'There's Aunt Jaycinth,' he pointed out.

'But I imagine she has her own things to do.'

'She rides that horse Uncle John keeps for her at the big house.' He nodded. 'And she's going to marry...'

He screwed up his face and thought for a moment. 'Charles. Only she doesn't like him much.'

She suppressed a smile at this intriguing piece of information. 'Go to sleep now,' she said firmly, but as she went out she felt an unexpected rush of warmth towards this lonely, insecure little boy and was suddenly determined to do all she could to draw him out of his shell. It seemed she had taken the first step towards accepting this new life into which she had so impulsively pitched herself.

When she crawled into her own bed that night it should have been to sleep like a babe herself. Her future, if not precisely glittering with prospects, at least looked rather brighter than at any time since James had first mentioned marriage and William Carlisle. Yet, although she was tired to the point of exhaustion, her head was spinning. It had been a very long day and there was too much to take in. Her impressions were confused, and she was still full of doubts, but already she had learned enough about this unconventional family to fire her lively curiosity. And giving free rein to her imagination left her sleepless well into the night.

CHAPTER THREE

EMMA awoke, however, with a feeling of well-being as she snuggled further into the warm softness cocooning her, smiling blissfully at the luxury of a bed that did not end at her ankles and elbows. How Kit, who was considerably taller and broader than she, ever managed to sleep in that tiny cot she would never know.

Finally she coaxed her eyes open and observed Jinny making up the fire. 'Good morning, Jinny. What time is it?'

'Nearly ten o'clock, Miss Emma. But,' she added soothingly at Emma's dismayed exclamation, 'it's all right. I wouldn't have disturbed you only the seamstress is coming at eleven. I brought up a tray for your breakfast.'

Murmuring thanks, she threw back the covers and sat on the edge of the bed. The seamstress was coming. Everything seemed to be happening so quickly! 'What are the usual arrangements for breakfast, Jinny?'

'Well, the mistress always breakfasts in her room. Miss Jaycinth never eats anything before noon and ever since the old nurse left and Master John married Matthew takes his in the kitchen with us.'

'What of my brother?' she asked, pouring water from the jug into the bowl on the wash-stand.

'Oh, he was up early, miss, and went out. He said to tell you he'd gone to see the merchants and Master John.'

Emma nodded, splashing water on her face and determining to be up early enough to at least join Kit for breakfast while he was here. After that she supposed she would eat that meal with Matthew in the nursery.

Another of Beth's gowns had been found for her, this time of pale blue. 'I noticed the lavender was a bit loose round the waist, Miss Emma, so I took this one in a bit. And this...' She took up a crumpled emerald-green gown with a small rent in the shoulder. 'Miss Beth gave it to me to make something for my sisters, but I never got round to it. I thought, perhaps, I could mend the tear and drape some lace over the shoulder, and once it's well pressed it might be all right to wear tonight...' The girl looked at her with a mixture of doubt and hope.

'It will be lovely,' Emma reassured her. 'But surely you will have more than enough to do in the kitchen? And I'm sure——'

'Oh, no, miss!' she protested, eager to please. 'It won't take but a few minutes. And I'm sure the other two will look as fine as peacocks and you ought to look just as nice!'

'Very well, then! But as soon as maybe you shall have it back and I will help you make some things for your sisters.'

Her session with the fussy little Frenchwoman who arrived a little later was wearing in the extreme. She was measured every which way and talked about as though she were not there, until she was dangerously close to an ungracious protest. Only the startling extent of Cousin Maybelle's generosity as they pored over pattern books and fabric samples held her in check. She was to have a collection of modest day gowns, slippers to match, underwear in fine lawn, nightwear and a serviceable wool cloak—all at the earliest opportunity. There was even a suggestion of something more elegant for 'social' occasions, although when she would have cause to wear such a thing she could not imagine.

When Jinny helped her dress for dinner, she was well pleased with the transformation of the green gown. It was a colour that suited her and the few alterations Jinny had made had produced a very flattering gown. She had even found a length of matching velvet ribbon, which threaded through her ringlets to great effect. The neckline was low, and a small emerald pendant on a fine gold chain that had been her mother's added just the right finishing touch.

A pang of misgiving assailed her as she surveyed her reflection in the mirror. Surely she looked too fine for someone in her betwixt-and-between position? She should look more demure, more subdued—less elegant! But she was anxious to look her best and could not regret the fact that she did.

Comforting herself with the excuse that she had little choice, and might as well make the most of the opportunity, she declared herself satisfied and told Jinny to run along before she got into trouble. Bobbing a curtsy, the girl dimpled and whispered, 'You look a picture, Miss Emma. Enough to ruffle Mistress Ann's feathers, I shouldn't wonder!'

But it was not Mistress Ann who had been at the back of Emma's thoughts as she dressed, and when she entered the drawing-room her gaze was drawn irresistibly to the far side of the room where Ben Sullivan was deep in conversation with her brother. Her breath caught in her throat. How handsome he looked, in a dark blue coat and breeches, the colour adding a new depth to the vividness of his eyes.

As Maybelle was not yet down, John stepped forward and introduced himself. 'Your arrival has been timely, Miss Wyatt—Emma,' he said. 'I was anxious to indulge my mother in her desire to keep Matthew with her, since they both wished it, but her health is so fragile.' He smiled briefly. 'If you need anything you have only to ask, although I am sure she is taking good care of you. She will not permit me to rule her life,' he added with a touch of humour, 'but merely expects me to pay her bills!'

'You are all being very kind and generous,' she replied, feeling faintly embarrassed by this last comment
and wondering what he would say when he received the
dressmaker's account. He merely nodded and drew his
wife forward, excusing himself as Mr Sullivan called him
away.

'So. You are Emma.' Ann's diminutive figure and
golden prettiness lent her a fragile beauty, but the blue
gaze that swept over her was hard and calculating, giving
the lie to her doll-like appearance. 'You are very pretty.'

The false surprise in her voice made it almost an insult
and Emma took an instant dislike to her, refusing to
utter the simpering thanks that were clearly expected.
Instead she said nothing, merely returning the haughty
gaze steadily.

'No doubt you are aware, Miss Wyatt,' she continued
in a voice threaded with ice, 'that my husband is the
boy's legal guardian and, although we should have pre-
ferred to have been consulted about you, he seems
content to indulge his mother. And you will find that
this family knows its duty to its less fortunate relatives,
however remote. But let me make one thing quite clear.'
Her voice hardened imperceptibly. 'You are not at all
what we had in mind for Matthew, and I have serious
doubts about the wisdom of entrusting such a task to a
young woman who would shirk her responsibilities and
run away, leaving her family to face ruin and scandal.
In my opinion, Miss Wyatt, you are unlikely to be a
suitable influence over my nephew.'

The contempt in her tone fanned Emma's rising annoyance. 'You are entitled to your opinion, of course,'
she conceded, controlling her voice with difficulty.
'However, I rather think it is your husband's view which
matters most in this instance.'

Ann arched her fine eyebrows at such bold manners.
'Have a care, Miss Wyatt,' she said softly, her eyes

gleaming. 'If you think you can cross me with impunity, you are mistaken.'

Emma bit her lips together, and took a steadying breath. 'I had no wish to appear ungrateful or insolent,' she forced out. 'Perhaps you would not think so harshly of me if you understood the reasons——'

'I understand,' Ann interrupted coldly, 'that you arrived without a stitch of clothing to your name and threw yourself on our charity! Only a fool—or a scheming little opportunist—would flee without even pausing to pack a trunk!'

Emma's anger suddenly flared. 'Only a fool, Mistress Winston, would judge a person's character by her lack of wardrobe!' she retorted hotly. 'And only a greater fool would condemn someone's actions without being in possession of all the facts!'

Rewarded by a sharp intake of breath and a look of shock, she swung round, intending to make a swift exit to cool her temper outside. But her way was suddenly blocked by Mr Sullivan, who regarded her with a gleam of something between admiration and amusement. 'Do not quit the field yet, Miss Wyatt,' he murmured, 'for you will lose the advantage of your victory.' He took her arm and drew her to the window, as Ann stood staring at them, tapping her fan into her palm with barely controlled fury.

'Victory?' Avoiding Kit's questioning look from the far side of the room, she withdrew her arm and looked up at him bleakly, already bitterly regretting her outburst. 'I have probably ruined everything with my wretched temper!'

He raised an eyebrow. 'If your temper is so easily aroused, Miss Wyatt, I would advise you against venting it on Ann. The lady is a viper and well practised in the use of her venom. She will make you a formidable enemy.'

'Thank you!' she said caustically, 'but your advice is a little late!'

'So it would appear.' There was a shadow of a smile hovering on his mouth. 'Had I realised you were so temperamental, I should have offered it sooner.'

He seemed to find the whole thing highly amusing! But as she flicked her gaze past him to where Ann had drawn her husband from Kit's side and was speaking to him in urgent undertones her annoyance dissolved in a heavy sigh. 'Well, I doubt I shall be here long enough to cross swords with her again,' she sighed gloomily.

Watching the conflicting play of emotions across her face, he took pity on her. 'Nonsense! If Ann wishes to be rid of you, she will have Maybelle to deal with.'

The prospect of such a battle brought a sudden sparkle to her eyes, and without pausing to think she exclaimed with feeling, 'Poor John!'

Mr Sullivan threw back his head and laughed. 'Poor John, indeed!' He looked down at her for a moment, a devil dancing in the blue depths. 'And I suspect that you, Miss Wyatt, are going to be an enlivening addition to this household. I shall enjoy watching the fireworks!'

This time she swallowed back the smart rejoinder that sprang to her lips. Clearly he was already anticipating that her ready tongue would afford him a great deal of amusement and she was not about to oblige him further! She was saved from having to find something else to say by the timely arrival of Cousin Maybelle and Jaycinth, and the announcement of dinner. As she allowed Mr Sullivan to escort her into the dining-room, she could not avoid the icy glitter in Ann's eyes or the frowning disapproval in Kit's, and she was full of self-reproach as she sat down at the table.

It was only a small relief that Mr Sullivan was seated between herself and Ann, shielding her from the malicious scorn in the other woman's eyes, nor could she draw much comfort from John's unreadable expression.

Fortunately, as the conversation flowed freely round the table, she was not called upon to contribute very much, and ate her fish soup morosely. Her first day and already she had found it impossible to keep a curb on her tongue! It was not a very auspicious start.

'We are holding a soirée at the end of the month,' Ann announced as Jinny cleared the plates. 'You will come, Mama?' She looked down the table at Maybelle. 'You have not seen the house finished, and it is six months since Beth died. We thought it time to entertain again—modestly, of course.'

'I agree!' Maybelle declared with alacrity. 'And of course we shall come.'

'And you, Ben?' Ann turned to Mr Sullivan. 'We all know how busy you are, but you are quite forbidden to arrange anything else for that evening.'

'It is a fortnight hence!' he protested. 'I never arrange my life so far in advance.'

'Oh, but you must!' She was all cloying sweetness now, Emma observed as she leaned forward to take her wine glass, the malicious gleam gone from her eyes and the thin-lipped tartness of her voice replaced by a persuasive caress. 'I shall take it as a personal insult if you do not come. We see so little of you at Cedars.'

'I would not dream of insulting you,' he replied with more than a touch of irony. 'I shall do my utmost to attend, I promise.'

'Are you filling the house with Redcoats?' Jaycinth demanded. 'Ben might care to be a hypocrite and mix with them, but I would rather not.'

'Hypocrite?' There was a tremor of amusement in Ben Sullivan's voice. 'And what of you, my dear Jaycinth? You refuse to drink tea, yet you do not scorn your silk gowns for homespun.'

'Few people bother with that now,' she argued defensively, 'and the tea is different—there is still a duty on it to protest about!'

'Anyway, you are not excused on any grounds,' John told her severely. The Arnolds will be there and you will be civil to Charles, and not have one of your convenient headaches!'

As her mother agreed with him, Jaycinth pulled a face and flashed her green eyes at Kit. 'Will you be there then, Kit?'

He shook his head. 'Afraid not. I should sail within the week.'

Emma shot him a look of dismay. Only a week! She had thought he would be here longer. He half smiled at her and gave an apologetic shrug.

'That is a pity.' Maybelle turned and patted Emma's arm. 'But it will give you an opportunity to meet a few people, my dear, and enjoy a taste of Boston society.'

She returned the smile, but before she could respond, Ann hissed a breath between her teeth and said sharply, 'Emma will surely be required to remain here with Matthew. I hardly think——'

'I doubt that will be necessary,' John interrupted surprisingly. 'I'm sure he can be safely left in the care of Jinny and Ellen.'

'Of course he can,' Cousin Maybelle asserted, and, firmly dismissing the subject, smiled at Emma. 'You look delightful tonight. Jinny has done wonders with that gown. Tell me, are hoops still narrower in England this year?'

As the duck in plum sauce was served, Emma was glad to turn her attention to so innocuous a subject. Jaycinth was apparently engrossed in Kit's theories on improving colonial trade, and Ann was far more interested in whether the latest scandal concerning Mr Sullivan and a certain Martha McIntyre had any foundation in truth.

Keeping half an ear on this latter conversation out of a compulsive curiosity, Emma noted that Mr Sullivan was tellingly evasive. Neither could she help but notice, as dinner progressed to the orange syllabub, that Ann drank more wine than was considered prudent for a lady and was beginning to flirt outrageously with him.

For his part, Mr Sullivan seemed to parry her coquetry with practised ease and even seemed to be amused by it despite the increasingly stormy glances that John cast at his wife who, resting an elbow on the table and setting her chin into her palm, seemed to fairly melt towards Sullivan.

'I hear you won a superb black gelding from Captain Hunt on the turn of a card the other night,' she observed. 'Is it true?'

'Of course. But he was playing like a fool and should not complain.'

'He was heard to remark that the beast would unseat you at the earliest opportunity. I trust——' she lowered her voice to a seductive purr, seemingly unaware that a natural lull in the other conversations made her remarks perfectly audible to eveyone '—I trust your performance in the saddle is equal to your performance . . . elsewhere.'

This was evidently going too far even for Mr Sullivan, who was fully awake to the fact that everyone was listening. 'He has not unseated me yet,' he said tautly, and turned away, a muscle tensing at the corner of his mouth. 'Do you ride, Miss Wyatt?'

'What? Oh, yes,' she stammered, momentarily taken unawares by the suddeness of his question. 'I love riding. I have a—that is, I had a horse called Sir Francis at home.' Caught by a fleeting memory of wild gallops across the Hoe, she glanced across at Kit. 'You will look after him, Kit?'

'Of course,' he said too quickly, and her heart contracted at the thought that James probably would not keep her darling Sir Francis.

'Jack should bring you all to Eastwood one day,' Sullivan offered. 'I have a particularly fine bay mare I should be happy to put at your disposal, Miss Wyatt.'

'That's very kind of you!' she exclaimed, but the rush
of pleasure was almost immediately tempered by caution.
Cousin Maybelle might not consider such an expedition
seemly. 'Should such an opportunity prove possible, sir,'
she said carefully, 'I should very much enjoy the chance
to ride again.'

'We might contrive to arrange something,' Cousin
Maybelle conceded. 'It must have been difficult for you
to leave your——'

A clatter interrupted her as Ann upset her glass,
spilling wine over her gown and over Sullivan and suc-
cessfully diverting his attention—and that of everyone
else—back to herself.

When the damage was repaired, Maybelle turned back
to Emma and continued her question. There were fine-
drawn lines about her mouth and it was clear that she
was unimpressed by her daughter-in-law's behaviour.
That little love was lost between them was obvious.
Perhaps Ann was the reason that she was reluctant to
give Matthew up to their care. What, Emma wondered,
had persuaded John to marry such a creature?

Her opinion was not altered by the short interlude the
ladies spent in the parlour while the men lingered over
the brandy. Ann persisted in turning the conversation
round to people and events of which Emma could have
no knowledge, and, despite Maybelle's continually attempting to draw her in, she spent a very uncomfortable
half-hour. At the end of it she was in no doubt that she
had made an enemy, and would have to be careful if she
wanted to remain in the Winston household.

She could only feel relieved when the men rejoined
them and John announced that they should leave. 'It's
a dark night and it would be as well to go by the Common
earlier rather than later,' he said.

'I must take my leave also,' Mr Sullivan declared.

'You surely will not attempt to go back to Eastwood
at this late hour?' Ann exclaimed. 'Would you care to

pass the night at Cedars? Or may we give you a ride somewhere?'

A little smile curled his mouth. 'Neither, thank you.'

'Then I presume you will not accept our hospitality either.' Maybelle smiled reproachfully at him. 'Though I do not care to know where you are going.'

The enigmatic smile deepened and Emma could only assume he had a mistress. Martha McIntyre, perhaps? He probably has several, she decided, since she could not imagine him wanting for willing bed-mates! And later, helping her prepare for bed, Jinny confirmed that he had something of a reputation where women were concerned.

''Cording to Hannah,' the girl said as she moved the warming-pan about in the bed, 'he turned up about ten years ago out of nowhere. A bit of a rogue he was...' she giggled '...drinking and gambling and women, you know. I don't suppose he's changed very much, really! You should have a care, Miss Emma; he's got quite a reputation for the ladies, you know, and you looked real pretty tonight!'

Emma shot her a reproachful look, but, unperturbed, Jinny went on, 'Well, the master gave him a job at the mill and, when he was really good at it, made him a partner, which set Master John off in a real temper. That's about when he started paying attention to Miss Beth, and, just when everyone started thinking they'd get wed, all of a sudden it was all off! Mr Sullivan's fault, they say. He didn't come near the house for months.'

'But he seems very friendly with the family now,' she prompted, startled by this revelation.

'Oh, yes.' Leaving the warming-pan in the bed, Jinny began to stoke up the fire, obviously enjoying the opportunity to gossip. 'But the mistress was real poorly over it. Hannah says it was that caused her heart trouble. Miss Beth turned round and wed the next man that asked her and that was that. When the master died, they all seemed to get back to being friendly again.' She shrugged philosophically and laid out Emma's nightgown. 'Queer family, when all's said. Mr Sullivan has taken a real shine to Matthew since Miss Beth died, though. Feels sorry for him, I dare say.'

That a man like Ben Sullivan should have any interest at all in a four-year-old child seemed unlikely enough to Emma, but when he obviously went out of his way to be kind to the boy her curiosity about the man was aroused still further. He arrived mid-way through the morning a few days later with an enormous crab's claw. Matthew pounced on it with delight and dashed off to the kitchen to terrorise Jinny.

'You should not encourage him, Ben,' Maybelle chided. 'His room is full of such grisly relics!'

'Nonsense! It is a small boy's prerogative to collect such things! I have to check some timber at the warehouse—I am sure he would like to come with me. And as I should not be above a few minutes attending to business I would very much like to show Miss Wyatt something of the town.' He turned an enquiring gaze on Emma, and she immediately looked away, unaccountably flustered, the vague protest on her lips forestalled by Maybelle.

'I am sure Emma would enjoy that, would you not, my dear?' She smiled brightly. 'Kit will not be back for some hours, I imagine, and Matthew would certainly enjoy the outing. Jinny can go with you.'

So it was settled without Emma even having to open her mouth. Already she was coming to realise that Cousin Maybelle had a happy knack of organising everything, and after several years ordering her day-to-day life to suit herself she was not at all sure she would find it easy to submit to being managed.

However, for the moment the thought of an outing in the company of Mr Sullivan overrode any such concern and she ushered Matthew upstairs to get ready with a treacherous thread of anticipation tingling in her veins.

Settled in Maybelle's carriage with Jinny beside her and Matthew tucked in the corner eagerly watching the passing traffic, she was acutely conscious of his speculative gaze upon her. 'It was kind of you to give up some of your valuable time to introduce me to my new home,' she said, covering her confusion with cool courtesy.

He smiled a lazy smile that set her heart quivering. 'I can always find an excuse to spend an hour or two with an attractive woman, Miss Wyatt.'

I am sure you can, she thought uncharitably and returned his smile sweetly. 'You flatter me, sir. I had hoped Kit would have more time to show me the sights——'

'He has much to do to finalise his cargo for the return voyage.'

Her cool demeanour evaporated at the stark reminder of his imminent departure. 'I know that. But I have seen very little of him and there are so few days left!'

The days were indeed being eaten up with alarming speed. Even when Kit was at home, she could not claim his time. Jaycinth had borne him off to Cedars all yesterday afternoon where they had gone riding on the Common while she had endured another session with the dressmaker. And Matthew took up much of her time, for already she found him left almost totally in her charge. And it did not help that Ben Sullivan took Kit off in the evenings on 'matters of business' which she rather suspected were conducted in some tavern.

Some of the resentment she felt must have shown in her face as she regarded the man opposite her for he threw up a hand. 'I know I am guilty, Miss Wyatt! But if I promise to desist from luring him out in the evenings will you stop scowling at me?'

'I was not scowling!' she protested.

'Good. Such an attractive face should not be marred by so unbecoming an expression.'

He was laughing at her! She sent him a reproachful look. 'I will bear that in mind!'

He inclined his head with the hint of a smile playing about his mouth, but any further exchange was prevented as the carriage drew to a halt in front of a warehouse, the fading sign over which proclaimed it the property of George Winston & Sons.

'I shall not be more than a few minutes,' he assured her. 'Matt, do you want to come with me, or shall you wait with Miss Wyatt and Jinny?'

The answer to that was predictable enough and Matthew tumbled out of the carriage to disappear with Mr Sullivan into the ageing building. '"And Sons"?' Emma quoted, glancing enquiringly at Jinny. 'Surely John is the only son?'

Jinny nodded and shrugged. 'That sign's been there an awful long time, miss. P'raps it was wishful thinking!'

'Probably.' Inevitably her thoughts returned to Plymouth and the sign above the door of the tiny office just off the quayside. 'Wyatt Shipping Company.' No mention of sons there, and yet Thomas Wyatt had had four of them. Once Kit left Boston, would she ever see any of them again?

True to his word, Ben and Matthew emerged within a few minutes, Matthew clamouring to go to the harbour. 'What, again?' Ben exclaimed in mock horror, depositing the boy in the carriage and climbing in after him. 'Do you never tire of it?'

'Never! Can we?'

'If Miss Wyatt does not object. I doubt harbours hold quite the same fascination for her.' His eyes smiled into hers, doing strange things to her stomach.

'On the contrary.' She shifted her gaze to Matthew and smiled at him. 'I love watching ships loading and sailing off to exotic places. I always try to imagine where they are going and what they are carrying.'

She was rewarded by a beaming grin from Matthew and—did she mistake it?—a gleam of approval in Ben's blue eyes. 'The harbour it is, then.'

The *Emma Louise* rode at anchor out in the bay and when Emma pointed her out to Matthew he besieged her with a stream of increasingly unanswerable questions, much to Mr Sullivan's evident amusement. Finally she said, 'Would you like to go on board? I expect she will be coming in to load in the next day or so.'

Matthew's blue eyes widened like saucers. 'Can I really?'

She laughed and stroked his hair. 'Well, I cannot promise, of course. I shall have to ask the captain. But since he is my brother and he always does what I ask, I dare say I shall be able to persuade him to take you.'

This time there was no mistaking the approval in Mr Sullivan's gaze, and her blood quickened. It was totally irrational, of course. It could not matter whether he approved or disapproved of the way she handled Matthew—and yet she had the feeling that he was watching her, assessing her, and it made her feel very self-conscious.

Back in the carriage, they made a circuitous tour of the town. Ben proved to be a well-informed and amusing guide, contriving to keep Matthew entertained at the same time, and she could not help but admire the ease with which he took on both roles. They passed the fine Faneuil Hall given to the town thirty years ago by Peter Faneuil, and turned into King Street. 'It was there,' he said, directing her gaze to the Customhouse, 'that the Redcoats killed five of the townspeople three years ago. The so-called "massacre".'

'What exactly happened?' she queried. 'I have always thought it was started by a riot, that——'

'A riot?' He raised an eyebrow. 'British propaganda, Miss Wyatt. It was hardly that.' He paused, and seemed to choose his words with care. 'When the Townshend duties led us to ban British imports in protest, the resulting hardships caused a lot of resentment against the British. There were four regiments here then and they were very free with their money and their favours—some of our more pious citizens accused them of corrupting both manners and morals. I am not sure I agree with *that* but the commanding officers could certainly have done more to ease the tensions. Some of the duties were repealed, and half the troops were withdrawn. That encouraged a number of our more naïve and reckless patriots into thinking a total victory was possible, and they subjected the company guarding the Customhouse to a great deal of verbal and physical abuse. Someone's temper snapped and they opened fire. Had they not then hastily withdrawn, there might well have been a riot—and a massacre of the soldiers.'

Behind the carefully measured words lurked an intensity that hinted of deeper feelings and she longed to probe further. But he immediately drew her attention to something else. Turning up Milk Street, they passed the South Church, a meeting place for the patriots and dissenters, and then into School Street with its Latin School. In answer to Matthew's request, they drove along the edge of the Common, but Ben had to resist his demands to stop. 'Next time,' he promised. 'I really do have to see your uncle this afternoon. Besides, Kit may be home by now and Miss Wyatt has a promise to keep.'

He flashed her an enigmatic look, which seemed almost to hold a glimmer of warning. Did he think she would forget? Or break her word to so insecure a child? Irritation nudged aside the other odd feelings coursing through her veins, but none the less she was sorry when Jack turned the carriage in through the gates of Maybelle's house.

'Thank you,' she said, her throat unexpectedly dry as he handed her down. 'That was interesting. I enjoyed it very much.'

The blue eyes held hers for a long moment. 'Good.' He seemed about to say something more, but changed his mind and turned to assist Jinny and Matthew. He left soon afterwards, but she found him lingering in her thoughts, distracting her for the remainder of the afternoon with annoying persistence.

Kit was easily persuaded into taking Matthew on board his ship, and was thus elevated to the position of hero in the little boy's heart. Emma, however, had cause to regret it since she was excluded from the outing—and valuable time with her brother—because Cousin Maybelle had arranged to take tea with a particular friend and both she and Jaycinth were expected to accompany her.

She found herself struggling to suppress a rising panic, and biting her tongue against an ungracious outburst of protest at the web of almost overwhelming kindness and generosity being woven around her. Whatever her own feelings, Maybelle had taken pity on her, had taken her firmly under her wing and was determined that she should feel like one of the family.

All this, and a further session with the seamstress, conspired to give her very little time with her brother, and as the days were eaten up she found herself biting her tongue and keeping a tight rein on her temper. And this only a week into her stay in Boston!

'Oh, it's undeniably pleasant to have fine clothes and every comfort,' she conceded when finally she had Kit to herself long enough to voice her disquiet, 'but I do not want to be mothered! I do not want to feel so—so tied, so beholden to Cousin Maybelle that I can never leave. I want to have a little independence, make my own decisions. But—but everything has been taken out of my control!'

'Then find a good man and get married,' he advised unsympathetically.

Cousin Maybelle will probably arrange that too, given time, she thought ungraciously, but kept that observation to herself. As far as Kit was concerned, she had been lucky—and of course he was right. Yet with Maybelle treating her like a daughter on one hand, and Ann determined to restrict her to the role of obsequious nursemaid on the other, the immediate prospect did not look comfortable.

His last night was upon them all too soon. Ben Sullivan, with whom he had spent the afternoon, was persuaded to join them for dinner, and Emma sat beside him at the table with very mixed feelings. All week, fleeting encounters with him had jarred her already unsettled nerves. He made her feel defensive and nervous, constantly on her guard against the mockery and sardonic humour he used like a rapier. She might almost have believed she disliked him intensely, except that she was not so innocent. She knew well enough that what she felt was the stirring of a primitive response to his powerful physical attraction. Yet neither was she a fool. Ben Sullivan, with his devastating good looks, wry wit and disarming charm, tempered with his arrogance and supreme self-confidence, would be dangerously attractive to any woman, and in her limited experience such men were careless with the emotions of their victims.

Since she was not a romantic, impressionable halfwit, she was not going to commit the fatal mistake of losing her heart to such a man. Nevertheless, she felt decidedly tense over dinner, despite the fact that it was an altogether more pleasant and relaxed affair without Ann frosting the atmosphere, but she put this down to Kit's imminent departure and the thought of being abandoned to her fate, perhaps never to see her family again.

Desperate for a few minutes alone with him, it was with great reluctance that she climbed the stairs to bed with Cousin Maybelle and Jaycinth, leaving him to enjoy a last glass of brandy with Ben, who this time had not refused Maybelle's hospitality for the night.

She made no attempt to sleep, but sat up in bed with her knees drawn under her chin, watching the flickering shadows cast by her candle. Eventually the sound of barely subdued laughter and masculine voices reached her, and as she heard the two men part company and doors close, she reached for her robe and slid out of bed.

Kit was gathering the last of his things together and she sat on the end of his bed and watched him for a few minutes. 'What will you do if—Wyatt's is finished?' she asked at last.

'Come back here, of course!' he reassured her. 'Sullivan has already offered me work—of sorts!' He flashed her a look of devilment and her heart sank. He was far from drunk, but he had had too much to be sensitive to her mood. Neither did she now seem able to put into words all the guilt she was feeling. There was not a man among the crew who would not be eager to talk for the price of a tankard of ale, and James would know where she had gone within an hour of the *Emma Louise*'s putting into Plymouth, if he had not already guessed. And the full force of his wrath would fall on Kit's head. The knowledge that he was well able to take care of himself did not assuage her conscience.

'I've something for you,' he announced, producing a leather pouch. 'Fifty pounds. Not a fortune, I know, but——'

She gasped as he dropped it into her hand, and in some alarm she stared up at him. 'But where—Kit, what have you done?'

He grinned at her. 'Nothing, yet. But a little business for Sullivan in New York before I sail for home. Nothing for you to concern yourself about.'

'Oh!' She looked down at the bag, dreading to think what her brother had been drawn into.

'He is a good man, Em. If you need anything—if anything happens and you want to come home, go to him. He would help you and you can trust him.' A mist of tears suddenly blurred her vision and she could not immediately answer. 'Promise me, Emma,' he insisted, watching her closely.

She murmured her promise. But climbing back into bed some minutes later she thought it rather unlikely that she would trust either herself or her gold to a man who was both a womaniser and a gambler, and a smuggler, however physically attractive she might find him!

Sleep evaded her. Kit had sworn to wake her so that she could go down to the harbour with him before dawn and see him leave, but she knew he would slip away without doing so if he could. So she lay in a drowsy half-world as the candle sputtered out in its own pool of wax, afraid to let herself sleep.

Did she imagine in her drowsiness that she heard a distant door click open and stealthy footsteps in the corridor? A door creaked nearby—Jaycinth's, surely?—and were they whispering voices she heard or merely the wind in the trees outside? Was it a masculine chuckle and a groaning bed? Or simply the natural sounds of a strange house settling for the night?

Ironically, it was those indistinct sounds, and not her resolve to see Kit sail for home, that kept her awake until the first pale light lifted the edges of darkness.

She stood on the quayside determined to watch until the ship that bore her name was gone from sight. The sunrise was fading, promising a cold, bright morning, and she hugged her cloak closer around her.

Eventually, with a shuddering sigh, she turned away and walked back along the wharf, over giant hooks and thickly coiled ropes so recently discarded, to where Jack waited by the carriage. Conscious of the curious stares directed towards her by a group of seamen with heavy heads and unsteady feet, she brushed away her tears and lifted her skirts clear of the filth at her feet, quickening her pace.

But she was in no mood to go directly back to the house. 'Take the carriage home, Jack,' she commanded, swallowing a lump in her throat. 'I will walk back.'

Quite horrified at his suggestion, Jack protested at length until she cut him off impatiently. 'Please do as I say! I shall come to no harm!' He looked mutinous and she felt quite unable at that moment to assert herself. Why couldn't the man do as he was told without a fuss? At home, Phillips had always obeyed her instantly.

'It's all right, Jack, you may do as she says.' The familiar voice sounded faintly amused and she swung round to find Ben Sullivan behind her. What was he doing here? He had not come to see Kit off otherwise he would have joined them in the carriage, surely. 'I will escort Miss Wyatt home,' he said.

Poor Jack looked as though he considered that infinitely worse, and began to protest once more. 'I can't allow it, sir. The mistress——'

'Go home, man!' There was a faint impatience in his voice. 'Miss Wyatt will be quite safe with me.' After a moment's indecision, Jack gave a brief nod, and without further argument climbed up into his seat, clicking the reins.

'How dare you dismiss my cousin's servant like that?' she cried as he drove away, whipping up her anger so that her tears might subside.

He looked at her with raised eyebrows. 'Forgive me! I must have misunderstood. I was under the impression that you wished him dismissed.'

'I needed no assistance from you, sir!'

'My mistake,' he conceded. 'However, I am sure you and Jack will be in far less trouble with your cousin if you accept my escort.'

He was laughing at her. 'I rather doubt that, but it seems I have little choice,' she complained irritably.

'True.' A little shiver ran through her at the touch of his hand on her arm and she drew away, pulling her cloak more tightly around her as they walked away from the quayside. 'Are you in the habit of walking the streets unescorted?' he demanded.

'Only when I wish to be alone!' she threw back at him, and with a little sigh of annoyance added, 'I have four older brothers, Mr Sullivan, and I know well enough how to defend myself should the need arise! However, if I must have you for a companion, perhaps you would be good enough to be quiet!'

'Certainly, as you now seem far less inclined to tears.'

She shot him a startled look as they paused on a corner to allow a laden cart to trundle past, but his expression was impassive and they went on in silence.

'You are abroad early, sir,' she said eventually, regretting her scathing rudeness, and finding that she wanted him to talk to her.

'It is an unfortunate habit I seem to have acquired of late,' he told her wryly.

Recalling those stealthy footsteps in the night, and in no doubt to whom they belonged, she said tartly, 'I should have thought you were more used to late nights than early mornings!'

'They are very often the same thing, you know.'

'In some occupations, perhaps!' At the thought of smuggling, she remembered the fifty pounds Kit had left her and suddenly burst out, 'I wish you had not involved Kit in your contraband dealings!'

He looked at her in some surprise. 'My dear girl, it was his idea to smuggle tea. I merely provided the market. I hardly think I can be blamed——'

'I am referring to New York!'

'As to that...' he shrugged '...I wanted something carried, he offered to take it.'

'He only did it so that he could leave me some money.' Her voice trembled dangerously.

'Then he obviously cares a great deal for you,' he said rather more kindly.

She bit her lip and they lapsed into silence until they turned into Tremont Street. As they reached the house he suddenly stepped round in front of her and, before she could draw breath, pulled her against him and claimed her mouth in a kiss. Shock rendered her momentarily powerless, as his mouth moved purposefully over hers, his tongue parting her lips.

Before she could recover her wits, and just as abruptly, he released her. 'I have been wanting to do that all week!' he said with some satisfaction. 'And you may also take it as a warning of what can happen to young ladies who walk the streets unescorted, however well they think they can defend themselves!' There was a wicked gleam in the blue eyes. 'I will join you for breakfast.' And, with a formal bow, he walked away down the street.

She stared after him, speechless. Oh, but he was arrogant! A glance round reassured her that no one had seen, but it was not embarrassment that brought a flare of heat to her cheeks but anger at herself. Her pulses were racing, her stomach fluttering and there was no denying that she had enjoyed the experience, however hard she tried!

CHAPTER FOUR

THE house was still quiet, only a muffled giggle and the rattle of crockery coming from the kitchen as she went straight upstairs in the hope of an hour's respite in which to gather her tangled emotions into some sort of order.

She was not so lucky. Barely had she removed her gown and lain down upon the bed when an urgent tap on the door preceded the entrance of an anxious-looking Hannah.

'Sorry to disturb you, Miss Emma, only it's the mistress——'

She sat up at once. 'What is it?'

'She's awful white, miss, and she's got a pain in her chest which she won't complain of only to say it aches a bit and that she's a bit tired—only I haven't seen her so white before, miss, and sort of blue around the lips. I think it's her heart again——'

'All right, Hannah.' Emma stopped the incoherent flow and reached for her dressing-robe. 'Have you told Miss Jaycinth?'

'Oh, no, miss! Not yet! I wouldn't want to wake her at this hour, not if it's nothing at all. And seeing as you've been up——'

She smiled faintly. 'Of course. I will come at once.'

One look at Cousin Maybelle was enough, for she looked old and drawn and her breathing was laboured as she began to protest that it was nothing but too much rich food the night before. 'Go and tell Jack to make ready to fetch the physician,' she whispered, unwilling to give the direct order. 'I will wake Miss Jaycinth.'

She tapped on Jaycinth's door and went in immediately. The room was in chaos and she had to pick her way between the discarded garments that littered the floor. Clearly Jinny had been dismissed before her mistress had retired! Unceremoniously she shook her cousin awake.

'Jaycinth! Your mother is ill; I think you should send for the physician!'

After a moment, from beneath the lace-edged pillows and a tangle of bedcovers, came a snapped, 'Then go and send for the damned physician!'

Shocked at such lack of concern, Emma turned away. But as she reached the door a voice emerging from the covers called her back. 'Hand me my nightgown and robe, will you?' Emma turned around as the other girl sat up in bed, holding the counterpane against her and obviously without a stitch of clothing on.

Finding the required items and giving them to her silently, she again recalled those furtive footsteps in the night and Jaycinth's door creaking. She had been trying not to think of it, Jaycinth and Ben Sullivan, and in Maybelle's own house, but now disgust brought a bad taste into her mouth and she turned away.

'I will be with your mother,' she murmured, and left the room quickly. Why she felt so disturbed, she did not know. The realisation that Jaycinth was no innocent should not surprise her. She had been flirting unashamedly with her brother all week. And she would surely be a hard temptation for any man to resist—let alone one with Sullivan's reputation. She herself had known him little more than a week and he had kissed her twice and thrown her usually level emotions into confusion. So why should she feel so shocked that Jaycinth had succumbed to his persuasive charms? If Jinny was to be believed, he had been attracted to Beth, almost to the point of marriage, so why not to the sister who apparently so closely resembled her?

Resolutely thrusting her disturbing thoughts aside, she
dispatched Jack for the physician and took Matthew
back up to the nursery, spending the next half-hour trying
to persuade him to settle down to something con-
structive. Although he was gradually losing his suspicion of her, he was cross at having been dragged from
the kitchen and seemed intent on thwarting all her efforts, wanting only to toy with his collection of fish-jaws
and shells. She heard Hannah bring the doctor upstairs
and after a few minutes abandoned Matthew to his play-
things and went downstairs to wait.

She had all but forgotten Sullivan's promise to join
them for breakfast. He was there before her, apparently
engrossed in the *Boston Gazette*. He looked up as she
entered and put aside his paper. 'Was that Cornwallis I
saw coming in?'

'Yes,' she answered shortly, the memory of his
snatched kiss souring beneath the conviction that only
hours before he had been in Jaycinth's bed. 'Did no one
tell you? Cousin Maybelle is unwell. And, as Jaycinth
is with her and Matthew has already eaten, I am afraid
that if you want any breakfast you will probably have
to go and fetch it yourself.' Realising that she sounded
extremely ungracious and deciding that he deserved it,
she avoided his speculating gaze and went to stand by
the window.

'I will do that.' He got to his feet. 'How is she? For
Jaycinth to be up at this hour——'

Glancing at him, she saw genuine concern in the slight
frown between his brows and softened a little. 'She protests it is nothing. But we must await the physician's
opinion.'

He gave her a brief nod and turned towards the door,
pausing to look back at her. 'Have you eaten, Miss
Wyatt?'

'I am not hungry, thank you.'

'That is not what I asked.' The penetrating blue gaze regarded her steadily for a moment, before he went out, leaving her to stare disconsolately out of the window. How could he be so concerned for Maybelle on one hand yet blatantly abuse her hospitality by seducing and compromising her daughter on the other? Obviously he had neither scruples nor conscience. The thought made her unreasonably angry and matters were not improved when he returned a few minutes later with a tray bearing two plates and two cups of tea.

'I said I did not want anything!' she began heatedly. 'I told Jinny——'

'You scarcely ate anything at dinner last night,' he observed, setting down the tray and ignoring her hostile glare. 'And if Maybelle is ill the last thing anyone needs is you fainting!'

'I never faint! And I find your "concern" for my cousin rather difficult to swallow since, not content with being the cause of her ill-health in the first place, you abuse her hospitality——'

His brows drew together sharply. 'What are you talking about?'

The narrowed eyes gleamed, and she regretted the outburst. Whatever had made her say such a thing? But she could not withdraw it now. 'I was told—that is, I understand that you and Beth——'

She got no further and broke off in a cry as his hand gripped her arm, a muscle tightening in his jaw. 'Prattling gossips,' he said in a voice harsh with anger. 'They made much mischief over a simple friendship that had no more substance than my acquaintance with the rest of the family. Circumstances warranted that I keep my distance once the wagging tongues started marriage plans for us, Miss Wyatt. I was not at liberty to disclose my reasons then and I do not intend to do so now!' He released her arm abruptly. 'I suggest you spend more time attending to your duties, and less gossiping with the servants!' He turned away, and before she could say anything the physician appeared in the doorway.

'Ah, Sullivan. She said you would be around somewhere. Miss Wyatt?' He moved to take her hand, holding it briefly as she nodded, her stomach still churning. 'Sorry we do not meet in lighter circumstances.' He was a comfortably rounded man who wore a wig and owned a deep rich voice.

She passed her tongue over dry lips and found her voice. 'How is she?'

'Tired.' He set his bag down and regarded her gravely. 'As you undoubtedly know, her heart is weak. I would go so far as to say dangerously weak. Yes, dangerously weak. Another such attack may well be her last.'

Dismayed, she chewed her lip and gave a despairing gesture. 'What can I do?'

'If you are up to the task of dealing with young Matthew, you will be doing a great deal! She is a very stubborn woman. She'll not rest more than absolutely necessary and she has refused to move into that fine new house of young John's, though we have all begged her to. Maybelle Winston,' he continued, 'will do as she wishes and put herself in an early grave despite anything I, or anyone else, may say to her.' He shrugged his shoulders. 'However, I will tell you the same as I told Miss Jaycinth. Keep her in bed as long as you can and do not let her do anything more strenuous than needlepoint. And I wish you well of the task.' He turned to Sullivan. 'Have you seen the *Gazette* this morning, Sullivan? This Tea Act business?'

'I have. God knows there have been enough rumours about it these past months.'

'And is this finally the truth of it?'

Ben shrugged non-committally. 'I hear the same rumours you do, Cornwallis.'

'Yes, but usually well in advance of anyone else,' the doctor commented drily. 'It will stir up trouble.'

'Probably. But it will be trouble long overdue.' There
was a grimness behind the words that flicked at Emma's
curiosity, but his expression was unreadable.

'Well, since I shall get nothing out of you as usual,'
the doctor complained mildly, 'I think I will go down
to the *Gazette* office. Perhaps they know more than they
have printed.'

'Then you can give me a ride in that atrocious old
carriage of yours.' Ben reached down and gulped a
mouthful of tea. 'I am going that way.'

'Be glad of the company.' He turned to Emma and
bowed rather stiffly. 'Your servant, Miss Wyatt.'

Ben followed him out with a preoccupied frown and
not so much as a nod in her direction. Heavy-hearted,
she moved away from the window, a small knot in the
pit of her stomach. Questions tumbled over one another
in her mind. Why had her careless gibe about Beth
angered him so? What would she do if anything happened to Maybelle now? Or if her illness forced her to
remove to Cedars? Why did Sullivan's curt suggestion
that she spend more time at her 'duties' rankle so much?

She had little leisure to dwell on such unsettling
thoughts amid all the comings and goings of the
morning, and her own activities with Matthew in the
nursery. John arrived, summoned from the mill, and
stayed until early afternoon when he went off to his
warehouse, considerately taking Matthew with him.
Jaycinth paced about for a while, and finally announced
that she was going to Cedars to ride Tempest. 'Mama
seems a little better,' she said, more in hope than certainty. 'Sit with her, will you? I dare say John will not
be long.'

For an hour she read to Cousin Maybelle from the
Bible she kept by the bed, and, when she drifted into
sleep, slipped quietly from the room and went downstairs. Jinny was polishing the little table. 'Shall I fetch

you a cup of tea into the parlour, Miss Emma? You look
as if you need it. Hannah will sit with the mistress.'

She accepted gratefully. The morning's news-sheet still
lay where Mr Sullivan had discarded it, and when Jinny
brought the tea she settled into the chair by the fire to
read the editorial that had caused so much concern between the two men. It concerned some scheme of the
East India Company to import tea direct from China,
but she had scarcely begun to make sense of it when
there were voices in the hall and John walked in with
Sullivan. 'How is my mother?' he demanded.

She jumped up, conscious of the heat flooding into
her cheeks at being found taking her ease. Annoyed with
herself for feeling guilty, she tilted her chin and said,
'She is sleeping. Hannah is with her. Shall I fetch you
some tea?'

John shook his head. 'Sit down, Emma. I am sure
you wish to finish your tea, and Matthew has gone to
beg scraps from Ellen and will be occupied for some
minutes, I am sure. I shall go to the kitchen myself—
Ben is in need of a packet of food to sustain him until
he reaches Dedham tonight.'

Unwilling to be left alone with Mr Sullivan after their
earlier encounter, it was with some reluctance that she
sat down again as John departed. Standing with his back
to the fire, he seemed to tower over her and she could
not think of a single thing to say to him. A surreptitious
glance through her lashes revealed that he showed no
signs of the anger he had displayed earlier. Indeed, with
his thumbs thrust casually into the top of his breeches,
he was regarding her almost quizzically. Disconcerted,
she said quickly, 'You are going to Dedham? Where is
that? Is it far?'

He shook his head. 'Ten miles, south-west. I shall be
away for a day or two, I imagine—mill business. Have
you been reading that?' He indicated the *Gazette* on the
table beside her.

'I was reading the article about the East India Company tea,' she answered, wishing she could control the erratic pounding of her heart as their eyes met fleetingly.

'And did you understand it?' he demanded mockingly. 'Or are you one of those decorative but witless females who leave politics to men?'

She bridled at his question and rose to the challenge in the crystal blue eyes. 'I am not witless, sir! I understand perfectly that you all think you are very hard done by and that you continually complain about all the taxes and import duties you have to pay. I must confess, however, that the details of petty colonial grievances have never been my main interest!' His brows drew together sharply and a look of disgust passed fleetingly across his face. Hastily she bit back her anger. Did she want to prove that she was indeed quite witless and had no understanding of what was behind the colonists' discontent? Casting her mind back to their discussion of the massacre, she realised she had said nothing to make him think otherwise.

Drawing a long breath, she made a placating gesture. 'Discussions of American politics at home were restricted to how they would affect our trade,' she explained meekly. 'I know your non-importation protests affected us quite badly and our dealings this side of the Atlantic dried up until the Act was repealed and we started to trade again.'

'Not completely repealed,' he corrected, the blue eyes gleaming. 'The duty on tea remains. Which is why most people with any conscience still refuse to drink dutied tea!' She glanced involuntarily at her half-empty cup. 'There is no duty paid on that!' he assured her, a wry smile lightening his expression. 'Though I am uncertain whether Maybelle is aware of it and I have no intention of enlightening her about its origins. Besides, I should hate to deprive Jaycinth of her grand gesture!'

As he moved from the fire, she frowned in puzzlement. His relationship with Jaycinth was hard to fathom. He did not appear to regard her with anything more than a casual affection. How could Jaycinth be so blind, and so heedless of her reputation, as to allow him to use her with such indifference?

Picking up the news-sheet, he dropped into the chair opposite her. 'Officially we import a negligible amount of tea, you know, yet we drink hundreds of chests of it every year!'

She dragged her thoughts back, but could not keep the indignation from her voice. 'And you, sir, profit handsomely!'

He shrugged indifferently. 'It avoids filling the coffers of the British with American money, and the profit is not so great.' He glanced over the *Gazette's* editorial again, and she watched the muscle along his jaw harden. 'The East India Company have made an agreement with Parliament to help them out of their financial predicament. This is what this . . .' he flicked the paper with his finger '. . . is all about. Their surplus supplies of tea can be sold direct to us—they do not have to pay middlemen in England to handle it and, although duty is paid on its importation here, they avoid paying anything to Britain. And several of our merchants—including Governor Hutchinson's sons, Thomas and Elisha—have been appointed by the Company to act as agents.' A look of disgust momentarily hardened his features. 'The scheme will probably cut the cost of tea from twenty shillings a pound to around ten.'

For a moment she said nothing, her nimble brain considering the effects of such drastic price reductions. 'If it is made so cheap even those who at present still refuse to drink it as a matter of principle will be tempted?' she suggested.

'That is very astute of you,' he commended drily, 'And it is certainly what Parliament and the East India Company hope.'

'Correct me if I am wrong, Mr Sullivan,' she went on thoughtfully, 'but will it not be cheaper than even your smuggled Dutch tea? Your profits—however modest—will suffer badly, I suspect. No wonder you are so put out——'

She was unprepared for the sudden anger that glittered in his eyes. 'You think like the rest of your countrymen, Miss Wyatt!' he accused her scornfully, and, getting to his feet, he walked to the window. 'Shortsighted, bigoted fools, most of them,' he muttered, 'who can see us as no more than a rabble complaining about taxes and wanting something for nothing!' Abruptly he turned round, and then came back to stand over her, his eyes seeming to burn into hers. 'Certainly those of us involved in the free trade are indignant, but most of us are sensitive to the underlying dangers. A few of our merchants, acting in collusion with the East India Company, could monopolise our tea trade. And where will that end? With monopolies on all our foreign trade?'

Bending his tall frame, he sat on the edge of the chair and leaned forward, warming to a subject that was obviously his passion. 'Think of the wider issues! Tea is only a part of it. Is it not absurd that we are ruled by a Parliament three thousand miles away? Decisions that need to be made within hours or days take weeks and months, and then are made by ignorant fools who cannot see what is really going on and apparently make little attempt to find out! Those decisions that are made here are made by government officers who are paid from Customhouse receipts, including tea duty. That is British money, Emma; it makes them independent of us and lackeys of the British government. So we are bound by British standards and British justice. As far as Parliament is concerned, we are merely colonists, to be taxed until we are saturated with taxes and bled of all our resources. What do we get in return? Damned little. Except more taxes, more laws and more oppression—and a garrison to keep us in line!'

He sat back in the chair with an expression of contempt darkening the handsome features. She searched for some reply, an intelligent question, but was momentarily nonplussed by his vehemence, and the blazing light of passion in his eyes. She picked up her half-empty cup, and nearly dropped it again as he gave a sudden shout of laughter. 'I am sorry, Miss Wyatt! I have thrown you into confusion!'

'Your usual pastime, Ben!' John accused him from the doorway.

'I have been educating Miss Wyatt on the subject of colonial politics.'

John threw up his hand. 'I do not intend to get into that argument! Ben is quite aggressive on the subject, Emma.' He smiled. 'And you would be advised to stay away from it in his hearing. His views have been known to border on the treasonous.'

'And John has a somewhat different outlook on things...' Ben grinned goodnaturedly at the younger man '...since he counts a number of the British soldiery among his friends...!'

Jinny tapped on the door and walked in with a tray laden with bread, cold meats and Ellen's pickled plums, and Emma excused herself to go and deal with Matthew. Every encounter with Ben Sullivan produced something else to surprise her. Now it seemed he was a fervent patriot. What else was there, she wondered, beneath that mocking, arrogant exterior? There was little enough to recommend him so far, she told herself. The man was a rogue, and only his obvious affection for Matthew redeemed him.

He was an enigma, handsome and dangerous and undeniably fascinating. Perhaps that was the reason she

·

did not sleep very well that night, despite an over-whelming tiredness. She had been up since before dawn, and at midnight was still awake, unable to dismiss the insignificant fact that in the midst of his impassioned speech he had unwittingly used her Christian name. Visions of him plagued her and would not go away, whatever else she tried to focus her drowsy mind on.

Finally she drifted into sleep, worrying what would happen to her should Maybelle fail to recover. Kit's words of advice to find a good man and get married kept coming back to her, and she slept only to dream of a succession of prospective husbands, each one worse than the last, images so disturbing that she tossed and turned in feverish panic until Ben Sullivan called her name and held out his hand...

She started up, her heart pounding and his name on her lips. It had been so real that for a moment she listened intently in the darkness. But there was nothing except the wind whispering in the trees outside. The house seemed deathly quiet. The awful vision of William Carlisle and others like him gradually receded, and she gave herself a mental shake. What a fool she was! Then, as she was settling down again, a sudden rattle against the window set her bolt upright, her breath caught in her throat.

Tentatively she pushed aside the covers and got up, creeping to the window. He was standing in the moon-light below, gesticulating violently. A shiver snaked down her spine at the sight of him, so like her dream that her hand shook as she opened the window.

'For God's sake open the kitchen door,' he hissed up at her. 'And hurry!'

Without quite knowing why, she did as he bid her un-hesitatingly, without pausing to light the candle, feeling her way down the stairs and along the passageway to the kitchen. And when she had let him in he shot the bolt on the door and said, 'Upstairs' in a tone that warned against further questions, although from his attire she guessed he had been seeing in some more contraband.

His hand on her back added to his urgency as he guided her up the stairs ahead of him. When she hesitated at the door of her room, he opened it, pushed her inside and followed her in.

'The Excise followed me,' he murmured, closing the door softly. 'They will be here in a minute.'

'I thought you were going to Dedham!' she accused him, her voice a low hiss.

'So did everyone else. At least,' he added with a wry grimace, 'that was the intention.'

'Well, you have been busy!' she taunted derisively. 'You see my brother go to New York this morning with one load, and tonight you are receiving another!'

'No, merely moving it to a safer place,' he corrected. 'It was an ill night to do it with the moon up, but there was no choice. I intended that they follow me,' he added, advancing into the room, 'since both my men and the contraband went in the other direction, but they proved rather more tenacious than normal.'

'Well, you cannot stay in here!' she whispered violently, watching in horror as he sat on the edge of the bed and tested its softness.

He looked at her reproachfully. 'That is cold comfort for a man who has had no sleep for two nights!'

'Your sleeping habits are no concern of mine, sir! You might have been better received in Jaycinth's room!' she added with a snap.

His brows drew sharply together, and the mockery faded from his eyes. 'This family knows no more than rumour tells them about my more dubious activities,' he said stiffly, 'And I have no intention——' A loud banging on the door downstairs interrupted him. Calmly he picked up her dressing robe and held it out to her. 'You will need this,' he suggested with a swift appraisal of her scantily clad figure, which was clearly defined in the moonlight.

With an embarrassed gasp, she snatched it from him and wriggled into it. At the sound of more thumping downstairs and muffled demands that they open up to His Majesty's officers, she moved to the door. He crossed the room in two strides and barred her way, grasping her wrist. 'Wait.' He looked down and held her gaze. 'And do not underestimate me, should it cross your mind to alert them to my presence.'

A strange tremor ran over her as he held her mesmerised. 'I would not do that,' she murmured, not realising, for a moment, that she had even spoken.

'No,' he said softly, 'I rather thought not.' Someone else finally obliged the irate officers and he opened the door for her.

Jaycinth emerged from her room at the same time, muttering sleepily, and Emma followed her downstairs, absently rubbing her wrist where Sullivan had held it and trying to still a trembling that had nothing to do with the cold. The hall was illuminated by the candle which Ellen held aloft in the open doorway, where two men were demanding to search the house.

'You will not!' Jaycinth's scathing voice cut into Ellen's protest and she waved away Hannah to go and reassure her mistress. 'My mother is very ill and I will not have her frightened or intimidated at this hour of the night! What is all this about?'

'Miss Winston, we followed Ben Sullivan half across town——'

'Whatever for?'

'We believe he has been involved in importing goods with the intention of avoiding payment of duty,' came the pompous reply.

'What nonsense! He went to Dedham this afternoon on mill business for my brother. Obviously you were mistaken, gentlemen, and I would suggest that as you have now wasted several minutes here you will not catch the unfortunate fellow you were chasing anyway.'

Both men grew visibly uncertain under the confident scorn of her green eyes, and within a few minutes took themselves off, conceding that she was probably right and complaining bitterly at having lost their quarry, doubtless to the warmth of a woman's bed.

Jaycinth despatched Ellen to explain the disturbance to Maybelle and, roundly condemning all such lackeys of the government, went back to bed. Emma, satisfying herself that Matthew still slept, returned to her own room, hoping Sullivan had somehow disappeared.

But he was lying stretched out on the bed, his hands linked behind his head and a pistol by his side. Arrogantly confident, he had lit the candle, its flickering light illuminating his face. Her heart seemed to miss a beat and her throat went dry. 'You can leave now,' she whispered huskily, walking to the window. 'They have gone.'

Regarding her through half-closed eyes, he shook his head. 'They will be waiting around the corner, lurking in some shadow. I shall have to stay at least till dawn.' He patted the bed beside him. Would you care to join me?' There was laughter in the blue eyes and a teasing challenge behind the words.

'Go away!' she hissed angrily, aware that Jaycinth was probably still wakeful in the room next door. 'Before someone hears you!'

For a long moment he lay there looking at her, his eyes raking her up and down, taking in every curve and contour beneath the robe and nightgown, clearly imagining what he could not see. She felt her cheeks glow warm and moved away from the window. 'Go away!' she insisted.

Reluctantly he sat up and swung his legs around. 'Well, perhaps another time.' Getting to his feet with a sigh, he thrust the pistol back into his belt and looked at her with a speculative gleam in his eyes. 'You are very tempting when you are angry,' he said softly. And, reaching out, he pulled her towards him and kissed her.

She stood quite still as his mouth moved over hers, gently persuasive, his tongue teasing her lips apart and probing her mouth. She seemed powerless to stop him as the resistance drained out of her. A tingling shiver snaked through her, crystallising into a warm, liquid sensation as his hand moved slowly down over her shoulder, brushing aside the robe and lingering over her breast, burning through the flimsy nightgown.

With a gasp, she tore her mouth free and abruptly thrust him away, her cheeks flaming and her whole body shaking. 'If you seek to seduce me, sir,' she whispered hoarsely, 'and add me to your list of conquests, you will be sorely disappointed!'

'I wonder.' With a slow smile, he let his gaze slide down over her. 'It would be interesting to prove you wrong...'

'Get out before I scream!' she threatened fiercely, and walked quickly to the door.

He inclined his head with an amused quirk of his mouth, enjoying himself immensely. 'Certainly, temptress, for I should hate to put you to so much trouble!' Then, in almost a single movement, he threw open the window, climbed through and dropped out of sight.

She gasped. The fool! It was a terrifying drop! Rushing to the window, she looked down, half-expecting to see his crumpled body on the ground below. But there was no sign of him. Her knees went weak with relief, and she went back to bed, her heart pounding. Snuffing the candle, she lay for a long time in the darkness, her thoughts in a whirl. She ought to be furious, but she could not whip up enough anger. Damn the man! He had put her in such a confusion that she scarcely knew whether to be flattered or insulted by his half-hearted attempt at seduction! The sheer audacity of him—and the arrogance! And yet her lips still tingled at the memory of his kiss, his hand upon her breast——

She cut the thought off abruptly. She would *not* fall prey to his compliments and kisses and luring charms. Jaycinth might have succumbed but she was not so easy a victim. Neither was she a fool. An involvement with him had very little to offer as far as she could see except a great deal of heartache and the ruin of her reputation and any chance of finding a respectable husband. Ben Sullivan would have to look elsewhere for a new bedfellow.

She would have liked to forget the whole incident— or at least push it to the back of her mind and refuse to think about it. But he was not an easy man to forget or ignore and the next morning the servants were full of the night's interruption and speculating freely on whether or not it had indeed been Mr Sullivan whom the officers were chasing.

Even closeted in the nursery she could not concentrate on Matthew's letters and so preoccupied was she that she did not hear the commotion downstairs until Jinny put her head round the door and whispered, 'I thought I'd better tell you, Miss Emma. Mistress Ann's just arrived and she's brought her trunk!'

'Her trunk?' Emma stared at her blankly.

'She says she's going to stay until the mistress is better,' the girl confided, casting a swift glance over her shoulder. 'And just when we'd got used to only having one mistress here!'

'Jinny!' The admonishment was wasted, for the girl had ducked out again and Emma was left staring at the closed door with a sinking heart. She was no craven but it seemed advisable to keep out of Ann's way as far as possible, and Ann evidently had the same notion because she sent up a tray at noon with the message that Emma should take her meals in the nursery or in her room.

'It's not right!' Jinny was indignant as she set down the tray. 'If the mistress knew——'

Emma put a hand on her arm and smiled. 'Do not mention it to her, Jinny. She must not be distressed and it does not signify. In truth...' she lowered her voice with a glance at Matthew '... I shall prefer his company to Mistress Ann's.'

The maid's troubled face cleared. 'Well, there's that for it, I suppose. But it's not right...'

Halfway through the afternoon, with Matthew happily engaged in the yard with Jack, and Jaycinth and Ann taking tea in the parlour, Emma sat with Cousin Maybelle reading quietly to her while she drifted in and out of sleep, the bluish tinge faded from her lips but her breathing still ragged and uneven. Suddenly a muffled cry and a splintering crash shattered the hush of the house and brought Emma to her feet. Maybelle flinched but did not wake and Emma left the room swiftly to investigate.

A frozen tableau met her gaze as she started down the stairs. Jinny was standing amid a pile of broken crockery with Matthew cowering at her feet, staring white-faced at Ann, who was glaring furiously at him from the parlour doorway. 'You wretched child!' she cried. 'Look what you have done!'

Seeing Emma, Matthew scrambled to his feet and burst out 'I didn't mean to! I was coming to find you and——'

'He bumped right into me!' Jinny exclaimed, bending down to collect the larger shards.

'You will clear it up immediately!' Ann ordered Matthew angrily, before turning her glittering gaze on Emma. 'If you cannot control this boy and prevent him from running wild all over the house, I shall be forced to find someone who can! Kindly keep him upstairs where he belongs!'

'He's only a child!' she protested hotly, running down the remaining stairs. 'It was obviously an accident. There is no need to——'

'How dare you be so insolent? Clear this mess up at once!' And with a look of icy contempt she swung round and went back into the parlour.

Emma let out a breath in a little sigh of annoyance, and turned to hold out her hand to Matthew. 'We shall ask Ellen for a broom.' She smiled reassuringly. 'It will only take a minute.' Matthew's hand gripped hers tightly and her dislike of Ann deepened. He was clearly terrified of her. Had she always treated him so harshly? No wonder Maybelle had wished to remain here and keep him with her.

He stayed close to her for what remained of the day and the following morning, anxious to further dissolve his distrust, she went in search of Ann and found her going through the week's menus with Ellen. 'Would it be possible to have the use of the carriage for an hour this afternoon?' she asked, swallowing her pride and injecting a note of deference into her voice.

'For what reason?' Ann's brows arched upwards.

'I should like to take Matthew out, perhaps on to the Common. He would benefit from the fresh air and exercise, and I am sure he would settle more readily to quieter pursuits in the house if he were allowed time to expend his energy outdoors.'

A long look of mutual dislike hung in the air between them. 'Very well.' Immediately the brief consent was uttered, Ann turned back to the menus, dismissing her.

Irrationally feeling as though she had won a small victory, Emma hastened back to the nursery. 'We'll make a kite,' she declared, remembering how James had made one for her when she was a child little older than Matthew was now. 'I'm sure Ellen will have some fabric and string.'

The project threatened to fail at the first hurdle when Jack could not produce any wood suitable enough, and she stood in the yard wondering how to get around the problem when Ben Sullivan arrived on a huge, beautifully proportioned black horse.

'Mr Sullivan might find you somethin' at the mill,' Jack suggested helpfully.

'What might I find?' he demanded, springing to the ground with the ease and agility of a cat.

Suppressing a reluctance to ask him for anything, she outlined her plan to make a kite. 'But I have promised to take him on the Common this afternoon and he has set his heart on having the kite finished.'

'A kite? And you know how to make such a thing?' He looked at her with a mocking respect. 'Well, I am on my way to the warehouse. There are always odd splinters of wood lying around. I will see what I can find. I called in to see if Matthew wished to go with me.'

'As to that, you must ask Mistress Ann.'

He looked at her for a moment. 'John said she was staying here for a few days.' His eyes regarded her steadily, as though he was trying to judge her reaction to Ann's descent upon them, but she carefully kept her face expressionless. 'I think I'll leave Matthew to you for now,' he went on. 'But if I find what you need I will be back later.' He flashed her that disarming smile. 'Perhaps I will join you on the Common to see if it flies!'

'Of course it will fly!' she responded with spirit. 'Unless you supply me with only oak or elm!'

'Only the lightest cedar!' he promised, and she watched with a curdling in her stomach as he hauled his long, muscular body back into the saddle.

When he returned, some two hours later, she and Matthew were happily engaged tying bows of pink silk on to a long length of twine for the kite's tail. The door snapped open and she twisted her head round to see him standing in the doorway bearing a laden tray, a quiver of amusement playing around his mouth at the sight of her sprawling so inelegantly on the floor.

Damn him! Feeling the warmth of an embarrassed flush staining her cheeks, she scrambled to her feet and glared at him. Matthew sprang forward and tugged at the wooden diamond dangling from his arm. 'Is this it? Is this for our kite?'

'Wait!' he protested. 'You'll upset your luncheon all over the floor and then I shall be in trouble.'

'*I'm* already in trouble!' he declared proudly, waiting while Ben set down the tray and disengaged the frame from his arm. 'I broke all the plates yesterday but Emma shouted at Aunt Ann and——'

'I did nothing of the sort!'

'Is that why you are confined to the nursery?' The blue eyes rested on her speculatively. 'Jinny said——'

'Jinny says a good deal too much!' she snapped. 'And I am not confined to the nursery.' Turning away from the too-perceptive gaze, she began to rummage in a pile of fabric scraps.

'As I have nothing to attend to this afternoon that cannot wait,' he went on, 'I shall come and watch you fly your kite. But for now...' He paused. 'I am invited to lunch—downstairs.' Smiling blandly at the look she threw at him, he turned for the door.

As he did so, it opened abruptly and Ann walked in. After a brief glance at Ben she turned to Emma. 'I have need of the carriage this afternoon after all, Emma. I am sorry, but Jaycinth and I have a call to make. I am afraid your little excursion will have to wait.'

Disgust brought an angry protest to her lips as young Matthew's face fell into a mask of disappointment. She had done it on purpose! To hurt Matthew, or to spite her, it did not much matter; the result was the same. Seething, she fought down the impulse to give vent to her feelings and clenched her fists impotently in the folds of her skirts as a look of satisfaction passed fleetingly across Ann's face.

'Well, he will just have to come up on Blade with me,' Ben said quietly and although Emma could not see the look he gave Ann there must have been displeasure in it for she lifted her chin defensively. He turned to Matthew and cheerfully ruffled the boy's hair. 'We cannot have you missing the enjoyment of flying Miss Wyatt's kite!'

Despite Matthew's whoop of pleasure and her own reluctant rush of gratitude, she could not help an exclamation of dismay. 'Not that animal you were riding earlier? It's not safe for him!'

'Your concern does you credit, Miss Wyatt, but he will come to no harm, I promise.'

She turned to Ann, raising her eyebrows in silent query, reminding her that responsibility was ultimately hers. Ann waved a hand dismissively. 'I know you will take care of him, Ben. Shall we return to the parlour?' And, linking her hand through his arm, she bore him out of the nursery.

'Oh, wretched woman!' she gritted through her teeth, her nails digging into her palms. And, as she took out her anger on the stitches she stabbed into the blue silk stretched across the cedar frame, she wondered despairingly how much longer she would be able to hold her temper in check. Sooner or later, she reflected grimly, Mistress Ann was going to discover that no Wyatt would be treated with such contempt for long without retaliating!

CHAPTER FIVE

EMMA was in the kitchen helping Jinny and Ellen when Matthew burst in, flushed and triumphant and scarcely able to contain his glee. 'It was wonderful!' he cried. 'It went up and up and up—and right over the trees and then it got caught in the branches and Ben had to climb up to get it and——'

'He did *what*?' A gurgle of laughter bubbled up in her at the thought of Ben Sullivan climbing trees on the Common.

'Oh, he never did!' Jinny exclaimed with a giggle.

'I most certainly did!' Ben walked in with the kite in his hand, and shot Jinny a reproachful look. 'I am not yet too old to climb trees, child, and anyway...' he flicked his gaze to Emma '...we did not dare return without it!'

The happy mood was infectious. 'I should think not!' she rejoined, and added with some satisfaction, 'I told you it would fly.'

'Certainly you did,' he agreed, 'but then...' he examined the kite with a gleam of mischief in his eyes '...the frame is just the right size and weight.'

'A frame on its own is not a kite!' she declared, refusing to let him get away with that. 'It requires silk stretched across and expertly stitched in place if it is not to come apart at the first gust of wind. And a tail the correct length——'

'And a kite will not fly without wind, Miss Wyatt, and someone to fly it who knows how. To say nothing of an ability to climb trees!'

76

'I certainly know how to fly a kite,' she assured him with feeling, 'and if necessary I am quite capable of climbing trees!' Almost as soon as the words were out, she wished she could snatch them back, for his eyebrows rose and a speculative gleam crept into his eyes.

'I am sure you are,' he murmured. 'And I confess I should enjoy the sight immensely!' Her cheeks flamed with heat and he relented and composed his features. 'But you will have to concede that a lack of wind could have defeated both our efforts.'

'I concede that much willingly,' she agreed, and, in an effort to still the fluttering in her stomach, turned to Ellen. 'Is there any tea left, Ellen? I am sure Mr Sullivan is in need of reviving after such a strenuous afternoon——' She broke off and looked up at him. 'Unless you would prefer something stronger? I am afraid Ann is not back yet but I am sure you are used to helping yourself——'

He shook his head and said wickedly, 'I have a great fondness for tea, Miss Wyatt! But I insist you join me——'

'I'm sorry, but, with Hannah upstairs with Cousin Maybelle, I am needed to help here.'

'Oh, no, Miss Emma,' Ellen interrupted. 'You go along with Mr Sullivan. He can't sit in the parlour by himself and I can't get anything done with a kitchen full of bodies.'

'May I have an oatcake, please?' Matthew pleaded, eyeing the tray of fat biscuits on the table.

'You get along with Miss Emma and I'll see what I've got to spare.'

Matthew flung himself on the couch beside Emma, munching his oatcake and excitedly recounting the kite's adventures and demanding when they could go again.

'Soon,' she promised. 'When your aunt does not need the carriage. Why don't you take the kite upstairs now?

She will be back soon and she will not like to see it in here.'

'He seems to have taken to you,' Mr Sullivan remarked when the trailing silk bows had disappeared through the doorway.

'I hope so. I have grown fond of him.'

He regarded her thoughtfully for a moment. 'Is Ann making life difficult for you?'

The sudden seriousness of the question surprised her. 'Not at all,' she lied cheerfully. 'Matthew and I keep out of her way as much as possible—which has allowed us to get to know each other better. He is a very lively and intelligent child. And,' she added with a smile, 'I have learned to keep a better guard on my tongue since our first encounter.'

He raised an eyebrow. 'Apart from defending Matthew?'

She shrugged. 'I did nothing but protest that she was being a little harsh on him. He seems terrified of her.'

'He has a child's instinct in such matters. She does not like children and has no idea how to deal with them. Whereas you, I suspect, have a natural ability in that direction.'

A flush warmed her cheeks, much to her chagrin. 'If that is true,' she murmured diffidently, 'I have no idea where it comes from. I have had little experience of children.'

'You have hidden talents, Miss Wyatt.'

The smiling gaze that held hers so steadily sent disturbing tremors through her veins. Did he approve of her? Was he flirting with her? What was he thinking of behind those penetrating eyes?

The sounds of a carriage outside brought her back to earth. Ann would not be best pleased to find her entertaining him alone like this. But she was there at his invitation and she would not be intimidated. It would give her no small satisfaction to see Ann put out. So she settled back and smiled at him. 'I am afraid my talents are limited. I had little in the way of tutoring in the feminine accomplishments and a simple tune on the harpsichord is all I can manage.'

'I am sure you underestimate yourself,' he replied gallantly. 'Besides, there are other talents besides those accepted in fashionable drawing-rooms——'

Ann walked in and took in the cosy scene at a glance. 'Ben, I am glad you waited for us!' she exclaimed. 'I trust you enjoyed indulging the little boy in you this afternoon?'

'Of course! I have just been telling Miss Wyatt that she makes an excellent kite. A pity she could not see it.'

Ann turned her icy gaze on Emma. 'It was good of you to entertain Mr Sullivan in our absence, Emma,' she said frostily, 'but you may return to your duties now.'

'I do not believe she has quite finished her tea,' he pointed out smoothly.

Ann opened her mouth to say something and then shut it again, compressing her lips. She sat down, folded her hands in her lap and waited. Jaycinth murmured something about seeing how her mother was and disappeared, leaving Emma to finish her tea as slowly as she dared, avoiding the gleam of amusement in Mr Sullivan's eyes. He continued to extol the virtues of her kite, and praised her for the change that was already apparent in Matthew—even going so far as to seek Ann's agreement that Maybelle was very fortunate she had agreed to stay.

He was obviously enjoying himself at Ann's expense, but the sight of that young lady struggling with her temper beneath all this praise for someone she disliked intensely and thought scarcely fit even for the role of nursemaid was so rewarding that she forgave him for using her to do it.

Finally she set down her cup and rose. 'I must see what has become of Matthew,' she said as he too got to his feet. 'Thank you for taking him, Mr Sullivan. I should not have liked to see him disappointed.'

'It was my pleasure, Miss Wyatt.'

She found Matthew still playing with his kite in the nursery. That toy had dissolved any lingering remnants of distrust, and as they conspired together during that week to keep out of Ann's way he began to focus on her the love and trust he so badly needed to express, and in the process crept inexorably into her heart.

Although the time she spent in the nursery kept her pleasantly occupied, she failed to prevent Ben Sullivan intruding upon her thoughts. It annoyed her to think that, despite her resolve, she was unable to prevent the treacherous quivering of her stomach or the quickening of her blood whenever she saw him. And in the following days he came several times to the house. She was not safe even in the nursery, for he always had something for Matthew and would appear without warning, setting her heart pounding. Keeping the pleasure from her expression and the warmth from her voice was far more of a struggle than she would have liked. But she was too sensible, too awake to her own vulnerability at the moment to fall under the spell of a pair of piercing blue eyes, a lazy half-smile and a few careless compliments.

Yet it would have helped had he not found so many reasons to call at the house: to deliver a message for Ann from John, or to take Matthew with him on an errand to do with the mill, or simply to enquire after Maybelle. He, who was no relative at all, seemed more anxious for her well-being than her own son. Indeed, his concern for her, and his affection for Matthew, nagged at her thoughts, as though there was something here that was not quite right.

'A real gentleman,' was Ellen's verdict. 'Despite what people say about him. Not so high and mighty as some and always a kind word for us. Oh, his morals might

not be all they should be, but he's got a way with him . . .
A real gentleman, Mr Sullivan, and don't you let no one
tell you any different.'

He might be a respectable gentleman by day, Emma
thought wryly, their encounter in her bedchamber still
vivid in her memory, but at night he was something quite
different. By moonlight, Ben Sullivan was handsome and
dangerous, a rebel and a rogue. And as for his morals,
she could only speculate . . .

She was speculating on that very subject the evening
after the kite's success, and failing to keep her attention
on the Boston news-sheet she was attempting to read.
Ann had gone to bed with a headache, leaving the two
girls alone in the parlour, and after a little while Jaycinth,
who had been playing idly on the harpsichord, abruptly
stopped. 'What are you reading?'

Emma looked up. 'An article about the East India
Company tea.'

'Oh, that. I think it's disgraceful.'

'Mr Sullivan gave me a lecture on the subject,' she
smiled.

'He would!' The younger girl swivelled round on the
stool and eyed her thoughtfully. 'I do not hate the
British, you know. Merely the soldiers they keep here to
watch us. And the way they refuse to allow us any say
in matters that affect us.'

Emma hid a faint smile at the echo of Sullivan's views.
It was Jaycinth, she had discovered, who sent Jack out
to fetch the many newspapers and periodicals Boston
boasted, and was an avid reader of them all. She could
not help but wonder if her belief in colonial self-rule had
more to do with Ben's influence than any real interest
in politics.

'I have not been very friendly, have I?' Jaycinth got
up and came to sit beside her. 'I'm sorry. Do you—think
we might be friends?'

Emma smiled readily. 'Of course!'

'Ann has behaved badly, too, I don't understand it. She is not usually so abrasive.' She pulled a face. 'I do not know why she had to come here, anyway. I am perfectly capable of running the house while Mama is ill.'

'Perhaps,' Emma suggested placatingly, 'she does not like to think that you can manage without her guidance.'

Jaycinth smiled and visibly relaxed. 'Yes, of course you are right! It's just that she is so—irritating sometimes!'

The ice, once broken, melted rapidly and they spent the evening in somewhat unfeminine discussion about the rights and wrongs of colonial grievances.

Unwilling though she was to admit it, Ben's speech had lit a spark of interest and over the following days she became as eager a reader of the news-sheets as Jaycinth. Articles on the subject of the tea argued every which way, with the Hutchinsons and the Clarkes—most notable among the merchants involved in the scheme—bearing the brunt of the criticism.

'The Clarkes have always been pro-British,' Jaycinth told her disparagingly. 'The Customhouse is full of their tea. They probably pay the salaries of half the officials in Boston on their own. The Governor's sons cannot be expected to do anything else and Faneuil and the rest involved in this will follow where the others lead!'

'No one likes taxes,' Emma conceded, 'but surely you agree America has to give something in return for the security and protection offered by Britain? I can't believe independence is a serious proposition. How could you survive?'

'Not total independence, perhaps, but at least some real say in how we are governed. "No taxation without representation"!' she quoted. 'Why should we Americans constantly bend to British domination?'

Emma had to admit a certain sympathy for the colonists' position and could quite understand how galling it must be to be ruled by such a distant Parliament. It was easy to imagine, reading the inflammatory news-letters and bills Jack secretly brought in, how minor injustices such as the tea could be blown up into something far more symbolic and serious than they really were. While correspondents on the pages of one publication argued that there was little point making a noise over these particular shipments of tea when dutied tea and other commodities had been coming in virtually unchallenged for years, patriots on the pages of others made vehement demands for the tea to be sent back as soon as it arrived, or else burnt. And warnings about monopolisation and rising prices came from the merchants not chosen as agents for the Company and the whole discussion quickly became very heated.

An awful lot of bad feeling, Emma thought, is being whipped up over a few chests of tea. No wonder the government thought fit to keep a small garrison here. This latter, however, was one thought she wisely kept to herself!

In little over a week Maybelle was well enough to insist that Ann should return to Cedars, which, fortunately, she was finally persuaded to do. And almost immediately Jaycinth resumed her habit of going there every afternoon to ride her beloved Tempest. After one such outing, she breezed into the parlour waving an invitation aloft.

'For the soirée!' she announced. 'They delayed it a week because of Mama, but now that she is recovering...' She pulled off her cloak. 'Half the town will be invited. Do you think we shall go?'

Emma, having quite forgotten about it, looked at her in surprise. 'I doubt your Mama will be well enough.'

'No, of course not. But you and I——'

'Not I!' she disclaimed.

'Oh, I know what Ann said. But John insisted. He said it would not look right, and he had it from Dr Cornwallis that there is now no immediate danger for

Mama. Ellen can look to Matthew and Jack can ride to Cedars—or to the physician—in no time if necessary——'

'You should perhaps ask first,' Emma interrupted, putting a sobering caution into the other girl's exuberance. 'In any event I shall not go. I shall remain with your mother.'

Maybelle, however, with a return of her usual spirit, had different ideas. 'We shall all go! 'Tis just what I need to liven my spirits again.'

The two girls exchanged horrified glances. 'But Dr Cornwallis will never allow it, Mama!'

'I am sure "enlivening the spirit" goes against everything he has ordered!' Emma protested.

'Nevertheless, I intend to go, if only to keep an eye on that impossible minx John has married! And I should much prefer to die on my feet enjoying myself and not expire of boredom in my bed, thank you!' She turned to Emma. 'What do you say, my dear? Shall you enjoy meeting some of our finest citizens? I wonder if Madame Leclerc can be persuaded to finish your evening gown in time?'

'There is no need for that,' Emma assured her hastily. 'I can easily make do with what I have. But I really do not think——'

'Now, Emma, if you are going to argue with me, I shall become quite out of temper with you! And Cornwallis was adamant that I should not be upset!' This artful ruse succeeded and Emma subsided into thoughtful silence.

A soirée would be a welcome diversion, she had to admit, besides being a perfect opportunity for her to assess the possibilities of finding a man of modest means to marry! And hard on the heels of this thought came another. Ben Sullivan would doubtless be there...

*   *   *

Cedars was lit by dozens of candles and crowded with people when they arrived. Though 'half the town' proved to be an exaggeration there was certainly a crush and John led them immediately to the comparative quiet of the parlour and ensconced them in seats in a corner.

'*I* am not convalescent!' Jaycinth protested peevishly, dazzling in cream and ivory silk that shimmered as she walked.

'Then you may wander at will,' he told her. 'There are card tables in the library if you care to watch some of our more distinguished gamblers, refreshments are laid out in the back parlour, and in a little while a group of travelling players from Philadelphia will be performing a short play in the drawing-room—until which time the harpsichord is at the disposal of anyone who cares to entertain! In the meantime, I shall tell young Charles Arnold where to find you, my dear sister, since he has been enquiring.'

Jaycinth groaned and grimaced at Emma behind her mother's back. Her sparkling attire had won Maybelle's approval as being sufficient to jolt Charles into thoughts of marriage. 'I should not mind so much,' she had confided to Emma as they left the house earlier, 'if he did not have almost as many Redcoats for friends as John!'

'Only one or two officers, dear,' Maybelle chided gently over her shoulder. 'That is all.'

One such officer accompanied Mr Arnold into the parlour a few minutes later, fair-haired and gleaming in the scarlet coat and white breeches of the British Army.

'I am surprised to see you here, Captain Hunt,' Jaycinth exclaimed when the necessary introductions had been made for Emma's benefit. 'I should have thought you were better employed pursuing rebels and smugglers!' Her dislike was ill-concealed and earned her a frown from her mother. 'Or do you seek them here,' she went on, unperturbed, 'in parlours and drawing-rooms?'

'It is not a pastime that amuses me, Miss Winston, I assure you,' the captain told her, apparently unmoved. 'I prefer gentler sport.'

'Indeed? Then I am sure you and my cousin will deal very well together.' She walked away, leaving Emma feeling faintly aggrieved at such an unwarranted remark.

'I apologise for my daughter's manners, Captain Hunt,' said Maybelle. 'I fear she is a little out of sorts this evening.'

'No apology is necessary, ma'am.' The captain smiled as he answered, his voice revealing the faintest trace of a Scots accent.

'Will you excuse me?' Charles Arnold, seeing his mother advancing on them, went after Jaycinth, and while Maybelle was engaged in conversation with Mistress Arnold Captain Hunt turned to Emma.

'What brings you to Boston, Miss Wyatt?' he asked with a smile as he seated himself beside her.

'A disagreement with my brother on the subject of my marriage, sir,' she explained briefly. 'I am afraid I could not bring myself to agree with his choice.'

'Ah.' He looked at her with a sharper eye, but did not give in to his curiosity. 'Well, Plymouth's loss is most certainly Boston's gain. I hope you intend to stay here?'

'I believe I will, Captain. Mistress Winston has been very kind to me. Indeed, there is little enough to tempt me back and a great deal to encourage me to stay.' She cast down her eyes with deceptive meekness and peeked up at him through her lashes, excusing herself with the thought that if she were to secure any man's interest she would have to flirt a little. 'And from the little I have seen of the town itself I believe it is not so very different from Plymouth that I should be overly homesick.' He was also handsome and charming, and if she was looking for a husband it could not hurt to start with a captain!

'Oh, there is the river and the busy harbour to be compared, certainly,' he agreed. 'But, with respect, I think that when you have been here longer you will find it a very different sort of town.'

Something in his tone made her ask, 'You do not like Boston?'

'On the contrary. With no family ties in England—or even Scotland where I was born—I thought to make my home here. But...' he lowered his voice a little '...as an army officer life is not altogether as congenial as it might be. Many of the townspeople are resentful of the garrison here and there is a great deal of bad feeling directed towards us.'

'I have already come to realise that, Captain. And to learn a little of the politics of this place. I confess to a sinful ignorance.'

'Oh, well, there are a few extremists preaching revolution and principles are everything. There is always a lot of hot air in Boston about something or other, and the latest is the news about the tea, of course. And if there are protests in New York and Philadelphia about it the patriots of Boston will not wish to be left out. But then...' he broke off with a smile '...'tis not a subject to concern a pretty young lady.'

'I thank you for the compliment, Captain,' she murmured, and looked up to meet his gaze, 'but we are not all empty headed. I am interested. I have been reading the newspapers and it seems to me that it is becoming a fairly major issue for a great many of the people here. Do you think it might cause trouble?'

There was a glimmer of something that might have been a deepening interest in his eyes before he shrugged and said, 'If tempers get frayed and extremists like Sam Adams stir the pot sufficiently, anything could happen. But I doubt it. The people most likely to be upset are those smuggling Indian tea via Holland. China tea is arguably far better and will be cheaper if this scheme succeeds!'

Charles Arnold returned then, to bear the captain off to the card tables. 'Forgive me, Miss Wyatt,' he said, 'but there are one or two friends anxious to take a few hands of whist or roll the dice. Sullivan's among them, Alex, and you'll want your revenge, no doubt!'

A strange expression played briefly across the captain's face, but it was gone in an instant and he had risen and was bowing over her hand. 'Beauty and an inquisitive mind,' he murmured. 'I hope we may have an opportunity to speak again.'

She smiled absently. The mention of Ben Sullivan had quickened her pulse, and she found herself looking for him every time someone entered the room, despite the knowledge that he was playing cards in the library.

Ann flitted around her guests, pausing only briefly to enquire if Maybelle needed anything, and, but for a haughty glance over Emma's attire, ignored her completely. Which made Emma glad that there had been no time for the seamstress to finish her evening gown and she was dressed in an uncluttered gown of russet and cream.

Jaycinth returned in a little while to announce, 'The players are about to begin. Though I doubt it will be better entertainment than we have seen at the cards. Ben has won a handsome sum off Captain Hunt—and Charles says he is still furious about losing that black horse!'

'Ben should not gamble so much,' Maybelle commented disapprovingly.

'Why not? He has the devil's own luck in everything. Shall you come and watch the players, Mama?'

She declined, but insisted that Emma should go. 'I shall be very well here, enjoying the gossip,' she assured her.

All the seats that had been arranged in a semicircle in one half of the large drawing-room were occupied and most of the remaining guests crowded in behind. Charles assured them of at least space to breathe, and Emma found Captain Hunt beside her. She thought he looked a little less congenial than earlier—there was a grimness about his mouth—but he smiled when he saw her and his features relaxed slightly. As the players began, her eyes scanned the room, and found Ben standing by the window on the far side, devastating in dove-grey waistcoat and breeches, and a white shirt with lace at neck and wrist. Her heart missed a beat. She could not help herself; he was so handsome and aroused treacherous excitement in her veins that would not be put down, whatever common sense told her.

The man beside her had followed her gaze. 'So you, too, fall victim to Ben Sullivan,' he murmured.

She started, dismayed. 'Oh, no!' she began in some confusion even as she silently admitted the truth of it. But she drew a steadying breath. 'I am not easily moved by such fickle charm as his, Captain,' she whispered, sounding far more certain than she felt. 'If half what is said of him is true, I am well warned to guard my heart!'

He nodded. 'I imagine that if you believe a half of it you will come somewhere near the truth! But his reputation for gambling and...charming the ladies serves him well, for half the town promotes it. I have known him be in two women's beds at the same hour, half the town apart—an impossibility even for him!' He broke off and gave an apologetic smile. 'Forgive my plain speaking, Miss Wyatt. But I find the man's total disregard for both law and morality quite galling.'

'I am sure that is quite understandable,' she murmured. And it was tempting to suggest that perhaps Mr Sullivan's reputation for success in gambling was not so exaggerated! But she thought better of it and turned her attention to the play. She could not, however, prevent herself from glancing across the room occasionally, once or twice finding Sullivan watching her, frowning, and it annoyed her to think of his sitting in judgement of her simply because she was having a conversation with a British officer, his adversary.

When the play was done, she caught sight of Ann making her way to Ben's side, and the way she held herself and the tilt of her head as she laughed up at him were clear indications of what she was saying—at least with her body, if not her words!

'Why does she behave so badly?' she whispered to Jaycinth. 'Why does John permit it?'

'It was Ben she wanted to marry,' Jaycinth whispered back. 'But he would have none of her—though I could not swear to it that he didn't bed her once or twice before she finally married John.'

'Jaycinth!'

The younger girl ignored the hushed exclamation and went on, 'And as for John . . .' She shrugged. 'Too much opposition is likely to make her worse and I imagine he knows well enough that Ben would not make a fool of him.'

As Charles drew her away, Emma marvelled at her indifference, her ability to let Sullivan into her bed without apparently caring very much how many other women had succumbed to his seduction before her. Could Ann, too, be numbered among his conquests? Had every woman in Boston fallen victim to his insatiable appetite?

Captain Hunt touched her arm. 'Would you care for some refreshment, Miss Wyatt? If you will allow me . . .'

'Oh, yes, please.' She was beginning to find the heat of the room, and her thoughts, rather uncomfortable. A glass of lemon water, or even wine, would be welcome. But before she could say anything further Ben, having extricated himself from Ann, came towards them on his way out, and paused.

'Good evening, Emma. I trust you are enjoying yourself?'

Her heart quivered, despite herself, at the sound of her name on his lips and her voice was brittle. 'Thank you, yes.'

'I believe Mistress Winston has come this evening, despite everything.' His own voice sounded taut. 'Allow me to escort you back to her.'

'Thank you,' she forced out again, her eyes gleaming with anger at his peremptory tone. 'But Captain Hunt has just suggested a little refreshment and——'

'Then I shall be happy to relieve him of the task.'

'I believe you have relieved me of quite enough of late, Sullivan,' the captain said darkly, and offered her his arm. She hesitated for a fraction of a second, as her heart leapt treacherously. But she must make it clear to him that she would not fall victim either to his dubious charms or his arrogance, and she put her hand lightly on the red sleeve. As they walked away, his eyes burned into her back, and she acknowledged a tiny glow of satisfaction.

'Would you care for a little air?' the captain suggested, smiling down at her. 'I believe it would not be improper,' he added reassuringly as she hesitated. 'There seem to be a great many people wandering the garden!'

She agreed readily, infinitely preferring his company to that of the older ladies gathered in the parlour to gossip. He proved a charming and gallant companion, sufficiently concerned for her reputation not to venture far from the open doors and lighted windows. He kept up a steady flow of easy conversation and she found herself telling him the story of her life without learning very much at all about him.

The chill of the night air was beginning to make her shiver, and she was about to suggest they return inside when, somehow, an uneven patch of ground caught her unawares, and turned her ankle. She stumbled and would have fallen, but for the swift support of his arms that caught her up and steadied her. His hands tightened about her waist, holding her closer than was strictly necessary once she had regained her balance, his voice full of gentle concern. 'Are you hurt? Let me see...'

Ben Sullivan, coming in search of her, came upon a scene that could only lead him to one conclusion: that Alex Hunt either had just kissed her, or was just about to. He could not blame the man. She seemed unaware that the colour of the gown perfectly complemented her own golden colouring, or that the simple narrow hoop accentuated her slender figure. The swift stab of annoyance he felt at Hunt's lingering hands on her waist put an edge in his voice as he strode towards them. 'Emma, your cousin is ready to leave.'

'Thank you.' She disengaged herself from Captain Hunt's hold, conscious that disapproval smouldered in Ben's eyes. 'Will you excuse me, Captain?'

'Of course.' He took her hand and raised it to his lips. 'We will meet again soon—perhaps I shall call on you.'

Aware of Ben's frowning gaze, she smiled back. 'I will look forward to it. Goodnight, Captain.'

Ben's hand at her elbow guided her back to the house. 'You would do as well to avoid him,' he said in uncompromising tone.

'Thank you.' She smiled brightly, annoyance gleaming in her eyes. 'But you need not be concerned on my account. I am sure your own affairs are sufficiently worrisome.'

He stopped in the doorway. 'I promised your brother I would keep an eye to your well-being——'

'What?' she gasped.

'And I do not consider that encouraging you to have any contact with Alex Hunt would be doing justice to that promise.'

She swallowed hard, forced her voice. 'So because you and the captain have gambling differences I should not encourage him?'

'It has nothing to do with that.' He drew her away into the shadows beside the doorway and lowered his voice to a harsh whisper. 'He uses people for his own ends and he will use you.'

'Ah! Suddenly it is clear!' Her voice cracked with ice. 'You were afraid he might learn something from me about your little smuggling activities, is that it?'

She winced as his fingers tightened on her arm and his eyes glinted dangerously. 'Don't be a fool! There is more at stake than contraband. He spends precious little time with his regiment at Castle William, but a great deal socialising at events like this, gathering information.' He emphasised the words with a scornful twist of his mouth. 'I doubt you could tell him anything about the contraband or anything else that he does not already suspect, and you have no more real proof than he. But he is a dangerous man, Emma, and——'

'To you, no doubt, since you make no secret of your—treasonous views!' She pulled her arm free. 'Certainly not to me. And I would thank you to concern yourself with your own dubious affairs and leave me to mine!'

As she stalked into the parlour, Jaycinth broke off from her conversation with Charles and looked up. 'What have you done with Captain Hunt? You seem to have made something of an impression on him!'

There was a faint accusation behind the words, and Emma gave herself a mental shake, determined not to be dictated to by anyone. With a defiant tilt of her chin, she shot Jaycinth a speaking look and turned to Cousin Maybelle. 'He asked if he might call.'

Jaycinth made a sound of disgust. 'Since he never seems to spend any time at his duties, perhaps you can bring him with you tomorrow, Charles!'

Cousin Maybelle either failed to notice the heavy sarcasm in her daughter's voice, or else chose to ignore it. 'That is an excellent idea,' she smiled. 'Charles, perhaps you would mention it to the captain. Now, I think I am ready to go home...'

As they waited for their carriage to be brought round, Emma caught a glimpse of Ben through an open door. His head was bent towards the dark curls of an extremely pretty girl and they were both laughing. The sight sent a stab of pain to Emma's heart and she turned swiftly away, hating herself. Surely it was not jealousy? How could she even begin to feel anything at all for such a despicable man? Every little show of concern that she had foolishly imagined to be for her own sake was now exposed as nothing more than the result of a promise to Kit! And his kisses? She could not even deceive herself that he kissed her because he found her attractive. Doubtless he had kissed every woman in Boston! Obviously he was as careless in bestowing his kisses as he was diligent in honouring his promises!

A bitter self-reproach simmered in her heart as she stared out at the night.

'You cannot mean for Emma to encourage Alex Hunt, Mama!' Jaycinth's voice broke into her thoughts.

'It can do no harm.' Maybelle's voice was weary and the smile she gave Emma had not quite the strength to reach her eyes.

'But a Redcoat, Mama!'

'Jaycinth, your aggression on the subject of the British garrison is both unfeminine and unjust and I weary of it.' The usually soft voice had a sharp edge to it. 'The sooner you are wed, the better, I think. You will set your mind less on politics and more on marriage, if you please!'

Jaycinth subsided into mutinous silence and Emma huddled into her cloak, wondering ruefully why the first man to show a genuine interest in her had to be of a profession guaranteed to alienate her new-found friend.

The evening had tired Cousin Maybelle considerably and the following morning she asked Emma to go to the apothecary for a particular herbal that always seemed beneficial.

Jinny and Matthew went with her, and as they walked down School Street, they were greeted by the sight of a group of people standing outside the school, clustered around the gate.

She paused, holding Jinny's arm. 'What is it?'

'Mischief, probably. We'd best not linger, Miss Emma.'

'No, wait. Stay here with Matthew.' Ignoring the maid's cry of protest, she crossed the street and tried to see what was attracting so much attention. A notice was posted on the gate, but she could see nothing of it and after a few minutes gave up.

'If it's anything interesting, miss, Jack's bound to know,' Jinny told her as she rejoined them.

'Yes, of course. Is the apothecary much farther?'

'Just down aways, not far.'

The interior of the shop was gloomy, and acrid with the odours of herbs and spices. He had made up preparations for Mistress Winston for years so Emma had little difficulty procuring the mixture of wild tansy, rosehip and purslane she wanted and had only to wait a few minutes. Which was just as well, since Matthew was fascinated by all the little bottles and the dozens of carefully labelled drawers lining the little shop, and looked set to cause havoc!

As they emerged into daylight and fresh air, a horse was suddenly drawn to a skidding halt in front of them, and Captain Hunt sprang to the ground. 'Miss Wyatt! What a pleasure! What brings you abroad so early?'

'An errand for my cousin at the apothecary.' She smiled.

'Then she is in good hands—he is a skilled man. His son runs errands and messages for me sometimes. In fact, this is a timely coincidence, for I was about to ask him to deliver a message to Mistress Winston.'

'Oh? Then I can save him the trouble.'

'Indeed. I fear I must decline her kind invitation for me to join the Arnolds in calling on you this afternoon. My duties will not now permit it, I am afraid.'

She was genuinely disappointed. 'I am sorry, Captain.'

His eyes met hers. 'Are you? I am gratified. But one or two of the merchants concerned with this tea business have been threatened and this——' he waved a crumpled piece of paper at her '—means trouble, and I must forgo the pleasure of this afternoon's visit.'

'What is it?'

With a sardonic curl of his lip he gave it to her. 'I've just removed it from the school gate. The Liberty boys are trying to gather a mob together and do not stop at using intimidation to gain their ends.' Matthew was trying to pat his horse, and he lifted him into the saddle and held him while Emma straightened out the bill and read it. It was an invitation to the town to witness the public resignation of the offending merchants as recipients for the East India tea, at the so-called 'Liberty tree' at noon the following day, Wednesday the third of November. And a footnote warned of the dire consequences should anyone try to remove the notice, a fact which apparently had not deterred Captain Hunt.

The tree, she already knew, was, like the Green Dragon Tavern at the north end of town, a rallying point for the active militants and patriots calling themselves the Sons of Liberty. The Liberty tree at noon. The drama of it caught at her imagination.

'Will they agree?' she asked, handing back the notice.

'I doubt it.' He turned to Matthew. 'Now, laddie, if you can persuade Miss Wyatt to bring you up on the Common one Thursday afternoon I'll give you a real ride on him! I always ride once around the Common on

Thursdays!' The long look he gave Emma was almost predatory, and there was no mistaking the suggestion of a clandestine meeting behind the words. 'Well, I must not tarry. Do not venture on the streets any more than is necessary.'

When he rode away, Jinny's pale features were clouded with disapproval. 'I don't like soldiers and he's a sly one. A sight too familiar, if you ask me.'

Emma shot her a reproving look. 'I didn't.' She took firm hold of Matthew's hand and set off for home.

Jaycinth, at least, was not disappointed at Captain Hunt's message of regret. But her green eyes gleamed at the mention of the handbill. 'Good! Something positive at last!'

'It's so arrogant, it's laughable!' Charles Arnold declared later when the matter was discussed over tea and ratafia biscuits. 'I can't see Clarke or the Hutchinsons agreeing to it.'

'But they should agree,' Jaycinth said decisively. 'Sam Adams and the others will not let this pass without a fight. They have been waiting too long for such an opportunity. Of late his correspondence committee has had precious little real meat to pass on to our outlying neighbours in their circular letters.'

'You have been listening to Sullivan,' he accused her, and Emma wondered at Maybelle's desire for a match between them. They would surely have a stormy marriage.

Louisa, Charles's sister, suddenly voiced a petulant protest. 'Oh, let's not discuss the wretched tea! It really is too boring.'

Much to the evident relief of the two older women, the conversation turned to Louisa's recently announced betrothal. Jaycinth adroitly contrived to deflect any hints about her own engagement and Emma could not help but think that she would stand a far better chance of happiness with Ben Sullivan than she would with Charles,

for at least their politics were in harmony! But the thought
did not sit easily with her and she thrust it away hurriedly.

John arrived unexpectedly next morning and, gathering them all into the drawing-room, said grimly, 'I
would be happier if no one went out today. There were
hotheads and trouble-makers gathering on every corner
last night and there are already a few people waiting by
the tree. If a crowd turns out it would not take much to
start a riot. That includes you,' he added, with a warning
look directed towards his sister. 'Do not go out.'

It was enough to set Emma pondering on the possibilities of doing just that. She needed *some* sort of excitement to divert her thoughts from the curdling in her
stomach that would not go away. If she could find some
excuse to slip out ...

As the morning advanced, church bells began to toll
until it seemed that every bell in the town was ringing a
summons and a strange excitement began to course
through her veins. She had almost made up her mind to
risk it when, with but half an hour to noon, Jaycinth
drew her from the nursery. 'Have you mettle enough to
go?' she demanded in hushed tones.

'But John said——' she began cautiously.

'Never mind John! It's not far and we can contrive
to slip away. I shall go and I'd as soon not go alone,
though I shall if necessary!'

That tipped the balance. 'No, you will not! I will plead
a headache and ask Ellen to mind Matthew while I lie
down.'

'Jinny will cover for us, and we need not be long,'
Jaycinth added eagerly.

'Then I will meet you at the gate directly.' She hastened
to her room, where she pulled out her cloak and, with
only a moment's hesitation, dropped it out of the window
to retrieve later—a trick learned early in her turbulent
childhood. Then she returned to the nursery for Matthew
and, leaving him to Ellen's mercies in the kitchen, slipped
out unseen.

CHAPTER SIX

MINUTES later, Emma was hurrying away from the house with Jaycinth, guilt and misgiving thrown to the wind amid growing excitement. As they left Tremont Street and cut across the Common, they were joined by scores of people, coming from all directions, drawn by the bells and the Crier. The townspeople were massing in their hundreds, milling about, waving banners and shouting with a patriotic fervour which Emma had scarcely suspected. The tree itself was splendidly adorned with flags and ribbons, fluttering defiantly, and there was almost a festive atmosphere about the scene.

'There.' Jaycinth stood on her toes. 'Beneath the tree. That is Sam Adams, and beside him John Hancock. I cannot make out the others. Oh, curse this crush! Can we move along here?'

They edged round a little, and, through a gap in the throng, Emma caught a glimpse of another figure standing a little apart from the patriot leaders, with his arms folded across his chest. It was a fleeting glimpse only, for her view was quickly obscured, but she carried his image around with her all the time and there was no doubt that it was him.

The crowd was thickening by the minute and they could get no nearer. Nor could she get another sight of the group beneath the tree. Instead she scanned the people around her. Every manner of citizen seemed to have turned out—some as well dressed as she and Jaycinth, some with painted faces and elaborate wigs, many in plain homespun and some in clothes no better than rags.

'What is happening?' she whispered. 'Can you see anything?' Jaycinth shook her head and she repeated her question to a youth in a worn leather jerkin standing in front of her. He barely turned his head to answer. 'They're not coming, mistress. Leastways, they haven't yet. Seems like they're all closeted together in Clarke's place down on King Street.'

'They're too ashamed to show their treacherous faces,' snarled a man beside her. 'Damn right, too!'

A ripple ran through the crowd. 'It's time we stood together,' shouted somebody nearby.

'Fight the British, not each other!' a high-pitched female voice demanded.

'We've put up with this treachery long enough!'

'Cowards and traitors!'

'Bring them out to answer for it!'

The voices rose all around.

'Are we Americans or lapdogs?'

The fervent demands for some sort of action grew wilder and, although a cry that the offenders be brought to the elm tree and unceremoniously hanged was laughed down as somewhat excessive, a little tremor of apprehension ran down Emma's spine.

A momentary hush indicated that something was finally happening, but even on her toes she could see little. 'Now what?' Jaycinth murmured to her neighbour, a man at least a foot taller. He shrugged. 'Looks like someone is going to tell 'em they'd better come out.'

Then a cheer went up. 'To the store! To King Street, patriots!'

The crowd had not seemed particularly threatening until then, despite the vocal abuse; indeed there was a great deal of ribaldry and good humour. But now there was a collective roar of approval that held a note of menace. A shiver of fear slid through Emma as she realised with a shock that revolution was indeed beginning to stir in the blood of these people.

'I believe we should go,' she whispered, and was relieved that Jaycinth nodded agreement. They were no longer on the fringe of the crowd, however, but swallowed up in its midst—a mass of several hundred people. And as they tried to edge their way through, they found themselves in a mêlée, as those hastening to join the rush towards King Street bludgeoned into the vast majority who were trying to leave. Emma found herself being relentlessly separated from Jaycinth.

Her heart began to pound with the beginnings of panic as she was bumped and jostled, all at once inexorably swept up and carried along until she was barely able to keep her feet.

A thick muscular arm curled about her waist and she cried out in alarm. 'Stay with me, little beauty,' the rough voice crooned in her ear, as his foul breath and the pungent odours from his wool shirt assailed her nostrils. 'You'll not go down—least not till we find a cosy ware'ouse corner!'

With a cry of horror, she struggled free of the grasp and managed to thrust herself out of his reach, his coarse laughter ringing in her ears. Thoroughly alarmed now, and bitterly regretting having left the security of the house, she pushed against the man in front of her, desperately trying to avoid being crushed. An elbow caught her sharply in the ribs, and she gasped, thrown off balance. Someone behind collided into her, cursing, and her knees buckled. In another moment, she would have gone down, trampled beneath dozens of heedless feet.

'You damned fool!' Iron fingers gripped her arm and hauled her up.

Ben! The familiar voice was momentarily music to her ears. She looked up gratefully, and encountered a stormy expression. He held her arm in a vicious grip and shouldered his way through the crowd with grim purpose, dragging her with him and totally impervious to the curses and insults hurled at him.

When finally they reached the quiet of a deserted side-
street, he swung her round to face him. 'What the devil
are you doing here?'

'I——' For a moment she quailed beneath the fury in
his blue eyes, her heart still pounding from the fright
she had had. Then she lifted her chin and looked at him
defiantly. 'I had no choice! I tried to get out of the way.
I was caught up when they started to leave the meeting——'

'But what were you doing there?' he persisted. 'What
possessed you to come out to a public meeting like that?'

'No doubt the same as you!' she snapped, struggling
free of his grasp. 'I went to see what was happening! I
was curious. I wanted to see for myself. Is that so
wrong?'

'It's damned irresponsible!' he exploded. 'Anything
could happen in a mob like that!' He looked at her with
a strange light glittering in his eyes. 'Maybelle is ill! Have
you no thought to the consequences if she discovers you
are involved in this?'

She was smitten by a pang of guilt, and a sinking sensation in the pit of her stomach that his concern had
nothing to do with her own safety. He was concerned
about Maybelle. As she should have been. 'I'm sorry. I
did not think,' she admitted meekly.

'Then perhaps you should! John is unlikely to be as
forgiving of your shortcomings as a responsible
nursemaid for Matthew as Maybelle might be. And you
should remember that she has only a limited income,
and it is ultimately John you have to thank for your
finery.' His gaze swept over her in a very pointed manner,
bringing colour to her cheeks and an indignant sparkle
to her eyes.

'I do not forget it!' she exclaimed hotly. 'But I did
not ask for their charity and I can do without all
this——' she flicked at her skirts '——if necessary. I'd as
soon have homespun and my independence!'

'Nonsense! There is not a woman alive who would choose homespun over silks and satins! Even our patriotic American women kept to their fine underwear beneath their homespun gowns.'

'Well, you would know about that!' she flung at him. 'But I came to Boston to avoid having my life arranged for me, to avoid a marriage my brother had all but agreed to before I even knew about it. Marriage to a man whose depravity and perversions were whispered about all over Plymouth!' She looked into blue eyes darkening as a frown furrowed between them. 'Kit did not tell you that? No, well, he might just have a vestige of conscience to trouble him! This was the only place I could come to. I am very grateful to Maybelle, and I am grown fond of Matthew. But—but I have always been wilful and used to doing as I please without being answerable to anyone very much. I—I am trying to accept...' Her voice began to falter as hot little tears threatened at the back of her eyes. 'I know I am fortunate. I know—— But I—oh! I do not expect you to understand!' She broke off with a frustrated little sigh and turned away, already bitterly regretting the outburst.

'I am not totally insensitive,' he said quietly.

She looked round at him. Was that compassion in his voice? But, though his expression had softened a little, there was conflict in the searching gaze and she could fathom nothing of his thoughts. Her heart began to pound erratically beneath the scrutiny and in some confusion she averted her eyes and pulled the cloak around her. 'I have to go back.'

'Do you wish to walk back alone?'

The now-familiar mockery was back in his voice and she could not help the defensive anger that leapt up to answer it. 'Are you offering to escort me? Surely you would rather see what goes on at the Clarkes' store? Your smuggling activities give you an interest, I think?'

'We shall hear soon enough. I would rather spare Maybelle further anxiety and see you safely within doors.'

'I do not need your escort!' she snapped ungraciously, irritated beyond measure that her heart ached to have his concern directed at her.

He raised an eyebrow. 'No?' A strange expression played across his features and he took a step towards her. She caught her breath as one hand pressed into the small of her back and the other entwined in her hair. Heedless of her cry of protest, he took her in a kiss that ravaged her mouth and sent her senses reeling.

Trapped against the wall, every fibre trembling, it was not fear that clutched so convulsively within her but something far more alarming. There was no will to resist him. A liquid warmth began in her loins and spread a tingling sensation all through her. Her lips began to move in response to his as a desperate need welled up in her and overcame all rational thought. His hand at her back pressed her closer, and her body arched, her hips thrusting against him as his tongue explored her mouth with increasing urgency. All manner of strange sensations coursed through her veins, but all coherent thought had fled. Somewhere within her was a desire to know more, to go wherever his kiss would take her, to give herself up to his will, to the unknown pleasures he could arouse...

Dimly she heard his muffled groan, felt his fingers tighten momentarily in her hair. His mouth stilled on hers. Then he drew away, releasing her. She groped unsteadily for the wall behind her, put a hand to her bruised lips, and could not meet his eyes.

'I warned you once what can happen to ladies who walk the streets alone.' His voice was uneven, oddly taut. 'Shall we go?'

She was shaking now, her stomach churning. He reached for her arm, but she shrank away instinctively, afraid to think what might happen, what she might do. If he touched her now, if he kissed her again, she would be lost. Dear God—that she was so powerless over her own body!

After a moment, his gaze holding hers, he caught her wrist firmly and drew her away from the wall. 'Be thankful it was me,' he said darkly. 'It could have been a good deal worse.'

He did not release her wrist, and she did not withdraw it as they walked in silence back to Tremont Street. She was too wrapped up in her own confusion to care who saw her in Ben Sullivan's unrelenting grip. His expression, too, when she summoned courage to glance at him, was equally unyielding.

Finally he pushed her firmly inside the gates, as though glad to be rid of her, and said curtly, 'I always have time to explain the politics and less romantic aspects of life in His Majesty's colonies, if you really want to know. You do not have to make a fool of yourself at every hothead meeting you hear about.'

'I rather think I should get a somewhat prejudiced account from you!' she accused him, hiding her turmoil behind a mask of anger.

He raised his eyebrows. 'Then I am sure Captain Hunt will oblige you with his views!' he retorted grimly, and, bowing rather stiffly, walked away.

Although his feet carried him back towards King Street, his thoughts were far from the mob outside Clarke's warehouse.

The sharp tug of anxiety he had experienced when he'd glimpsed her in the crowd at the tree had startled him considerably, and when he had pulled her to safety he had been overwhelmed by the need to crush her against him and kiss her. Yet when he had finally done so he had still been unprepared for the abrupt surge of desire and the sudden racing of his blood that threatened to blot out all else. It had been a long time since he had been surprised by such a swift and unexpected arousal. He was a man who liked to believe himself in control of his emotions and to be taken unawares like that was not merely disturbing, it was downright alarming.

But the memory of her responsive body instinctively moulding itself to his brought an involuntary smile to his lips. What unleashed passion lay beneath that innocent exterior? he wondered, and immediately caught himself up at the thought. Was that what it was, this sudden rush of heat to his blood? Surely he was not so jaded that he needed the challenge of an untried virgin to tempt him? He was acquainted with enough willing females who were both experienced and sufficiently inventive to keep him amused, surely? And anyway, he told himself impatiently, he had neither the time nor the patience at the moment to ease a little innocent into the ways of womanhood, however diverting a pastime that might be.

Crossing the street and purposefully lengthening his stride, he tried unsuccessfully to concentrate his mind on what he might find at the Clarkes' store. Despite his efforts, however, he could not rid his thoughts of the untamed spirit he had glimpsed lurking beneath the blushes and the confusion.

He had been watching her these past weeks, watching her with what he had dismissed as nothing more than a mild concern in keeping with his promise to her brother. Yet, if he was honest, it was also because she had interested him from the moment he had caught her lurking in the shadows of the *Emma Louise*, and her eyes had sparkled with angry indignation. Indeed, the impulse to kiss her the morning Kit had left had been little more than a mischevious desire to rekindle the fiery outrage in those hazel eyes.

Taking refuge in her bedchamber had been an impulse too, and he frowned to think how easily he had given in to it, had taken the risk. Yet it had been worth it if only for the sight of her slender body outlined in the moonlight. And she had reacted with admirable composure to an intrusion which would have reduced most innocent well-bred females to quivering terror!

A challenge had been laid down that night. And he was in no doubt, especially now, that if he put his mind to it he could win her into his bed easily enough. And yet—— Yet what? It would be too easy? Did he want something more than her responsive body? To know that she came to him not simply because he had seduced her and she had been unable to deny her body's awakening needs, but because——

He cut that thought off abruptly too, unwilling to explore it. Was he going soft? He gave himself a mental shake. What the devil was the matter with him? There were bigger things afoot to keep him busy and Emma Wyatt could only prove a diversion he could ill afford.

Emma found Jaycinth waiting for her in her room, pacing the floor in some agitation. 'Thank God!' she cried. 'What happened? Wherever have you been? Heavens, you look dreadful—are you all right?'

'I am perfectly all right,' she answered impatiently, throwing her cloak on to the bed, and briefly described what had happened, channelling her scattered emotions into indignation. 'He hauled me out of the crush,' she ended, 'gave me a lecture and insisted on escorting me back. He—he really is insufferable!'

Jaycinth stared at her for a moment, noting her heightened colour, and then said, 'Yes. Yes, he is. Will he tell Mama, do you think? Or John?'

'Not about you. He does not know.'

Jaycinth's eyes widened in surprise. 'Thank you for that! I doubt I should have been so loyal. Ben is rather—daunting when he is angry.' She went to the door and hesitated. 'Would you like to come to Cedars with me tomorrow? You can ride Tempest—I'll borrow one of

John's horses. Jinny will see to Matthew for an hour or two.'

Emma caught her breath in a little rush of pleasure. 'Do you mean it? I would love to.'

Jaycinth smiled. 'Well, then. I shall settle it with Mama.'

The thought of sitting a horse again helped in no small measure to temper the chaos of her thoughts. She had allowed herself to fall in love with Ben Sullivan and cursed herself roundly for it. He was dangerous and she could not trust herself—that much, at least, was painfully clear. And she had not forgotten what she had said in her room that night, though her brave words seemed empty enough now.

But the fact that she owed him a debt of thanks for pulling her from the crowd was brought home to her next morning when she collected Maybelle's breakfast from the kitchen. Jack came in bearing news of the previous afternoon's events.

'That meeting turned ugly,' he said darkly, warming his hands over the fire. 'Some of them went to Clarke's place. He and his friends had to shut themselves in upstairs. Countin' room, they say, an' I reckon they had time enough to count it,' he chuckled, 'and think on what they'll add to it when their tea ships come in!'

'Was anyone hurt?' Emma paused with her tray.

He shook his head. 'More's the pity.'

With Ben Faneuil, another of the offending merchants, living down the street, and other disturbances seeming likely, Maybelle was unhappy about the two girls riding on the Common. But, after eliciting promises from them both that they would not stray from the groom, and would return immediately upon any sign of trouble, she finally agreed.

As they alighted from the carriage outside the big house later that day a tall black horse being warily held by a groom, tossed its head and pawed impatiently at the ground.

'Ben is here!' Jaycinth exclaimed, springing to the ground. 'Look at that horse, Emma! Isn't he magnificent? No wonder Alex Hunt is said to be so sour about it!'

'He should not gamble with things he values so highly,' Emma murmured mechanically, and followed her into the house with a sense of dread lying in the pit of her stomach.

A maid took their cloaks and directed them to the drawing-room where Ben was standing with his back to the fire, a glass in his hand, talking to Ann. 'I will take what correspondence there is with me, then——'

He broke off as they entered and, despite having steeled herself for the meeting, she was powerless to prevent the sudden weakness in her knees as he looked at her, the penetrating directness of the blue gaze bringing a flush to her cheeks.

Ann, who did not miss either his look or her blush, glanced enquiringly towards the door. 'Have you brought the boy with you, Jaycinth?' she asked sweetly.

'Of course not——'

'Oh! Then perhaps there is some problem at home I may help Emma with?'

'Emma is coming riding with me. Ben...' She turned sparkling eyes to him. 'May I ride Blade? I am lending Emma Tempest.'

Ben grinned. 'Certainly not! You'll have to content yourself with one of John's cobs! Besides, I cannot delay any longer; I am late already.'

'You are going away?' Emma blurted the words out before she could stop herself, and felt the colour in her cheeks heighten.

He looked at her and raised his brows slightly, and she wished she could dissolve into the floor. 'I have to be in Benson Ford for a few days,' he said briefly.

'Have you any more news about what happened yesterday, Ben?' Ann interrupted, her eyes glittering.

'I've nothing to add to what John will have told you. Except that there will be another meeting tomorrow. An official one this time, in Faneuil Hall. Perhaps it will be more fruitful.'

'Let us hope so,' Jaycinth declared. 'Little enough came out of yesterday's fiasco except a few broken windows!'

Ann raised delicate eyebrows indignantly. 'Why should they relinquish their legitimate positions on the demand of an unruly mob?'

'Because such schemes are strangling the life out of us!'

Ben threw up his hand. 'Ladies, greatly though it would amuse me to hear you debate the subject, I must go.' He threw back the remainder of his drink, and added, 'Ann, I will need those papers.'

'I'll go and see that the horses are brought round,' Jaycinth declared, not bothering to ask Ann's permission to borrow a mount for herself. 'We shall ride a little way with you. I should like to see how you handle him!'

Emma could not resist the chance for revenge, and, carefully avoiding looking at Ann, turned innocent eyes on Ben. 'Perhaps, Mr Sullivan, we may see you unseated. Although I understand your ability in the saddle is legendary, and often remarked upon in parlours and dining-rooms.'

The corners of his mouth twitched dangerously. 'I like to believe I have some skill,' he remarked, and, as Jaycinth suppressed a giggle, Ann gave Emma a look so full of venom that her face was almost contorted by it, before angrily swishing her green taffeta skirts and leaving the room, apparently at a loss for words.

Jaycinth followed her out, her face a picture, leaving Emma standing rather uncomfortably in the middle of the room enduring a speculative gaze. 'I doubt that was entirely wise, you know,' he said, his eyes gleaming with amusement. 'Ann does not take kindly to that kind of remark from someone whom she considers should be totally beholden to her.'

She shrugged. 'As I told you yesterday, I can manage without her charity if necessary, and I do not intend to allow her to treat me like an insect.' A slow smile creased little lines at the corners of his eyes and completely disarmed her. Running her tongue over suddenly dry lips, she said hurriedly, 'I did not thank you for helping me yesterday. If you had not pulled me out of that mob...' Her voice trailed off as he raised one eyebrow.

'Are you always so reckless?'

She looked at him. 'Are you always so brutal?'

The blue eyes darkened slightly. 'Not always.' For a moment she could not tear her gaze away, lost to the sensuality in his voice that set her insides quivering. He turned to set his glass on the mantel-shelf and his voice was brisk as he went on, 'If you wish to send any letters home, have them ready by Monday. I am meeting a ship off Ridge Point that night. She'll return direct to London and her master is a friend of mine. He can be trusted to carry your letters and see them safely on their way to Plymouth.'

Taken by surprise, she lifted her gaze to his face. 'Oh, thank you. I—should like to try and make my peace with James, and——'

He nodded briefly. 'I will call on Monday, then.'

Footsteps beyond the open door prevented any further discussion on the subject as Ann returned with a sheaf of papers. And a few minutes later Jaycinth announced that the horses were ready and waiting at the front of the house.

Ann watched the three of them ride away, her lips set and a dangerous gleam in her eyes. That chit would have to go! She had seen the way Ben looked at her and she did not like it.

She had shared Ben's bed but once, before she married John, and more by her connivance than his, although he had been willing enough! And if only she could persuade him to get over his apparent reluctance to bed his partner's wife she would share it again. It was only a matter of time, she knew, but she grew impatient for the masterful, almost brutal lovemaking she had experienced with Ben and which John could not equal. There was just the faintest chance she was pregnant—God knew she had been lucky enough to escape this long—and a grimace of distaste darkened her features at the thought. If it were so, she had little enough time before her condition showed itself in which to win Ben back. And now this little opportunist and her quick tongue had caught his eye! If he was going to waste time amusing himself with an untried virgin it would delay his return to her. She did not care about the others—she was quite willing to share him—but not with an insolent, calculating little nobody she was forced to acknowledge almost as part of the family!

She would have to go—and soon.

Tempest felt eager and spirited beneath Emma and her own spirits soared as they gained the open common and broke into a canter. How she had missed it! Suddenly she wanted to gallop—to rid herself of the ache in her heart and the nagging unsettled feelings that troubled her, to feel carefree and happy and in harmony with the world. And, as Jaycinth complained about the hopeless sluggishness of her mount, a gurgle of laughter bubbled into her throat.

Tempest needed little encouragement. At a mere touch she lengthened her stride and they were soon flying across the ground, Jaycinth's cry of protest lost to the wind.

But she could hear the dull thrumming of hoofs behind her and did not need to glance back to know that Ben was following. He soon drew level with her and eased his horse back so that they galloped neck and neck and an exhilaration she had almost forgotten coursed through her veins. Everything was forgotten in the thrill of the race as the ground sped away beneath them and the wind whipped at her hair, stung her cheeks and brought the faint tang of salt to her lips.

With effortless ease, Ben drew in front, bringing Blade across her path some way ahead and finally coming to a halt at the edge of the Pond. She drew up beside him, laughing breathlessly. 'Even Sir Francis could not have matched him! He's beautiful!' she exclaimed appreciatively, and sent him a look of mock reproach. 'But had you been a gentleman, sir, you would have let me win!'

'Ah, but I am not a gentleman,' he replied solemnly, with the quiver of a smile. 'And I doubt you would be happy to win like that.'

'Just to ride at all is enough!' she declared happily, not even troubling to think of a clever response.

'And you ride very well,' he commended. 'You must come to Eastwood—Firefly would present you with few problems and there is some wonderful country for riding along the coast. You would enjoy——' He stopped, the little lines at the corners of his eyes deepening imperceptibly as he stared at her, seeming for a moment to look right through her.

'Is—is something wrong?'

He pulled himself together and shook his head. 'No. But I must be going.' He waited as Jaycinth came up to them with the expressionless groom trailing dutifully behind.

'That was unfair! I almost regret lending you Tempest!'

'I'm sorry!' She bent to pat the mare's neck. 'But I could not help myself. I think being able to ride every day is the only thing I miss about home.'

'Then I shall leave you to enjoy the opportunity today,' Ben put in, evidently anxious to be on his way. Turning his horse, he raised his hand in careless farewell and rode off.

They followed sedately in his wake for a while, Emma at least with a little regret, and then turned across the Common. Jaycinth took on the role of guide and rather unnecessarily pointed out the beacon, a tall, wooden structure with little to recommend it but which dominated the skyline and stood in stark contrast to the splendid Hancock mansion and the other fine houses beyond it.

As they turned into the wind and started back, another rider approached coming across their path.

'Look!' Jaycinth exclaimed. 'Is that not Captain Hunt?'

As he recognised them and turned his horse, Emma remembered it was Thursday. He reined in beside them and swept off his three-cornered hat. 'Miss Wyatt, Miss Winston. An unexpected pleasure!'

'Indeed, Captain.' Emma restrained her smile, for it was obvious from the look he gave her that he assumed she had contrived the meeting. What a conceited man he was, she thought with some amusement.

'We have just seen Ben Sullivan,' Jaycinth said with relish, casting critical eyes over his mount. 'And I must say that is a poor substitute for the magnificent beast you lost. You must miss him sorely.'

The captain's smile faded. 'I have not lost hope of having my revenge, Miss Winston, and having him restored to me.'

'Even after your experience the other night?' She raised her eyebrows. 'I assure you Ben will never give you the opportunity. He is very taken with the brute.

You would be better advised to withdraw gracefully to lick your wounds!'

'No retreat is graceful, Miss Winston,' he told her bluntly. 'Miss Wyatt, will you walk a little way with me?'

Her congenial mood undiminished, she agreed readily and, avoiding Jaycinth's glare of censure, dismounted and handed the reins to the groom. 'I apologise for Jaycinth's rudeness, Captain,' she said, picking her way carefully over the muddy ground beside him. 'I do not know what came over her.'

'It's of no consequence,' he assured her. 'It is no secret that Sullivan and I would come to blows if we were not both such gentlemen!'

'I do not believe he considers himself a gentleman,' she murmured.

'No? Well, perhaps even he is not that arrogant.' His brown eyes were studying her. 'And you? How do you consider him?'

'He is certainly arrogant,' she asserted, misliking the sudden personal turn of the conversation. 'And I try not to consider him at all.' And fail miserably, she added silently. Arrogant—and handsome, ruthless, outrageous, compassionate. Smuggler, seducer, gambler, rebel. What else? She knew so little about him, this enigmatic man who so monopolised her thoughts. Captain Hunt was still watching her, faintly sceptical, and she blushed. Was she so transparent?

'Be careful,' he warned in a low voice, not taking his eyes from hers. 'He is up to his neck in smuggling and I would not put it past him to conceal his contraband in Maybelle Winston's house.'

'I have heard rumours that he is involved in smuggling, Captain.' She widened her eyes at him. 'But I cannot believe it! Even less can I believe he would try to use my cousin's house! He would not dare, much less have the opportunity!'

He shrugged. 'Nothing is beyond him, Miss Wyatt.
The man is destined for a hangman's noose, one way or
another, and I should not like to think of you being involved with him.' He paused, and looked beyond her,
speaking more to himself than to her. 'In some quarters
it would be considered a triumph to catch him red-
handed now, and divert some attention away from the
furore building up over the tea—give the news-sheets
something else to print.'

'I hear there was some sort of disturbance after yesterday's meeting,' she put in quickly, glad to divert the
conversation.

He could tell her little more than Jack, apart from a
few details of the damage to the building. 'It seems only
to have been a few extremists,' he concluded grimly,
'intent on inciting trouble. Most of the crowd dispersed.
I dare say Sullivan was in the thick of that, too,' he
added, his brow darkening.

'If he is guilty of all you say, Captain,' she ventured,
'why is he still abroad? Surely you have proof, since you
are so sure?'

'He has the devil's own luck,' he swore bitterly, and
then shrugged. 'And it is simply not possible to effectively patrol all the coves, inlets and islands around the
bay. Someone will have to turn informer. But men seem
willing to give their lives for him, and women their repu-
tations. And I doubt he gives a fig for either!'

A protest sprang to her lips at that, an instinctive desire
to defend him. But she bit it back. It was probably true.
'I should go back, Captain,' she said quickly.

They turned and walked slowly back towards Jaycinth.
'What is the child like?' he asked suddenly.

'Matthew?' She cast a startled glance at him. 'Like
any other who has suffered the loss of both parents at
such an early age, I imagine. Why do you ask?'

He shook his head, but then said thoughtfully, 'Sullivan shows an undue interest in the boy, don't you think? I have often wondered if the rumours are true?'

She was puzzled. 'What rumours? I am afraid, Captain, that you have an advantage.'

'I am sorry.' He looked faintly embarrassed. 'I assumed you would have heard all the tales. It's somewhat indelicate, I fear.'

'Well, you will have to satisfy my curiosity now, you know.' She smiled bravely.

'You have heard Sullivan and Beth Winston were close? That they would marry? But there was an abrupt break in his dealings with the family and she married Edward Paxton very quickly afterwards.' He paused, seeming to hesitate. 'Of course, the dates preclude any scandal; the boy was born eleven months after the wedding. But if she was Sullivan's mistress after her marriage, as rumour suggests...'

Emma drew a sharp breath and stopped abruptly, staring up at him. What was he saying? That Matthew was Ben's son?

He took her arm, and began walking again. 'I'm sorry. I have shocked you.'

Silently she shook her head, her thoughts in confusion. When they reached the horses, he took her hand and she barely noticed that he brushed her fingers with his lips. 'Until next time, then.' She nodded mutely, too stunned to speak, and watched him ride away, the look of satisfaction on his face escaping her completely.

'Emma! Is anything wrong?'

'What?' She looked blankly at Jaycinth for a moment. 'Oh, no, nothing.'

'Did he upset you? What were you talking about?' Suspicion laced the younger girl's voice.

'No, it's not that. I have a slight headache, that is all.' And, summoning her brightest smile she added, 'It must be the exertion, after so long.'

Jaycinth shot her a look, but said no more, and they rode back to Cedars in silence, Emma having to acknowledge that what Captain Hunt had said was not impossible to believe. Matthew had blue eyes and dark hair; there could be a likeness of sorts. And the very vehemence of Ben's denial that there had been anything other than friendship between him and Beth could be construed as proof enough. And if Maybelle knew it would be just like her to allow him the freedom to visit his son whenever he wished, and that would explain the informality with which he came and went.

Of course, the captain did not like Ben, so his views were suspect, but, although a study of Matthew that evening could not decide her one way or another, the idea had taken root and would not be easily dislodged.

Shortly before noon on Monday Emma was drawing a picture of Noah's Ark when Ben came into the nursery unannounced carrying a carved wooden ship, which he gave into Matthew's eager young hands with a grin. 'One of the foresters I have been with these past few days carved it. It cost me a bottle of the best brandy, so mind you take care of it!'

'I will, I promise. Thank you!' The words were uttered with reverence, the young face glowing with pleasure, as he pulled up the rug into ripples and proceeded to sail the ship—instantly named the *Emma Louise*—over the makeshift waves.

Over his head, Emma regarded the man who uncharacteristically held a small boy in such affection. He was watching Matthew with an expression of mild indulgence that softened the sometimes harsh lines of his face. There was a resemblance, now that she studied them together. Nothing easily definable, but there nevertheless. Matthew's eyes were not so blue, nor his hair so dark, but in his smile, the shape of his mouth and even, perhaps, a promise of the same firm jawline. She was, of course, looking for such a similarity, unsure how she felt about it except that she was disappointed that he could risk blighting the life of a woman he loved by fathering a child upon her when she was wed to another. His reputation and general behaviour was testimony enough that she should not be at all surprised, but——

She suddenly realised that he was no longer watching Matthew but had turned those penetrating blue eyes on her. He raised a faintly questioning eyebrow, and she flushed. 'You are very kind to him,' she said softly, suddenly stricken by a sharp pang of sympathy. What an untenable position for him!

Ben shrugged. 'He has suffered too much tragedy for one so young,' he murmured, and raised his voice slightly. 'Matt, there is a bag of apples in the kitchen— if you go now you might rescue one or two from Jinny's clutches!'

This was greeted with a yelp of delight, and, clutching his ship to his chest, Matthew ran off eagerly.

'May I get you something?' she asked, only now taking in his travel-stained clothes and heavy-eyed appearance. Maybelle was resting in her room and Jaycinth would scarcely have risen yet, so the duties of hospitality fell on her. 'You look rather weary. Some brandy perhaps, or would you prefer tea?'

He cast an apologetic glance at his attire and smiled wryly. 'My dear girl, after three days of too much drinking, too much gambling and too little sleep, tea is not the answer. And I have little time to enjoy the revitalising effects of Maybelle's excellent brandy as I must go to Eastwood immediately. Have you attempted to make your peace with your brother? Though why you should wish to I cannot imagine.'

She nodded. 'I have tried. But I doubt he'll ever forgive me. I doubt he'll even accept the letter.' Glancing up at him, she encountered a look somewhere between sympathy and compassion, and mumbled hastily, 'I'll go and get it.'

When she returned clutching what had been the most difficult letter she had ever written, and another, somewhat easier, to Kit, he was standing with one foot on the hearth studying the tip of his mud-splattered boot. He looked up but made no move to take her letters. Instead, and she almost dared hope it was an excuse to linger a little longer, he said, 'I imagine you heard what happened at the meeting in Faneuil Hall on Friday?'

'Yes. The merchants refused to resign again.'

He nodded. 'This time an official request from a legal town meeting. And I heard last night that Governor Hutchinson, in his wisdom, has ordered the militia to stand ready. Since the colonel of the Corps is John Hancock, who is somewhat unlikely to take the order seriously, it seems a rather pointless exercise.'

'I should have said it makes him look rather foolish,' she observed. 'But I expect the—Liberty boys will enjoy it!'

He chuckled. 'There will be a certain amount of derision, I imagine.' He eyed her appreciatively and added, 'I rather suspect you of harbouring views sympathetic to the colonial cause, Miss Wyatt!'

This was surely the way to his heart, if there was one. And if she wanted one. 'I—have some sympathy with the frustrations of the situation, certainly,' she answered, truthfully enough.

'A careful answer!' He looked at her for a long moment, suddenly serious. 'How long do you think you can stand it? This . . . restrictive existence? You cannot possibly be happy. You have too much intelligence, too much spirit.'

Taken aback by his bluntness, she averted her gaze, moved to straighten the rug and pick up one of Matthew's toys. 'I am not unhappy.'

'That was not the impression I received last week.'

This was dangerous ground. The memory of that deserted side-street was still acutely disturbing and she took refuge in flippancy. 'Well, I do not intend this "restrictive existence", as you put it, to be a permanent state. As soon as possible I intend to take Kit's advice and find a husband.' She smiled brightly and moved forward, holding out her letters. 'Do you know of a likely candidate? A friend you could recommend, perhaps?'

Thrusting the letters into his pocket, he swept a speculative eye over her, a gleam creeping into the unhurried gaze. 'Tempting though such an offer is,' he said with a faint tinge of mockery, 'I am afraid I have neither the need, nor the desire, for a wife. Indeed, my lifestyle leaves little room for such an encumbrance. However, I doubt you will have any difficulty filling the post!' He left the fire and moved to the door. 'I will look around for a suitable applicant if you wish.'

Having blushed scarlet at his interpretation of her remarks, she recovered quickly. 'Please do. Preferably one of advanced years and a considerable fortune!'

'Mercenary child!' The look he threw her was full of reproach, but the harsh edge had gone from his voice, replaced by a tremor of amusement. 'But it narrows the field a little! Now, I must pay my respects to Maybelle and be away.'

'Good luck, then,' she said lightly. 'Though I doubt you need it. They say you have the devil on your side!'

He laughed as he pulled open the door, 'Ah, but even the devil needs a dark night, a calm sea and witless customs officers!'

Why she should find it so crushing that he considered a wife 'an encumbrance' she did not know. It was quite obvious, and whatever the state of her feelings she had harboured no illusions in *that* direction! Nevertheless she went about for the remainder of the day in considerably lowered spirits, which was incomprehensible allowing that the entire encounter had been remarkably friendly.

CHAPTER SEVEN

AT ABOUT the time Ben left Tremont Street, Captain Hunt received a despatch from New York. He scanned it idly until, his attention caught, he stifled an exclamation and read it again more carefully.

'Anything wrong, sir?' The young lieutenant raised his eyebrows enquiringly. 'Bad news?'

Hunt shook his head. 'Far from it. At least,' he amended hastily, 'not for us.' He flicked the corner of the paper and handed it across the desk.

The lieutenant gave a low whistle. 'Was he smuggling, do you think?'

'Of course! What else would he have been doing there? He spent a lot of time with Sullivan while he was here, if you recall. And Sullivan has friends in New York.'

'Shall I send someone to tell the sister?'

'No.' The captain took back the despatch and gazed at it thoughtfully. 'I have met her once or twice. I'll do it myself. We don't want to pass up an opportunity like this.'

'Sir?'

'Think, man! She is unlikely to know whether her brother was smuggling or not. If I can convince her Sullivan sent him to New York—in effect, sent him to his death—she might prove very useful. We need a pair of eyes in the Winston camp!'

The lieutenant sighed. He knew that his captain bore a grudge against Sullivan for personal reasons and it had become almost an obsession. It had started with a girl Hunt had taken a fancy to and had been bedding fairly frequently—until one night Sullivan had gone into the

tavern where she worked, and where the captain was
drinking. Sullivan had paid her a little careless attention, whispered an immoral suggestion in her ear, and,
after a lingering kiss that had the entire clientele of the
tavern cheering, had walked out with her on his arm in
a public humiliation the captain could never forgive.

From then on Sullivan had ruffled the captain's
feathers at every turn, smuggling with impunity,
flaunting his association with the likes of the militant
Sam Adams, and making no secret of his anti-British
views. Add to that his confounded luck at cards and
Hunt's inability to decline the challenges he frequently
threw down—and the situation was explosive.

It was not surprising, therefore, bearing in mind the
captain's fiery Scots temperament, that he had made it
his personal crusade to bring about Sullivan's downfall,
and would no doubt go to any lengths to achieve that
end.

'It seems a little harsh, sir,' the lieutenant ventured,
'to use the young lady's grief——'

'Scruples, Harry?' Hunt raised a sardonic eyebrow.
'You are in the wrong profession. Besides, Sullivan has
been showing an interest in her and I've a mind to beat
him to the spoils this time. If I can console her in her
grief, so much the better!'

'Sullivan is unlikely to tell her anything she can pass
on to us if he thinks you and she——'

The captain dismissed the objection. 'If he thinks I
want her, he will probably be all the more determined
to have her himself—and likely to get careless. We have
nothing to lose, after all, and I've a score to settle. And
this——' he tapped the despatch and regarded it
thoughtfully '—this could well be Sullivan's downfall.
We'll have him in the hangman's noose yet, Harry, lad!'

*   *   *

It was halfway through the afternoon when Jinny came to the nursery. 'Captain Hunt is downstairs, Miss Emma. The mistress sent me up to fetch you.'

At once flattered and disconcerted by this unexpected visit, Emma rose and smoothed her skirts. 'Stay here, Matthew—I'll not be long.' She went to the door and paused at the sight of Jinny's expression. 'Is anything the matter?'

'No, miss. Except the mistress looked—well, pale and peaky, you know.'

'She is probably just tired. As soon as Captain Hunt leaves, I will insist she lies down—she really should rest more.'

But as soon as she entered the drawing-room it was obvious that Captain Hunt's visit was not a social one. Her gaze darted swiftly from his unsmiling countenance to Maybelle, seated on the sofa looking pale and drawn, and then to Jaycinth, who turned from the window with such a shocked and ashen face that Emma was filled with sudden dread. Something had happened to Ben! 'What is it?' Her eyes searched Captain Hunt's. 'What has happened?'

'I am afraid I have come with bad news for you,' he said gravely. 'It—it is about your brother.'

'Kit?' Her face blanched and her hand went to her mouth as a thread of fear snaked through her. 'What is it?'

'I have just received news from New York,' he told her gently. 'His ship foundered on the rocks in bad weather. She—went down with all hands. No survivors have been reported. I am very sorry.'

A dozen memories darted swiftly into her mind and then were gone, leaving an overwhelming sense of loss. Dimly she was aware that she sat down abruptly on the couch beside Maybelle, of the older woman's reaching for her hand and squeezing it, uttering shocked words of condolence, and of Jaycinth's coming to stand behind her, a hand gripping her shoulder.

'We have no idea what he was doing in those waters so close inshore,' he went on quietly. 'But . . .' He hesitated, his voice tinged with regret. 'But it seems likely that he was hugging the coast for—for smuggling purposes. And, in unfamiliar waters, was driven on to the rocks when the squall hit them.'

'Smuggling!' Maybelle exclaimed in horror. 'Really, Captain, I do not think——'

He turned and raised his eyebrows. 'I am sorry, Mistress Winston, but I have my duty. It is well known that Captain Wyatt and Ben Sullivan spent a great deal of time together during his stay here. Since Sullivan is known to have associates of dubious character in New York and is himself under constant suspicion of illegal activities it is not unreasonable to assume that it was on Sullivan's instigation that Wyatt's ship diverted to New York.'

'This does not seem an appropriate time,' she told him acidly, 'to make accusations.'

Captain Hunt's expression hardened. It annoyed him that such inherently good people protected the likes of Sullivan. 'I accuse no one, ma'am,' he said grimly, 'but I do suggest that if, indeed, Wyatt was involved on business for Sullivan, then his death and the demise of the whole crew lie at Sullivan's door. The man is a menace and must be stopped before he causes the loss of other innocent lives. And those who protect him,' he added significantly, 'are equally guilty.'

Jaycinth found her voice, her hand closing convulsively on Emma's shoulder. 'How dare you insinuate such a thing? You have no——'

Emma suddenly stood up. 'I must go to New York,' she said in a hollow whisper. 'I must——'

Captain Hunt moved forward swiftly, forestalling Cousin Maybelle's less agile movement. 'No, Miss Wyatt, you must not.' He took both her hands in his. 'I am sorry, but I must tell you that although no survivors have been reported not all the bodies have been recovered and it seems that some are...' He stopped, looked down at her with pity in his eyes. 'I am sorry, Emma, there is no easy way to say this. Some of the bodies are unrecognisable. Is there—is there some way in which your brother might be identified?'

A hideous picture of Kit's face smashed out of all recognition on the rocks flashed through her mind and she shuddered. The captain pushed her gently back into her seat, and Cousin Maybelle's arm went consolingly around her shoulders.

'He—had a scar,' she forced out. 'Here, on his shoulder. And—and he always wore a thick gold chain round his neck. He was given it by a girl in Italy.' The memory of his sheepish grin when she had challenged his romantic weakness was too much, and she buried her face in her hands unable to cry but unable to bear the rush of memories crowding in on her.

The captain left, with repeated words of condolence and a promise to let her know at once if there was any further news. She scarcely heard the expressions of sympathy and comforting murmurs from Cousin Maybelle. Neither did she notice the catch in Jaycinth's voice and the hastily brushed away tears. Only one thought was in her mind. Kit was dead.

The only one of her brothers who cared anything for her, the only one who had voiced any opposition to the plans to marry her to Carlisle, the only one of her family she did not feel bitter towards, who had kept his place in her heart. He had risked James's wrath, ultimately his livelihood at Wyatt Shipping, to help her. Dear, funny Kit. He should not have gone to New York, should not have listened to Ben——

Ben. Ben was responsible for it, Ben had sent Kit to New York, to his death! A white, blinding anger sud-

denly swept over her, obliterating all else. She sprang to
her feet, and, heedless of the startled cries behind her,
ran from the room.

'Captain, wait!' She caught up with him outside as he
was about to ride away. He wheeled the horse and looked
down at her. 'Ben is expecting a ship tonight. Off Ridge
Point.'

A strange play of emotions crossed the captain's face
and a light gleamed in his eyes. He reached a hand down
for hers and grasped it briefly. 'Thank you. He will not
get away with playing God with people's lives, I promise
you.'

He rode away, and she went back inside drawing a
long, shuddering breath, her shoulders sagging and her
anger draining away as suddenly as it had come, leaving
nothing but a hollow emptiness inside her.

As Monday slipped through midnight into Tuesday, a
small cavalcade of men and mules moved carefully and
almost silently along a well-trodden rabbit path through
the gorse and scrub some few miles down the coast, and
just as quietly picked its way down a stony slope to a
narrow sheltered beach. Two flashes of light flared
briefly from a lantern held aloft at the sea's edge; almost
at once, from the dark expanse of sea, the answering
signal announced the presence of a waiting vessel.

In a very short space of time barrels, chests and oilskin
bundles were being unloaded from the rowing-boats that
slid up from the surf, and quickly secured to the mules.

The transfer was more than half complete when Ben
tied a final knot in the ropes of the lead mule and moved
down the beach to give Emma's letters to a man about
to return to the ship.

But the stealthy quiet was suddenly and violently
shattered. A clash of hooves, a slither of loose rocks and
a warning shout of ''Ware, Redcoats!' plunged the scene
into confusion. Even as the look-out wheeled his horse,

a single musket shot rang out, and he slumped across the saddle. Ben tugged the pistol from his belt, and jerked down to pull the knife from its hiding place in his boot. Another shot whistled past his ear. The man he had been talking to gave little more than a startled grunt, his own knife glancing across Ben's arm as he fell.

There was chaos. The air was rent by the sound of musket fire, as men scattered, shouting, some to push out the boats, others to drive the terrified mules into the path of the oncoming Redcoats.

A single glance at the man at his feet was enough to tell Ben he was dead. His mind worked swiftly. The tide was turning, and a narrow path was emerging at one end of the little cove. Ben yelled directions to the men ducking the musket fire. He knew these tiny inlets like the back of his hand and he was aware that if they could round the point they had a route along the beach inaccessible from above—then into the woods and away. There was a derelict hut a mile away, a few horses for just such an emergency.

There were already soldiers on the beach and Tom Ellis paused in his flight and grabbed Ben's arm. 'He's dead. Come on!'

Ben shook him off. 'Get out of here!'

'Don't be a fool, man! There's nothing you can do. If you're caught this whole operation is finished. And Sam Adams needs you, if we don't. You're no use to him dead. Come on!' He pulled insistently on his arm.

Another shot ricocheted off a boulder only a foot away. Ellis was right; there was little more he could do now anyway. Those men farther up the beach were already in the clutches of the Redcoats. He uttered an oath and started to run, Ellis beside him and a handful of others on their heels as they splashed through the water round the point.

It was not until they were sure they had shaken off their pursuers that they slowed their pace and made their

way to the hut and the waiting horses. 'Who was look-
out?' Ben demanded, vaulting into the saddle and taking
Ellis up behind him. 'Was he hit?'

'Josh Payne, I think. Aye, he was hit but he got away.
What the hell happened? Someone must have informed.'

'But who?' Another man pulled his horse alongside.
'We were all there, we've no one new, and none of us
can be bought . . .

Ben's face was set in rigid lines, the blue of his eyes
darkening with a dangerous gleam as he recalled the only
other person who knew their rendezvous. He dug his
heels into the flanks of his horse, and set a reckless pace
across the treacherous terrain that was a short cut to
town.

The other men, mostly two to a horse, exchanged
glances in the darkness. They knew that look and there
was not one of them who did not fear it. God help the
man on whom Sullivan's fury fell this night!

It was still dark, but Emma threw aside the covers and
sat up, her head aching relentlessly. She fumbled for the
candle, struggled to light it and then dragged on her robe.
Her limbs felt leaden as she got up, took the candle to
the dressing-table and slumped into the chair, staring at
her shadowy, dark-eyed reflection. What had she done?

Having obediently taken the sleeping draught Maybelle
had pressed on her, she had lain in her bed for hours in
an uneasy half-world, unable to prevent herself from relentlessly going over everything Captain Hunt had said.
And at some point the realisation had penetrated her
dulled senses that there was at least a forlorn possibility
that Kit had cheated the sea and lived. Without a body
there was hope, surely? And then she had begun to regret
what she had told Hunt. Even if Kit had perished, his
death was her fault, for he had gone to New York for
her sake, not to help Ben. Several times she had been
on the point of getting up, of seeking out Maybelle and

blurting out what she had done, begging for help in
finding a way to warn Ben. But her body felt like lead,
refused to obey her. And what if it brought about another heart seizure? What could Maybelle do anyway
without showing herself as condoning his activities,
putting herself in danger? It had been hours since Hunt
left, and she had also been forced to accept that it was
probably too late to stop him, to warn Ben...

Far from giving her the release of sleep, Maybelle's
powders had suspended her somewhere between, tormented by guilt and plagued by visions of what was happening at Ridge Point.

Now, as the night faded towards dawn and she stared
into the mirror, a hollow emptiness seemed to have come
over her; a numbness, she realised dully, that had more
to do with the possibility of Ben's death than Kit's.

Scarcely knowing what she was doing, she picked up
the hairbrush and began to draw it through the matted
tangles of her hair. A door banged somewhere downstairs, shattering the quiet. Moments later, her own door
crashed open, and she stared round violently, and almost
fainted with relief to see Ben in the doorway. But fear
swiftly followed the relief.

He stood, dishevelled and furious, his blue eyes cold
as ice in the unshaven greyness of his face. He knew!
Her mouth went dry, her heart pounded painfully. For
a moment there was utter stillness in the room. Then
she saw the dark stain of blood on the torn sleeve of his
shirt.

'You're hurt!' She started up, but a flicker in his eyes
stopped her. He pushed the door shut with a mud-
encrusted boot. His eyes never wavered from her face
and his voice was raw with a barely controlled fury.

'You treacherous bitch!' He almost spat the words at
her and she recoiled as if he had struck her, clutching
the chair-back for support. 'I trust you are happy with
your night's work!'

'Please—listen!' she pleaded desperately. 'I didn't mean to—I didn't know what I was doing. Alex said——'

The harsh crack of laughter made her wince. 'You could not resist running to him with the little scrap of information I let slip, could you? Half the damn army came down on us. My God, how could I have been so careless?'

'You don't understand!' she cried. 'I thought—I believed—— ' She broke off on a half-sob. 'Oh, Ben, I have been regretting it all night, I——' The words died on her lips beneath the look of disgust in his face.

'You expect me to believe that? One man dead, another dying, four more in the hands of the Redcoats and facing a rope. And as much on my conscience for my stupidity as on yours!' He thrust a hand into his shirt and drew out her letters. 'Here!' He crumpled them in his hand and tossed them down at her feet. 'You will have to find another ship.'

For a brief moment the glittering gaze held hers in a fathomless look, full of anger, accusation and pain. 'I hope Hunt paid you well,' he said bitterly, and, turning on his heel, threw the door wide and walked straight into a sleepy-eyed Jaycinth. 'You have not seen me,' he ground out. 'Do you understand?' She nodded mutely and he thrust past her, striding away.

Emma sprang forward with a cry and went after him. She could not let him go like this, hating her. 'Ben, wait!' She caught at his sleeve. 'I was upset about Kit. I didn't think. I am sorry, truly——'

But she doubted he even heard her. He thrust her aside and ran down the stairs, leaving her staring after him, a wave of utter despair sweeping over her.

The door beside her opened and Maybelle appeared. 'What is all this noise? Was that Ben?' A single glance at Emma's face brought a note of anxiety into her voice. 'What is it?'

'I betrayed him,' she whispered, turning desolate eyes to the older woman. 'I——' Tears spilled down her cheeks and, with a choked cry, she turned and ran back to her room, throwing herself on the bed and sobbing uncontrollably.

A few moments later, Maybelle came and sat beside her, resting a hand on her back. 'Emma.' The voice was gentle but firm. 'I think you had better tell me what happened. All of it.'

It was some minutes before she could pull herself together sufficiently to comply. 'Last week at Cedars— Ben asked me if I had any letters to send home,' she began tremulously, rubbing her eyes with Maybelle's handkerchief. 'He told me he was meeting a ship off Ridge Point and that her master was a friend of his and would carry my letters. When Captain Hunt told me about Kit—I couldn't think. I blamed Ben. Kit *was* smuggling for him, you see.' She glanced up at Maybelle, and realised at once that she knew all about Ben's clandestine activities. 'He only did it so that he could leave me some money. So—so it was not Ben's fault at all, it was mine. If I had not run away from Carlisle...' She stopped, knowing the futility of that line of thought, and drew a long shuddering breath, staring down at her hands twisting the handkerchief convulsively.

'You cannot blame yourself for Kit's decisions,' Maybelle murmured. 'He did not have to bring you here, and he did not have to go to New York.'

Emma looked at her miserably. 'But yesterday I could only blame Ben. It seemed as though everything Captain Hunt said was true. So—so I told him about Ridge Point. And—and they went there and—and one of Ben's men was killed. He said another is dying, four were captured....' Her voice faltered beneath the enormity of what she had done. 'He was so angry,' she whispered. 'So *cold*.'

Maybelle's arm tightened round her shoulder. 'He is not a man to take betrayal lightly,' she said gently. 'But I doubt he knows about Kit and, when he does, he will realise why you reacted in such a way.'

'But he will never forgive me.' She said it flatly, knowing that whatever foolish dreams she had nurtured they had been destroyed with the half-dozen words she had uttered so hastily to Captain Hunt. The last few hours had crystallised her love, her heart drawing in on itself all the emotions she had tried so hard to deny, and tying them up into such a knot of pain that she knew she would never be free of it.

Maybelle shook her head slightly. 'He is not such a monster,' she said softly, and, putting her hand beneath Emma's chin, turned her head to look into the tear-reddened eyes. 'Are you in love with him?' She could not answer, and pulled away, averting her gaze. 'Did he say where he was going?' Maybelle went on after a moment.

She shook her head, and raised anxious eyes to the older woman. 'He was hurt. It did not look serious, but he said it was enough to get him hanged. Do you think——?'

'No.' The fine-drawn lines around Maybelle's mouth belied the calm certainty in her tone. 'He has been in tight corners before and always contrived to extricate himself. He has many friends. We can do nothing but wait, I fear. I suggest you go back to bed and try to rest.'

Rest! As though she could! But, not knowing quite what else to do, she lay down and closed her eyes, the draught she had taken last night finally got the better of her and she did eventually drift into sleep.

She awoke several hours later, and although her head was no longer pounding she still felt sick with anxiety and guilt. Bracing herself to face the others, she splashed her face with cold water and went downstairs. Hearing John's voice from the parlour, she hesitated to go in.

'I may not agree with his politics and I may prefer not to know what he does with his nights,' he was saying with some spirit, 'but the man owns nearly half the mill and I count him a closer friend than any other—whatever you may think, Jaycinth! And if he is in trouble, I will do all I can to help. Besides which I do not care to have excise officials, magistrates and soldiers, and God knows who else, crawling all over my house and the mill without so much as a by-your-leave!'

He came out and barely paused when he saw Emma, only giving her a strange sort of look that was somewhere between irritation and pity. Just what he could do Emma failed to see, but she clutched at the straw and tried to banish from her mind the vision of Ben dangling at the end of a rope or rotting in some dark and stinking gaol.

Jaycinth's green eyes held only censure and blame in a face drained of colour and Jinny, who had been so solicitous the previous evening, now looked at her with eyes full of reproach. The others were worse. So she retreated to the nursery. But when she went to the door for the fourth time, alert for any sound that might herald news, even Matthew could not fail to notice her agitation.

'What's the matter?' he demanded crossly. 'What are you waiting for?'

'Ben is in trouble,' she told him, as lightly as she could. 'Your uncle has gone to help him.' She saw no point in telling him about Kit, at least not while there was still some doubt. But if only something would happen! Even a magistrate or army patrol hammering on the door would be preferable to this silence, a silence which seemed horribly ominous.

'Is that all?' Matthew dismissed her anxiety with a shrug, and all the faith of a four-year-old convinced of his hero's invincibility. 'He will be all right. He is very strong and clever and always gets out of trouble. Grandmama says so. Don't worry.'

She looked down at him, feeling as though a knife were twisting in her heart. Because of her the man who was probably his father might even now be in the hands of the authorities. Forcing a smile, she whispered, 'I am sure you're right, Matthew. I shall try not to worry.'

She sat in the parlour window-seat shortly before dinner, staring out at the darkness and seeing only visions of Kit's face bloody and mutilated, and Ben's, full of hate.

'Did you find him?' Jaycinth's anxious demand cut through her desolation, and she jerked her head round as John strode into the room, his face set in grim lines. Ann was behind him, casting off her cloak into Hannah's arms, a look of satisfaction flaring in her eyes as they met Emma's across the room.

John stirred the fire into a blaze. 'I do not think he will hang,' he said, warming his hands before turning back to them. 'Not one of the men being held will say that Ben was even with them on the beach. And Ben himself is lying dead drunk at the Ship and Compass with a dozen witnesses to say he has been there since noon yesterday. Fortunately the wound in his arm was caused by a knife not a musket ball which would have been far more damning. The story is being put about that it happened in a fight with Tom McGuire, whom he accused of cheating in a card game that lasted well into the early hours. McGuire readily admits it and I cannot see what they can do to Ben with the little evidence they have. And I don't think they dare fabricate anything the way feelings are running at the moment. Emma—you will have to say that what you told Hunt was simply something you overheard Ben and I discussing. I will make up a story to deal with any further questions.'

'Yes, of course,' she whispered, faint with relief.

'Thank God!' Maybelle breathed. 'And let us pray this teaches him some caution.'

'He would not be in such a predicament but for Emma,' Ann said coldly, moving to stand beside her husband and turning accusing eyes on her. 'I cannot believe such gross ingratitude! You owe every stitch on your back to this family and this is how you repay us! By almost bringing about the death of a close friend. I do not know how you have the effrontery to sit here! I should have thought you would at least have had the decency to pack your bags!'

'Ann!' John's voice held a sharp warning.

'You surely do not intend to defend her?'

Maybelle rose to her feet. 'This is still my house, though you choose to forget it, and if anyone leaves it will be you! You are an insensitive, selfish, malicious young woman——'

'Mother!' John interceded quickly. 'Do not distress yourself. Of course Emma will stay——'

'What?' Ann cried, glaring aghast at her husband. 'It is quite clear that she has been plotting this with Hunt since they met at Cedars!'

'That's ridiculous!' Emma found her voice at last, appalled at the heated exchange. 'I would never have betrayed Ben but for—but that I was upset about Kit and I could not think clearly! I just wanted—revenge——' She broke off. It sounded lame, even to her ears.

'What a scheming little slut you are!' Ann persisted viciously. 'My groom tells me you met Hunt on the Common after seeing Ben at Cedars last Thursday. Is that when you told him? What did he promise you in return for Ben's neck?'

Emma leapt to her feet, her control snapping. 'How dare you? How dare you suggest such a thing?'

'That's enough!' John's voice cut into her fury. 'It is folly to suggest Emma should leave, Ann. Apart from any other considerations, such an action would clearly indicate that we harbour anti-British feeling—after all, she was only doing her duty as an honest citizen. Casting her out would merely confirm the suspicions of the authorities that we are in league with Ben and all our efforts to appear on the best terms with the army would be undone. And that would help Ben not at all!'

'If you do not mind,' Emma found herself saying coldly, 'I do not care to be talked about as if I am not here. I will go to my room so that you may discuss me freely! If you wish me to leave, I will do so at once.'

Trembling with suppressed fury, she walked from the room with her head held high and her fists clenched. But before she reached the foot of the stairs a shattering crash from the drawing-room made her spin round in alarm. Moving swiftly to the door, she threw it open—and uttered a strangled cry at the sight that greeted her.

A crackling golden glow illuminated the room. The curtains were ablaze at the broken window and a torch lay burning beneath them, flames already licking at the couch.

'My God!' John pushed past her, and without pausing to think she followed him in, snatching up the rug as he tore down the curtains. Together they smothered the flames, and by the time the servants arrived it was all but out. They stood stunned in the smoking darkness staring at the smouldering remains of the draperies and the jagged hole in the window. Emma looked down at her hand, only now aware of a searing pain. The skin on the back of it was red raw and puckering where the flames had licked it. She nursed it against the cool folds of her skirt as Jaycinth voiced the question in all their minds.

'Dear heaven, who would do such a thing? And why?'

'Perhaps one of Ben's men.' Emma spun round at Ann's cool, unruffled voice from the doorway. There was no sign of horror or shock on her face, only a strange gleam of something that might almost have been triumph in her eyes. 'After last night, who could blame them for this? It was probably a member of one of the dead men's families...'

Emma stared at her, the implications of such a possibility making her blood run cold. But, before she could speak, Maybelle uttered a strange, strangled sound, her face blanched to a ghostly white and before anyone could reach her she crumpled and collapsed to the floor.

'Mama!' Jaycinth dropped to her knees and chafed the delicate hands.

'Jack, get the physician!' John bent over his mother. 'Loosen this damn bodice, Jaycinth. I'll get some brandy.'

'I'll get it.' Glad of something to do, Emma pushed past Ann, who was staring with a fixed fascination at the inert form of her mother-in-law, and ran to the parlour. Her hands were trembling as she splashed a generous measure of brandy into a glass.

When she returned to the drawing-room, John was shaking his head. 'She has not fainted. It's her heart.' He lifted her into his arms and looked at Emma. 'Bring that upstairs.'

'Give it to me.' Ann almost snatched the glass and hurried after her husband and Jaycinth, Ellen and Hannah trailing in their wake.

'Not much we can do with that lot up there,' Jinny said. 'Best come along with me and have a cup of tea.'

She sat down on the little wooden stool beside the kitchen fire while Jinny lifted the large heavy kettle on to the hook over the flames. She was shivering convulsively now, cold despite the proximity of the blaze. Dear God, was she to have Maybelle's death on her conscience too?

The kettle was already hot and started to boil immediately. 'Jack won't take long fetching the physician, Miss Emma. And the mistress has had bad turns before.' There was an anxious doubt in the girl's voice. 'Never as bad as this, though, and she did look an awful funny colour.' She took down the kettle and busied herself making tea, and, when she passed Emma a steaming mug, suddenly noticed the livid burn on her hand. 'You've burnt yourself! Oh, why didn't you say, miss? It looks a nasty one, too.' She went across to the dresser and took down a small jar of yellow-brown ointment. 'However did it start, that fire?'

Emma submitted with scarcely a wince of pain as Jinny applied the salve to the burn. 'Someone threw a torch through the window.'

'No! Why, who would do such a thing?' A fleeting recollection of Ann's expression came into Emma's mind as the girl bound a strip of clean linen round her hand and went on, 'But there are an awful lot of ruffians roaming the streets these days, and this tea business has given them a fine excuse for a lot of trouble-making!'

She didn't answer. Staring dully into the flames, a desolation seeped through her. Too much had happened too quickly, and she was to blame for all of it. It was too much to think about now, too much to bear.

Eventually the physician arrived, but it was only a few minutes later that Hannah came into the kitchen, weeping into her apron and telling them what Emma already knew. Dr Cornwallis had been too late. Maybelle was dead.

CHAPTER EIGHT

MAYBELLE was buried three days later.

Nothing was seen or heard of Ben in that time, except that he had been released from gaol and had disappeared. A great many people had come to the house to pay their respects or sent messages of condolence, but he had not been among them, and a swift glance about her on the cold, grey morning of the funeral dashed Emma's hope that he might appear at the graveside.

Neither was there any word about Kit. Daily she expected to hear that his body had been found, but when Captain Hunt sent his condolences he added a note to the effect that he had had no further news from New York.

Emma lived through those days in a dream, and it was Matthew who kept her mind from lingering on the guilt and sorrow nagging at her conscience and prevented her sinking into a black despair. He had retreated into a shell of silence and clung to her like a limpet, never leaving her side, as if he was terrified that she, too, would be taken from him. He did not want to go and live at Cedars with Ann, whom he disliked with an intensity alarming in one so young, and kept asking for reassurance that Emma would be going to Cedars too. But this, the one thing he needed most, she could not give him. For Ann regarded her with a haughty smugness that boded ill, and suggested that she was merely biding her time. The suspicion that she was somehow responsible for the fire—had perhaps let it be known in certain quarters who it was that had sent the soldiers to Ridge Point—still nagged at Emma's thoughts. She could not have anticipated Maybelle's death, of course, but nothing in her demeanour suggested she was altogether upset at the way things had turned out.

So when the will was read, and, having been made several years earlier, held no surprises, she was not entirely unprepared for the summons to attend Ann in the parlour.

'Ah, Emma,' she said sweetly, turning from her study of the garden outside and obviously relishing the task before her. 'Now that these harrowing few days are behind us, we must give some thought to your future. Sit down, please.'

Emma did not seem to have energy enough to summon any resistance to what she knew was coming and sank on to a chair, acknowledging a terrible weariness.

'It seems probable that I am—with child,' Ann went on, with such evident distaste for the condition that Emma could only pity the unborn child. 'If that is the case, we will be employing a nurse for our own baby, who will also have charge of Matthew until he attends the school or has tutors. I am afraid our plans cannot include you.'

'I see.' She had little wish anyway to go to Cedars as an unpaid servant, but there was poor Matthew to consider. His aversion to his uncle's wife was instinctive and unshakeable, and she shuddered to think of him in such unsympathetic hands. She swallowed her pride for his sake. 'Will I be able to stay until you employ someone else?'

Ann raised her eyebrows. 'I am afraid not. In deference to Maybelle and my husband's wishes, you may have until the end of next week to find some other employment, or a passage home.'

'Is it John's wish also?' Surely he was not so much under his wife's thumb that he would let her do this to Matthew? But if there was any hesitation in Ann's answer she could not detect it.

'It is.'

'I imagine I may not expect a reference?'

'You may not! You have caused three deaths this week, four if you include your own brother, and very nearly brought about a fifth. I do not think anyone would expect us to furnish you with references! Indeed, you should count yourself fortunate in the extreme not to have been thrown out on the street already!' She moved to the door and paused. 'Allow me to advise you, Emma. Alex Hunt is more than interested in you. Once he realises what your betrayal has cost you, I am sure you could——' her gaze slid meaningfully over Emma's slender frame '—persuade him to offer for you.' She gave a malicious little smile and as she went out added over her shoulder, 'You would make a good match.'

As she swept out, Matthew scuttled away from the door and fled upstairs, earning a stinging rebuke from his aunt, who cared not at all that his crumpled, tear-stained face was the result of understanding most of what he had just overheard.

Emma sat for a few minutes trying to collect her thoughts. What could she do? She could not remain in Boston—no family whose sympathies lay with the patriots would take her on once the story of her betrayal got around. Half the town probably already knew. And without a reference... Her fifty pounds and the little she had from James's safe would keep her for a while, but where and with whom? The awful prospect of having to go home with her tail between her legs loomed hideously before her.

But she could not think about it here. She left the room and went through the kitchen to the coach house. Usually the small stable housed only the carriage horse; now John's kept it company, and, although it seemed the sprightlier of the two and she was sorely tempted, she dared not take it. There was no sign of Jack, so she saddled the horse herself, and, with no clear idea of where she was going, was soon riding away at a pace which Jack, emerging from the house at the same time, later described as, 'Damned foolish'.

There were a few other riders on the Common, and a company of soldiers were drilling in red-coated ranks, watched by ragged boys and harassed by a few militant youths. Since she had neither hat nor escort, she was bound to attract attention, but she ignored the openly curious stares and spurred the sturdy creature across the muddy ground. She found herself glad that the horse had not more mettle, for her bandaged hand could only loosely hold the rein.

Finally they stopped by a fallen tree-trunk and she dismounted, staring back across the expanse of Common. The air was tangy with salt, and her hair, un-confined by hat or ribbon, flicked about her face as the wind caught it.

One thing was certain. She was not going back to England. Whatever else she had to do, however low she had to sink, she would not go back to beg forgiveness of James and face the shame and the scandal and the wrath of William Carlisle.

If she stayed in Boston, how could she bear it? Seeing him, hearing about him, perhaps meeting him by chance and finding only accusation and disgust in his eyes? Would leaving—never even seeing him at a distance again be worse? Perhaps she should try to go to New York, find out about Kit ... And what of little Matthew? How could she help him?

The questions went round and round. She felt like a small child, helpless and miserable, and could not pull herself out of it. Tears sprang to her eyes and fell un-checked down her cheeks. What a horrible, tragic mess she had made of everything.

'Emma?' She had not heard the rider's approach, and turned, brushing her damp cheeks, as Captain Hunt leapt from his horse. 'You are surely not out here alone?'

'Yes. And you, Captain? Is—is it Thursday? I have lost count of the days.'

'No. I have business in Milton—messages for the Governor.' He raised her chin and looked down at her. 'You have been crying. I am sorry, Emma. These past few days must have been wretched for you. And...' He hesitated. 'And I am afraid there is still no news of your brother. It is just possible——'

Suddenly she realised the futility of holding on to an impossible hope. 'No, Captain. He is dead. Just as Maybelle is dead and—and all because of me. Because I——' She broke off abruptly belatedly realising who—and what—she was talking to; she had been on the point of blurting out everything John had worked so hard to conceal these past few days. A wave of utter despair washed over her. Suddenly, perversely, she found herself clinging to Alex as the only available comfort. And his arms encircled her readily, holding her close against him.

After a moment, with a supreme effort, she pulled herself together, forced down the sobs and drew away. If she allowed herself to give way now she would not be able to stop; there was so much wretchedness inside her for the chain of events she had set in motion with so few impulsive words. And Captain Hunt was perhaps the one man with whom she dared not let down her guard. She had betrayed Ben once; she must not inadvertently do so again.

Gathering her horse's reins, she glanced at him fleetingly. 'I must go back. I will have been missed by now——'

'I will go with you, then,' he said immediately. 'You should not ride alone.'

'No, please! I really would rather you did not.'

Sudden comprehension dawned in his eyes. 'Of course. I'm sorry. It must have been very awkward for you.' He paused. 'Are you removing to Cedars? It will be easier there. I will call——'

'No, I will not be at Cedars.' She tossed the hair from her face and looked beyond him to the soldiers drilling in ranks on the far side. 'I must leave. They do not need me.'

He looked surprised. 'What will you do?'

'I do not know,' she admitted. 'I do not want to leave Boston. There is Matthew...' She finished on a shrug. 'I shall have to find some employment.'

He said nothing for a few moments, his expression unreadable. 'I must go to Milton,' he said finally and with obvious regret. 'But when I return we will talk about it. You do not need to leave Boston, my dear Emma. I feel at least in part responsible for your plight, but it is not simply that... You must know that in a remarkably short time and on such brief encounters I have come to think of you will admiration and not a little affection——' He put a finger to her lips as she opened her mouth to protest such an unwarranted declaration. 'Do not say anything now—this is not the time or the place to discuss such things. But while I am away, please give some thought to allowing me to take care of you.' Before she could stop him, he bent his head and kissed her on the lips. 'However little I have to offer,' he continued softly, 'it must be more than is facing you now. Consider it seriously, my dear, and we will discuss it when I return.'

She watched him ride away, still stunned by what was, in effect, a proposal. Ann had been right, then. She would consider it, of course. In her present predicament she had to consider all the possibilities.

Some distance away, Ben drew a totally incorrect conclusion from the touching scene he had witnessed and swore violently under his breath.

He had spent the days since his release from gaol in a friend's cabin up-river, trying to come to terms with a few unpleasant truths, and succeeding only in depleting the cabin's stock of smuggled brandy. Underlying his anger at Emma's betrayal had been a far more telling emotion—a bitter disappointment. It was also an unwelcome shock to realise that an emotion he had thought well under his control had crept up on him, and so affected his judgement and instinctive caution that he had caused the deaths of two of his men and put the lives of others at risk. He was unforgiving of carelessness in his men, and to find himself guilty of it was intolerable.

But then Tom Ellis had finally tracked him down, turning up at dusk last night, the bearer of bad news. Maybelle's death, and anxiety at what was happening at Tremont Street as a result, would have been enough to send him back to Boston. But by the circuitous grapevine that got information out of Castle William Tom had learned about the *Emma Louise*. With that news, Ben realised what had sent Emma to Hunt with her snippet of information, and if he could not forgive himself his carelessness he could at least forgive her.

So he had set off at first light, and if what he had found when he finally arrived at Tremont Street was not enough to fill him with angry disgust, he now had to see her in Alex Hunt's arms. The distasteful reality was that he was more than a little in love with a scheming hussy who was on intimate terms with a man he could only describe as an enemy, and it left a bitter taste in his mouth.

Jealousy and self-disgust were not emotions he was over-familiar with, and he sat watching them for a moment, trying to put his thoughts in order. It put quite a different light on everything. He had come looking for her knowing that a secret he had nursed for years could remain a secret no longer, and he would have to do what he had sworn never to do. That Emma had to be a part of it had tempered the decision with a pleasant anticipation. Now, however, the prospect was wholly unpalatable.

But there was no alternative. He would have to make it impossible for her to refuse. Whatever happened, he had to have her, and a small part of him was damned sure Alex Hunt would not!

As Emma turned her horse to ride back the way she had come, she caught sight of the unmistakable black horse and its equally unmistakable rider, and her heart missed a beat. She pulled up and waited for him, a nervous fluttering in her stomach.

His face was impassive, but there was a hardness in his eyes as he drew rein beside her and said curtly, 'Matthew has run away.'

All other thoughts fled as the impact of his words hit her. 'What?'

'I know where he will be, but you will have to come with me.'

A dozen questions flew through her mind, but his uncompromising expression prevented her voicing them, and anyway he jerked his horse's head round and set off at a gallop, not once glancing back to see if she followed. Her own stolid mount could not hope to keep up with the dashing Blade, and it was not until he reached the street and waited for her that she could ask where they were going.

'The harbour.' His tone did not invite conversation and everything she wanted to say to him evaporated as she glanced at his rigid profile. There was neither forgiveness nor understanding in it. He pulled ahead of her and they rode in silence until they left the busy thoroughfares and entered the narrower, gloomier backstreets around the harbour.

'Why do you need me?' she demanded finally, drawing alongside him. 'If you know where he is——'

'He ran away because he does not want to go to Cedars without you. He will need your reassurance that you are not going to leave him.'

'I cannot do that,' she said flatly. 'I am to leave by the end of the week.'

'They told me. Matthew apparently overheard the conversation.'

'Oh.' Her heart sank, and she looked at him helplessly. 'But what can I do? I don't imagine you will persuade Ann to keep me on! And she will not give me a reference or recommendation so even remaining in Boston at all looks—difficult.' Captain Hunt's proposal leapt to mind. But that would not help Matthew very much. 'Anyway...' She stared down at the reins in her hands. 'Anyway, he adjusted to me quickly enough, as no doubt he will to whoever John and Ann employ. He is more resilient than you would think——'

'You do not believe that,' he told her flatly. 'Do you want him to go to Ann and a nurse of her choosing?'

'Of course not! But he has you—he worships you.'

'That is not good enough, and you know it.'

'Well, I do not see what I can do about it!' She tossed her head angrily and stared ahead through a mist of tears. He was being unfair, using her affection for Matthew to punish her.

'You can tell him you are going to marry me.'

'*What?*' She jerked on the reins and stared at him. 'Are you mad?'

He looked at her for a long moment, his mouth twisted into a brief, sardonic smile. 'Probably. But you will tell him anyway.'

'I will not!' What was he trying to do to her? He dismounted and hailed a boy coming past with a handcart, tossing him a coin to mind the horses. Still staring at him, she allowed him to help her down, his hands on her waist sending a shiver down her back as he met her gaze and held it.

'Do you have a better idea?'

'But it wouldn't solve anything!' Her voice came out as little more than a harsh whisper. 'He would still have to live at Cedars. I cannot see——'

His blue eyes seemed to bore into hers. 'No. He would come and live with us.'

'But...' She searched his face, thrown into confusion. Did he have proof that Matthew was his son? 'But how? I don't understand.'

'Trust me.' The long look held a moment longer before he turned away. She followed him along the wharves, almost having to run to keep up with his long strides. She could not think. What was he up to? He could not seriously want as a wife the woman who had betrayed him to the British and caused so much trouble.

He stopped and nodded towards a pile of crates against a warehouse wall. An old man with an outrageous white beard was sitting on an upturned barrel mending nets, with Matthew at his feet. 'Wait here.'

'But——' But he was already striding away and she could only watch as Matthew greeted him with undisguised pleasure, and a few moments later spun round to see her. He leapt up and flew across the ground towards her. 'Is it true?' he demanded joyfully. 'You are going to marry Ben? And I'm going to live with you?'

Her heart contracted sharply. 'I...' She stared at him helplessly and then hugged him against her and over his head looked up at Ben with hatred and condemnation. The instant their eyes met she knew he had seen her in Alex's arms on the Common. What interpretation had he put on that? she wondered. Was this his way of having his revenge on both of them for Ridge Point? She could not believe it. And anyway, surely he would not use Matthew in such a way! How could he be so callous? So diabolically unscrupulous!

'For now it must be our secret, Matt,' Ben said, ignoring her contemptuous glare. 'You must not say anything to anyone until I tell you. Do you understand?'

Matthew pulled away from her and nodded, his eyes shining at being trusted with such a secret. 'Come, now. We must go back, for there is much to be done.' He lifted the boy on to his shoulders and strode back to the horses, leaving her to hurry after him, a sick disgust in her heart.

With Matthew up before him, he rode ahead of her all the way to Tremont Street, effectively preventing any discussion, and even when he sprang from the saddle and consigned Matthew to Jack he gave her little chance to speak.

'Wait for me in the drawing-room,' he said curtly. 'I will talk to John and ensure we are not disturbed.'

'But it's a mess,' she protested. 'There was a fire——'

'I know.' He gave her a long, measured look. 'I will only be a few minutes.'

Reluctantly, she went into the drawing-room. With one window temporarily boarded up, the failing light of late afternoon slanting in at the other cast eerie shadows into the corners and gave the room a faintly sinister atmosphere. She paced up and down, trying to keep out the memory of what had happened there, and rubbing at the bandage around her hand in some agitation. Why had he chosen this room? Was it another way of punishing her?

'Did that happen in the fire?'

She swung round to find him in the doorway, a decanter and glass in his hand. 'John said you helped him put the fire out. That was very brave of you.' Suddenly he wished he had not made her come in here, had not needed to test her, to see her reaction. 'Does it hurt?'

'Not really. Not now.' She stopped fussing with the bandage and looked at him. Was this concern? Certainly she could detect no mockery. Perhaps he regretted his moment of spite? Suddenly she heard herself blurting out, 'Ben, I'm sorry! I should never have told Alex. I do not know why I did except that I blamed you for Kit—I know you must despise me, but——'

'I do not despise you.' He pushed the door shut with his foot and walked across to the unlit fire, pouring himself a drink before setting the decanter down. 'I know about Kit,' he said, his voice less harsh than it had been, 'and I am very sorry. I do not blame you for what you did. It was my own fault; I was careless.' He paused, the blue eyes unreadable. 'It will not happen again.'

She flinched from the finality in his tone and fought back a rush of misery. She would not break down now, not here in front of Ben. Instead she masked her unhappiness with anger. 'Why did you tell Matthew we were to be married?' she demanded. 'You know it cannot be! How could you raise his hopes like that? I thought you cared for him! And if you have proof somehow that he is your son, then——'

'My son?' His voice cut sharply across her outburst. 'Where the devil did you get that notion?' He nodded towards a chair. 'Sit down.'

'He is not your son?' Obediently she dropped into the high-backed chair beside her. 'Then why——?'

'He is my nephew.'

She looked at him blankly, then wearily shook her head. 'I don't understand.'

'I am Maybelle's son. Beth was my sister.'

The words took a moment to register. 'But you can't be!' She stared at him, shocked. 'But—but Jaycinth! I heard—I thought——'

He raised his eyebrows. 'What?'

'I don't know.' She swallowed and frowned, looking away and trying to recall exactly what she had heard. 'The night Kit left, I heard footsteps—I heard Jaycinth's door and I thought—I assumed it was you...'

Shaking his head, he said gently, 'I rather think that if you heard anyone go into Jaycinth's room that night it was probably Kit.'

'Kit!' That possibility had not occurred to her. But she cast her mind back and realised that Jaycinth's distress, that she had attributed to anxiety over Ben, had begun when Alex broke the news about the *Emma Louise*. It was Kit she loved! Poor Jaycinth! To lose her mother and her lover within two days of each other... She raised her eyes to Ben's. 'I am sorry. I appear to have jumped to all the wrong conclusions.'

'Yes,' he agreed, a grimness about his mouth. 'And before there is any more confusion allow me to explain. When Maybelle married George it was against her father's wishes. He threatened to disown her if she went ahead with it, mostly because he was a poor farmer's son struggling on a failing farm, and, as far as her father was concerned, merely interested in using their money to save it. But she found herself pregnant and married him anyway. Within weeks George fell ill, and by the time I was born they were virtually penniless and scraping out a very meagre existence. When George was well enough he decided to give up the struggle and come to Boston to find work. Maybelle entrusted me to the nearest thing they had to friends—a childless couple on a neighbouring farm—and went with him.'

He paused, and swirled the brandy in his glass for a moment before continuing, 'Their fortunes changed rapidly once George got into the timber business. And then Maybelle's father died and they discovered that he had not carried out his threat and had, in fact, left her well provided for. But when they went back for me, they found we had disappeared. My new "parents" had changed their name and moved away.'

Emma gasped in dismay. 'Poor Maybelle! What did she do?'

'What could she do? They searched for weeks but all attempts to trace us failed. She was with child again, so finally they gave up and came home. My "mother" confessed the truth on her deathbed when I was fifteen, but

I did nothing about it for years, until I found myself in Boston. I persuaded George to take me on at the mill, without telling him who I was, and I actually began to enjoy earning a respectable living. I also had time to think about what being the eldest son in a relatively wealthy, respectable family would mean. I was more than content with my lot and involved in one or two things I had no desire to give up and I certainly did not want the responsibility, the restriction. But when the rumours about Beth and me started, I had to tell them, and they had very mixed feelings about it.' He gave a brief, rueful smile at the memory.

'But why?' she interrupted. 'They had been looking for you. Surely——?'

He shrugged. 'They had three children, prosperity, a settled, comfortable existence. Announcing a long-lost eldest son would cause a great deal of disruption and unpleasantness. I was happy to leave things as they were—and to keep my distance until Beth was safely married. I did not want the town's attention focused on me. And what is more, I still don't.' His eyes darkened a little as he drank his brandy, and then he raised his eyes and looked steadily at her. 'But now there is Matthew, and without you at Cedars his life will be miserable. You were right; Ann will not have you there and for some inexplicable reason John seems intent on giving in to her every whim.'

'I imagine it is because she thinks she is with child,' she murmured.

He raised an eyebrow, and, although he did not comment, his expression was eloquent enough. 'Matthew has suffered enough tragedy,' he went on. 'I am his uncle and I should be his legal guardian.'

'Can you prove it?' She looked at him doubtfully. 'John will not easily believe you——'

'I have all the necessary documents. Maybelle also made a new Will when Beth died confirming that I am her eldest son, therefore her heir, that she wished me to be acknowledged as such, with legal responsibility for Matthew. She had Cornwallis witness it, and she gave it to me, to use at my discretion.' His mouth twitched in a brief half-smile that had little satisfaction in it. 'I imagine John will agree to let me take Matthew without too much argument. He will not want a protracted legal wrangle over it any more than I do, and, apart from Matthew, I have no intention of causing him any upsets.'

As he finished his drink, she sat silently digesting the story. When he set the glass down and spoke again, his voice was brisk and business-like. 'I need your help, Emma. Clearly I cannot take Matthew on my own. It is equally clear that you cannot come to Eastwood in your present capacity. I am afraid your reputation would be in shreds within hours. So I suggest marriage as the obvious solution. Unless, of course, you have reason to expect an offer from another quarter?'

A tautly wound cord somewhere inside her suddenly snapped at the mocking challenge behind his words. Stung to anger by his high-handed arrogance, and his calculated assurance that she would fall victim to his emotional blackmail, she stood up abruptly. 'As a matter of fact,' she snapped hotly, 'Captain Hunt did offer to——' To what? Suddenly she realised that it was doubtful whether marriage was what Captain Hunt had in mind. Turning away to avoid his gaze, she walked across the room and stood looking out of the window. 'But I did not take his offer seriously,' she finished lightly.

Seeing her confusion as confirmation that she was, indeed, in love with Hunt, Ben hardened his heart against the emotions seething within him, quashing a pang of sympathy that all she got from Hunt in return was an offer to make her his mistress. The man was a fool.

'Well, then,' he said tersely, 'if you agree to become my wife, be assured I will make no unwelcome demands. But bear in mind that any—indiscretion on your part and I will be sure to hear of it. And I will not be made a fool of. Do you understand?'

She understood very well. He would be free to seek his pleasures while she must remain a dutiful wife. And he would make no demands. A knot of desolation tightened in her stomach.

'Do you agree?'

Reason cried out to her not to do this; that it would break her heart. Yet she loved him, and at least it would be preferable to becoming Hunt's mistress—or any of the other options open to her. Wouldn't it? This way she would be near him, at least, share some part of his life, and surely in time he would come to think less harshly of her.

'What choice have I?' She voiced the thought aloud as she turned from the window. 'You have already told Matthew we are going to be wed and I have nowhere else to go.'

He gave a brief nod. 'I have much to do, then, for I must track down Cornwallis and the lawyer.' He splashed more brandy into the glass and walked over to her with it. 'Here. You look as though you need it.'

She took the glass wordlessly, and he stood looking at her for a moment before turning on his heel and leaving her alone.

CHAPTER NINE

EMMA stood pale and very still, waiting to be married
and scarcely daring to move. Every tiny sound echoed
in the hollow silence of the church, seeming to mock
her.

How far removed was this sorry, spartan little ceremony from the elaborate arrangements that had been
made for her marriage to William Carlisle. There were
no flowers here, save the sad little posy Jinny had thrust
into her hand, no beautiful gown of white silk and clouds
of lace, no family and friends to crowd the pews...

Jaycinth sat alone in the front pew, paler than Emma,
her thoughts—whether on her mother or on Kit—certainly far from the impending ceremony. John stood
beside Ben to act as groomsman, his doubts about the
wisdom of this marriage, although unvoiced, clearly
mirrored in his face. He had taken all the shocks and
revelations of the past week surprisingly well. He had
even relinquished his role as Matthew's guardian with
scarcely a whimper of protest—a fact which at least reassured Emma that if nothing else her marriage to Ben
would save Matthew from Ann's uncaring charge.

At her elbow, Dr Cornwallis waited to give her away,
having volunteered his services in the absence of anyone
else. If Ann had had her way, the good doctor would
have been the only witness to this marriage, for she had
protested at length about holding a wedding barely a
week after Maybelle was buried. When John was adamant, she had pleaded sickness due to her condition and
remained at home.

Emma could only be relieved at her absence, for single-handedly she had made an awkward situation very nearly impossible, with her refusal to believe Ben's assurances that he had no intention of attempting to take over responsibility for the family, nor of getting involved in family matters except where it concerned Matthew. Then, yesterday, she had stalked into the parlour with a lawyer in tow, waving a piece of paper.

'If you are in earnest about keeping out of family affairs, Ben, dear,' she had said slyly, 'and making no financial claim on us, perhaps you will sign this document. Just to settle the matter, you understand.'

The document she had set in front of Ben was brief and to the point and effectively prevented him ever claiming any rights to the family's wealth and property. Not surprisingly, he had refused to sign it, as much to spite and humiliate Ann before the lawyer, Emma secretly thought, as from any real necessity to protect Matthew's future interests.

The church was as cold as it was empty and she shivered despite the wool cloak over her sombre grey gown. A glance at the man beside her did nothing to warm her, for he wore the look of an man inpatient to be done with the proceedings. And as the minister's impersonal voice wafted over the empty pews she had to admit that she, too, would be glad when it was over. Just how he had contrived to settle everything and make all the arrangements, including a waiving of the banns, in less than a week, she did not know and did not enquire. She could only be grateful.

For a few days Boston had buzzed with the news, scandalised at the thought of a wedding before Maybelle Winston was cold in her grave, and rife with gossip. But two days ago the *Hayley* had docked, bringing back from England Jonathan Clarke, son of offending merchant Richard, and that night a mob had gathered outside the Clarke house, heckling. A pistol had been fired and windows smashed, and the attention of the good folk of Boston was drawn back to issues far more important than the Winston scandal, for the tea ships could not now be far away.

On the few occasions when she had seen Ben these past few days he had seemed more interested in that than in his approaching marriage. He was like a polite stranger, treating her with a cool civility that kept her firmly at a distance, and she seemed incapable of showing him any of her own feelings. He always turned away or changed the subject before she could say anything that might ease the constraint between them.

As he spoke his responses to the minister, Emma raised her eyes to his rigid profile, willing him to look at her. But he did not so much as glance at her and she murmured her own vows in a small, tight voice hindered by a lump in her throat. Was it for this that she had fled William Carlisle? As the plain gold band slipped on to her finger she could hear again the scornful mockery in Ann's voice. 'You silly little fool! You'll never hold him! What have you to offer a man like Ben? He'll tire of you within a month—if he bothers with you at all!'

The touch of Ben's hand on her elbow recalled her. It was over. Briefly their eyes met, his seeming to search her face, hers quickly averted that he might not see the sudden blur of tears in her eyes.

Outside, Dr Cornwallis kissed her hand and shook Ben's, declined the offer to return to Tremont Street with them, and departed to attend his patients. The carriage swept them swiftly home, where the trunks and bags were packed and ready for their departure to Eastwood.

John immediately steered Ben to the parlour with the suggestion of a last drink before they left, and, as the door swung closed behind them, Ann came down the stairs and held out a slender white hand with feline disdain.

'So you are wed,' she murmured. 'You are to be con-gratulated—I did not think ever to call you sister-in-law.' She withdrew the hand Emma barely touched and her voice hardened. 'Do not be too complacent! Mere mar-riage vows will not bind Ben Sullivan to your bed—there are others, with pretty tricks and cunning ways, to lure him away, and you'll wish you had taken my advice and set your cap at Alex Hunt.'

Quashing a desire to slap her haughty face, Emma smiled sweetly instead. 'I shall pray for your condition to mellow your disposition as well as your figure, Ann, for you are in danger of becoming a shrew.'

Ann's eyes glittered dangerously. 'How *dare* you?' she spat.

Emma continued to smile. 'Please feel at liberty to visit Eastwood at any time.'

'How—gracious!' The words nearly strangled in Ann's throat. 'But you will be sorry you came to Boston, Emma, that I promise you!'

'Jack, you may take the trunks out now.' Emma turned away, blithely aware of Ann's darkly furious counten-ance as she swished her skirts around and swept upstairs.

Jaycinth moved forward with an expression hovering between amusement and anxiety. 'I wish you would not goad her, Emma. She is jealous and she will hurt you if she can.'

'Nonsense!' She gave the younger girl a brief hug and added, with a twinge of anxiety, 'You will be all right at Cedars?'

'Of course!' she exclaimed, a little too brightly. 'It will be deadly dull and I don't know why he wants you hidden away at Eastwood, but I shall survive without you, I dare say. You *could* live here much more conveniently——'

'It is his home, Jaycinth. Naturally he wants us to live there.' Resolutely thrusting aside the recurring thought that if she was at Eastwood he could continue with his life as if marriage had never happened, she injected a note of bravado into her voice. 'And you said yourself it is a perfect spot for a honeymoon! And after this last week I shall be glad of a little time alone with my husband——'

'I am very glad to hear it!' Emerging from the parlour in time to hear this, Ben's eyes held hers for a moment, the flare of light in them bringing a flush to her cheeks.

'You must bring her into town with you as often as possible, Ben,' Jaycinth went on. 'She will shrivel with boredom otherwise. Promise?'

Ben regarded his sister with a mixture of amusement and concern. 'I promise. Now, can we go?'

He had told her Eastwood was but an hour's ride away, but it proved to be nearer two. Jinny chatted on for most of it about her family—her brother Toby who worked for Ben, her mother who acted as a sort of part-time housekeeper for him, her handful of younger brothers and sisters. Between her and Matthew, Emma was required to say very little, and retreated into her own thoughts. Eventually, Ben turned the laden carriage off the uneven, pot-holed road on to a track through the woods which was in a far worse state. For the mile or so of its length they seemed in grave danger of overturning and it would be well-nigh impassable in really bad weather, she hazarded, contemplating weeks of being totally cut off while Ben was in Boston pursuing his pleasures.

The dog could be heard long before they emerged into the clearing, and as Ben opened the carriage door to hand her down she hesitated at the sight of a huge black beast leaping up and barking ferociously at her.

'Damn you, Lucifer, be still!' Ben's harsh command set the brute back on its haunches, though it bared pointed teeth and growled menacingly at her. 'He will not harm you,' he assured her, offering his hand.

'Though it might be better if he does not sense your nervousness.'

She glanced at him, but could not decide whether he was teasing, and stepped down boldly, carefully avoiding the dog's eye. A young man emerged from behind the stables with a musket cradled across his chest. When he saw who it was, he set the gun down against the wall, brushed his hands off on breeches already dusty with wood chips, and hurried forward.

'Emma, this is Tobias Tully, Jinny's brother. Toby, my wife, Emma.'

Before either of them could respond, Jinny came tumbling out of the carriage and so forgot herself as to hurl herself at her brother with a squeal of delight and a force that threatened to overset them both, despite his substantial build. 'Jinny, have done!' he muttered with obvious embarrassment, and, setting her forcefully away, turned to Emma. 'I'm pleased to meet you, ma'am. Never thought we'd see Mr Sullivan wed, but I'm real glad. We was all sorry to hear about Mistress Winston. A rare lady, she was, always sending little bits of things for the young 'uns, and good to Jinny here.'

As she shook the work-roughened hand, Emma smiled and nodded, quickly warming to this pleasant, unaffected young man. 'Jinny has told me all about you, Toby. Ben is lucky to have you here.'

'I reckon he knows that, ma'am.' The young man grinned, with a mischevious glance at Ben, who chose to ignore the lack of respect. 'Ma came over as soon as Tom brought his message, and fussed around a bit, tidyin' up the place. So it's all ready for you.'

'Oh, that's very kind,' she exclaimed. 'I am sure her own family is quite demanding enough——'

'Come and see the stream!' Matthew tugged her hand insistently.

'Yes, go on,' Ben encouraged them. 'We draw our water from it, via the well over there. It's crystal-clear and ice-cold and, despite what Matthew would have you believe, the fishing is poor sport!'

She followed Matthew down to a wooden bridge over the stream, and, as the little boy watched the deep clear water tumbling beneath them, she allowed her gaze to take in her surroundings. Nothing she had heard about Eastwood this past week had prepared her for the reality, and as she stood there surveying her new home she fell in love with it.

The house itself was modest enough, square-built and unpretentious, but, embraced on three sides by a horseshoe of woodland through which the breeze gently sighed, it faced a view of the sea that quite took her breath away. The trees beyond the stream sloped gently away to reveal the ocean stretched out beyond, white-capped and swaying, its greyness tinged with the pink and gold of the late afternoon sky above.

As Ben came towards them with Lucifer at his heels, she turned and exclaimed impulsively, 'Oh, Ben, it's beautiful!'

'Yes,' he said shortly, flicking his gaze from hers to survey his domain and the view it commanded. 'It is.'

Chewing her lip with disappointment at the abruptness of his tone, she, too, looked away. She could not know that to see her eyes glowing with appreciation had sent a knife to his heart. It was what he had always hoped for, to bring a woman here as his wife who would feel about Eastwood the way he did. But he had also envisaged that she would love him too. 'Can you cook?' he asked tersely.

She looked at him in some surprise. 'Yes.'

'And presumably you are capable of dressing yourself and seeing to your hair?'

'Perfectly capable!' she bristled.

He raised an eyebrow at her indignation. 'I was merely going to suggest that we send Jinny home to her family for a few days. Toby too.'

Cursing herself for being so swift to misjudge him, she said quickly, 'Yes, of course. It's a wonderful idea!' Suddenly another thought struck her. Could it mean he wanted to be alone with her after all? Her eyes darted to his face, but he was an expert at hiding his feelings and she could guess nothing of them. Anxious nevertheless to bridge the gulf between them and lighten the tension, she said teasingly, 'Why, I do believe you have a soft heart beneath that ruthless exterior after all!'

For a brief moment there was an answering gleam in his eyes; then his expression hardened. 'Do not credit me with that yet, Emma,' he said softly, 'for I shall disappoint you.' Her heart contracted painfully and she dropped her gaze as he went on briskly, 'Come, you will want to see your new home.'

Throwing a warning to Matthew over her shoulder to stay this side of the stream, she followed him towards the house. Toby emerged from the stable leading a graceful bay mare, and Ben paused. 'Your wedding gift, my love.'

The endearment was clearly added for Toby's benefit, but despite that a rush of surprise and pleasure brought a smile to her lips as she patted the velvety neck. 'She is lovely! Thank you.'

Ben met her gaze briefly and nodded before turning to Toby. 'Did Tom get Blade here safely?'

'Yessir, though he swears he'll not do it again!'

Ben laughed, gave Firefly a pat, and then strode away. Standing for a moment stroking the white patch between the doleful brown eyes, Emma felt irrationally close to tears. He had said he did not blame her for Ridge Point, but neither, it seemed, could he forgive her. 'Oh, damn him!' she muttered irritably, and then, finding Toby's eyes on her, flung away from the horse and went after him.

Within the walls of Eastwood, floors gleamed and fires blazed as evidence of Mistress Tully's endeavours. It was all simple and tasteful and functional, but as Ben helped Toby with the largest of the trunks and Emma wandered through the downstairs rooms it struck her that it lacked warmth, some signs of permanency. As if he guessed something of her thoughts, he paused at the foot of the stairs as he came back down and said wryly, 'I dare say it could do with a few...feminine embellishments. When we are next in town, order what you will and have the accounts directed to me.' He did not wait for her to comment but turned away and said, 'Come upstairs. I will show you your room.'

Having dismissed the first room as a guest-room, he allocated the second to Matthew and moved on to the third. 'This is my room,' he told her, and she stood in the doorway as he went in and shrugged off his coat. At least it had a more lived-in appearance, polished oak gleaming, a few masculine adornments on the dresser, a half-used candle beside the bed and a chair pulled up beside the fire burning in the hearth. He tossed his coat over the back of the chair and came out again.

'Your room is next door.' There was an air of indifference about him that cut her to the quick as he stood aside to let her precede him into the barely furnished room. Taking the key from the lock, he held it out to her. 'It's the only one. You will not be disturbed.'

Her stomach knotted. He had given Jinny leave to go home with Toby so that there would be no one to remark that they spent their wedding night apart! She took the key and swallowed her disappointment. Perhaps she ought, at least, to be appreciative of his consideration. Not that it was really necessary—Jinny might harbour romantic illusions, but even she knew the feelings her mistress had for Mr Sullivan were not reciprocated, that he had married her so that he could give Matthew a home, and she would not be too surprised to know that they spent their wedding night in separate rooms.

'I am sorry it is not more comfortable,' he apologised. 'But there was no time to do anything about it and I imagine you have your own ideas.'

She closed her fist around the key and forced a smile. 'What is through there?' she asked, nodding towards a door in the far wall.

'I suppose I intended it as a nursery or something of the sort,' he told her, with a suggestion of bitter irony in his voice, as he crossed to the door and opened it for her. A much smaller room was revealed, piled high with odd pieces of furniture and lumber, boxes of books and even a saddle and several bolts of cloth. 'We can clear it for Jinny,' he went on. 'I am sure you will want her near you and Toby has made himself comfortable above the kitchen.'

But the sudden vision of plump, gurgling babies was too much, and she could scarcely force a suitable comment before turning away and walking to the window, with its view over the trees to the sea. How she longed to hold him, to tell him she would fill the house with his children, that happy laughter would echo through the rooms of Eastwood. She wanted to take away the bitterness, the self-mockery that had crept several times into his voice since they arrived, and replace it with love.

Instead, she turned and smiled brightly at him. 'It's a lovely room. I shall soon have it comfortable.'

His eyes lingered on her a moment longer, but at the sound of Toby and Jinny coming up the stairs he moved towards the door. 'I'll leave you to unpack, then. Perhaps I'll take Matthew into the woods with Lucifer for a while—out of your way.'

'He will enjoy that.' She nodded, and as Toby came along with some more of the baggage he turned to the younger man.

'When you have finished, why don't you take Jinny home?' he suggested. 'We can do without the pair of you for the rest of the week and your mother will be glad of the help.'

Toby grinned, a knowing look in his eyes, and Jinny stuttered gleeful thanks, looking as though she would like to throw her arms around him.

An hour later, having watched the Tullys depart and Ben and Matthew making for the woods with an excited Lucifer running circles around them, she suddenly found herself quite alone. Her footsteps echoed on the polished floor, and she made a mental note to ask Ben for more rugs. In the kitchen she found that the cupboards were well stocked with bread and cheese, jars of pickled plums and apple chutney, and herbs hanging up to dry. And when she took a lamp to the cellar she discovered salt beef and sacks of flour and potatoes, fruit and vegetables to last a fortnight, a keg of ale and bottles of wine and brandy—though no more than any man would have and nothing to excite the Excise! If he kept a cache at Eastwood, it was well hidden.

She went through her repertoire of recipes, and was satisfied she could produce enough appetising meals to gratify her husband, and set about unpacking the supplies they had brought with them, easy about at least one aspect of the coming week.

'Can you use a pistol? Or a musket?'

She was folding linen the next morning, making a list of the items they would need. The question surprised her and she looked up at him, a sudden smile catching at her lips. 'I did fire James's pistol once. It was not a very successful attempt. I managed to miss everything— and everyone—and fell backwards into the gorse. Which caused them all so much merriment that I never touched it again. I think it was about then that my father decided to give in to pressure and allowed my aunt to come and take charge of me.'

He chuckled, a warm rich sound that sent a glow to her heart. 'I should think so! Well, I shall teach you—at a safe distance from anything as painful as gorse! And we will also teach Lucifer to obey your commands. Toby cannot always stay close to the house and when I am away I would like to know you can protect yourself, and Matthew. I have no intention of leaving you here alone unless it is unavoidable, but if we are short-handed Toby may have to come with us to help bring in a cargo, act as look-out, or some such thing. It does not happen very often...' He left the sentence unfinished and shrugged.

She felt the warmth drain out of her as thoughts rushed in on her of dark beaches and redcoat ambushes, of lying awake at night, worrying. The thought of him dangling in the hangman's noose had haunted her since that fateful night of her betrayal, and now she wanted him to hold her, to feel the strong arms crush her against his chest, reassuring her that he was, as Matthew already believed, invincible.

Ben looked into the luminous hazel eyes, and, seeing her stricken look, cursed his tactlessness. She had married him as a way out, as security, and already he was reminding her of the less laudable side of his character and the likelihood of his early demise. What would happen to her and Matthew should anything happen to him? Belatedly, the concern made him pause. John would take care of Matthew. But Emma...? Alex Hunt, perhaps? It was not a pretty thought and he thrust it aside. It was all he could do not to gather her in his arms and banish all thoughts of that treacherous Redcoat from her mind.

'We might as well start now,' he said briskly, and held out his musket.

Consoling herself with the knowledge that of necessity learning to use it would keep her in close proximity to him, she stopped what she was doing and took the gun from him.

His nearness, however, as he put his arms around her to position the weapon, his fingers on hers, his breath on her neck, was almost unbearable. Her flesh tingled, her pulse raced, her nervous tremblings sending her first shots impossibly wild. But he was patient, and she had a naturally good eye, and with a determined effort she quashed the turbulent flutterings of her stomach and summoned all her will-power to concentrate on the task in hand. His approval, when she quickly became adept at using both pistol and musket, and deft at reloading with powder and shot, brought a sparkle of satisfaction to her eyes and a glow of pleasure to her cheeks.

No less satisfying was her final winning over of Lucifer. Only Ben, she reflected with an inner smile, would give a dog such an outrageous name. It was no easy task to induce the brute to trust her, for he had been trained to forcibly deter strangers and continued to growl and bark at her for several days, despite Ben's admonishments. However, she won him round in the end, with the aid of a few surreptitious kitchen scraps, and it was then relatively easy, with Ben's help, to teach him to obey her commands.

On the third morning, Ben declared himself sufficiently convinced that she could at least terrify any unwanted callers with the musket and let Lucifer do the rest, and he went off to acquire a pony for Matthew from a neighbour and was gone for most of the morning. Then the three of them rode through the woods, touring Ben's modest 'estate' and following the stream down to the little cove, with Matthew being led at a sedate walk and clamouring optimistically to gallop, and Emma delighted with her lively Firefly.

The days passed relatively painlessly. Preparing meals and attending to chores kept Emma busy, and Matthew was sufficiently demanding that any idle moments were swiftly filled. And since he was tireless in his efforts to learn to ride, and asking to be taken to the beach, or fishing or hunting, Ben was also kept occupied. When they all rode together there was enough to remark upon, to encourage casual conversation, that these were pleasant, enjoyable interludes. Awkward moments between them were few.

Once Matthew was in bed it was not so easy. On the surface the evenings were companionably spent. She sewed, while he cleaned the guns; he entertained her with anecdotes from his rather lively past, and she talked of her family and childhood. They discussed politics, the likelihood of a serious confrontation over the tea, her growing sympathy with the Americans' demands for more say in the way the colonies were run. But there was a restraint between them, an uneasy tension, as though they were each trying too hard, each carefully subduing any show of real emotion, and the silences that fell between them in the evenings were uncomfortable.

Emma did not use the key that would have locked her bedroom door, wondering if he would try the handle one night, and scarcely daring to hope he would. But it remained firmly closed. Indeed, she usually left him with a glass of brandy and, however long she remained awake, did not hear him go to bed.

She could not know that he stayed long into the night with the dying fire, wrestling with an almost overwhelming urge to go upstairs, kick her door open and take her in his arms, willing or not, to arouse the response he had briefly tasted, to set a spark to the fire he knew lay dormant in her, to find release for the pent-up passions she aroused in him. She was driving him mad.

Why he held himself back so rigidly he did not know. Except that she flinched imperceptibly every time he put his arm around her to steady her aim with the musket, tensed every time he was close enough to catch the faint aroma of rosemary with which she rinsed her hair. He was tempted to seduce her anyway, if only to take her

from Alex Hunt, who was a bigger fool than he thought
if he was blind to all she had to offer. That he did not
trust his emotions, or his reasons, was perhaps what
made him put such an iron grip on himself.

He sat alone before the fire, and stared into the brandy
gently swirling in his glass, a wry irony giving the half-
smile on his lips a bitter twist. He drained the glass and
poured another from the decanter at his feet. What was
he thinking of, falling in love? More important things
were brewing and he did not want this distraction, this
tie, this responsibility. This nagging ache tugging at his
heart.

She had looked so lovely today, her hair pulling loose
from its ribbons and streaming out behind her as they
rode along the beach, her eyes sparkling and her lips
slightly parted as her breasts rose and fell with the
exertion... Then, caught by a sudden memory, she had
looked out to sea with such a sadness that he had moved
Blade beside her and would have reached out for her.
But she turned and looked at him with tear-filled eyes
and said, 'I wish they would find Kit's body and have
done with this uncertainty!'

Whether he could trust her or not, he had needed to
make her understand why he asked Kit to go to New
York. 'I had to ask him, Emma. I needed someone who
would not attract so much attention—my own people
were being watched. Even before the *Gazette* printed details, we'd had word from New York that the Tea Act
rumours were in fact reality. We needed to get word to
our friends there that we would be ready to support them
in total opposition to it. The information Kit carried was
a list of names, a network of couriers and trusted patriots
between New York and Boston. To send it with Kit
seemed quicker, safer...'

She had just looked at him, with eyes full of pain.
And then swiftly jerked Firefly round and rode off,
calling to Matthew. Even if she had not been in love

with Alex Hunt, Kit's death would always be between them.

Damn her, didn't she realise how guilty he felt? He filled and refilled his glass, cursing himself for a fool, cursing her for a witch and sinking into a morass of bitterness and self-pity. She had married him because of Matthew, because Ann was throwing her out and she had nowhere else to go, because Hunt was too stupid to marry her. Well, she *was* his wife and he was going to make damned sure she knew it.

Setting both the decanter and the glass down with undue care, he got to his feet and made for the stairs.

The sudden snap of the door woke her. She raised herself on her elbow as he came into the room, a shadowy figure in the darkness. A tremor went through her, a thrill of anticipation slaked with uncertainty. 'Ben?'

He came to the bed and stood looking down at her for a moment. She could not clearly see his face, but there was something in the way he stood there, a suppressed anger, that alarmed her. 'Ben?' she whispered again. Still he did not answer, but abruptly drew back the covers and lay down on the bed beside her. His mouth took hers, bruising her lips as he pushed the nightgown over her shoulder, seeking the soft flesh beneath.

There was brandy on his breath, and nothing gentle in the way his hand mauled her breast. She felt panic rising and began to pull away from him. But he shifted his weight on top of her, pinning her down, fumbling with his breeches and impatiently pulling her nightgown up over her thighs. She tried to stop him, tearing her mouth from his and pushing at his chest, writhing beneath him. But no words would come, crushed as she was beneath him, and it served merely to strengthen his determination. Heedless of her struggles, his knee forced her legs apart, and he eased himself between her thighs.

She closed her eyes, tears squeezing beneath her lashes. Not like this. Dear God, not like this, not when he was drunk and she could be just any woman. She wanted love and tenderness from him. She wanted him to make love to her, to *her*, not just her body, that could be any woman's. 'Ben, please...'

The words finally forced themselves out, only to be choked off in a cry as a sudden, piercing pain seared through her. She bit into his shoulder as he thrust into her again, and then, swiftly spent, he was still with his face buried against her neck, asleep almost immediately.

After a moment, she pushed against him, inch by inch eased her body free of his, and creeping to the far edge of the bed, turned her back on him and let silent tears fall into the pillow.

It was light when she woke, and early judging by the pale greyness suffusing the room. With the memory of last night forcing her awake, she turned to find the bed beside her empty.

Why had he come? she wondered, getting up slowly. Not out of love, that much was certain. Merely to satisfy his masculine lusts that had gone unquenched these past nights. She should be glad that at least he had come to her, his wife, and had not ridden into town to find a more rewarding bed-mate—although it had apparently taken a considerable amount of brandy to fortify him for the experience!

Making a hasty toilet, she dressed swiftly, glad that Jinny was not there. The door of his room was open as she went past, but of Ben there was no sign. Although his discarded clothes lay on the floor, the bed showed no signs of having been slept in. Matthew was still asleep when she looked in on him, so she went downstairs, assuming that Ben had gone out.

But he was in the kitchen, sitting with a mug of tea before the fire. She stopped abruptly in the doorway, her heart lurching painfully, unprepared for the encounter. Not knowing what to say, she turned to go in a sudden confusion, but he rose swiftly to stop her.

'Emma!' Her eyes met his, reluctantly. 'I am sorry about last night,' he said harshly. 'My behaviour was—inexcusable.'

She moistened her lips. 'You were drunk.'

'Yes.' He set his mug down on the table. 'But that does not excuse——'

'I am your wife,' she said stiffly. 'You are entitled——'

'No!' He slammed his fist down on the table with a force that made her start back in alarm. There was a violent anger in his eyes as he glared at her. But it died as swiftly as it had come and his voice was almost weary. 'I gave my word that I would make no unwelcome demands, promised you would not be disturbed. I broke that promise. It was unforgivable of me and I can only apologise—and swear that it will never happen again.'

She was silent, wanting to hate him for his brutal, selfish assault and finding that she could not. When she did not speak, he turned and strode to the door, snatched up his top coat and the musket and went out, leaving her staring forlornly after him.

He did not reappear all day. But she kept herself busy, refusing to think about last night or to be concerned at his prolonged absence. Ignoring the knot of confusion and desolation in her stomach, she made Matthew attend to his books for the first time since they had arrived at Eastwood and then allowed him to take out his ill-humour on the bread dough she made.

She was beginning to think of lighting the candles as the afternoon faded towards dusk when Ben finally returned, walking into the kitchen with the result of his hunting—a young deer—across his shoulders. He dropped it on to the table and said abruptly, 'I shall return to town tomorrow. I have neglected matters at the mill long enough and have things to attend to that will wait no longer.'

She stared at him, suddenly despairing. 'So—soon? Shall you... How long will you be away?'

'A few days, I imagine. I have been to the Tullys'— Jinny and Toby will return in the morning so you will not be alone.'

To mask her disappointment she voiced a thought that had been in her mind for a few days. 'I—should like to write to James again. There is Kit—I know he'll hear about it but I... There is so much to explain.'

A mere flicker in the blue eyes betrayed his recall of the fate of her last letter. 'Write it tonight, then,' he told her, going towards the door. 'I'll take it with me tomorrow.'

CHAPTER TEN

BEN paused in the doorway of the Green Dragon, and allowed his eyes to grow accustomed to the gloom before making his way across the noisy, crowded room to the far corner, where several tables had been drawn together. John Hancock hooked a stool from an adjacent table with his foot and pushed it towards him, nodding a casual greeting. 'Ben. We had almost given you up. You've had much else on your mind this past fortnight, it seems!'

A tankard of ale appeared in front of him. 'Aye! Suddenly he's related to the Winstons, who soirée with Redcoats, he's the guardian of a small boy, and he is married in indecent haste to a pretty young wench fresh out of England! Scarce the sort of behaviour you'd expect from a staunch patriot devoted to the cause!'

'Ay, Revere, but he was ever a devious bastard!' A roar of laughter greeted this and the young man who spoke was encouraged to continue, 'And with a new wife to break in you'd not have much appetite for anything else, eh, Sullivan? I dare say you've softer things to sink your teeth into now!'

This found a raw nerve and Ben suddenly lost his temper. His stool scraped on the floor as he half rose, spilling ale across the table. 'Damn you, O'Connor! Keep your accursed——'

A hand came down on his arm. 'Easy, Ben.' The low voice held a quiet authority that stilled Ben's anger. ''Tis only a jest, man. No one here doubts your commitment. Sit down.'

There was veiled strength in Sam Adams, a suppressed energy, a single-minded purposefulness that seemed to set him apart, a tireless force continually rallying the sometimes flagging fervour of Boston patriots. Ben sat down with an impatient gesture of apology at the man across the table, and Adams went on, 'The tea ships will be in the harbour before the month is out and we have not decided yet what we are to do about them. We must have some plan to put before the town.'

Ben's attention was only half on the discussions around the table. He voiced his views, but his mind was elsewhere, still full of self-disgust for what he had done to Emma.

He had hurt her. Drunk he may have been, but he knew that much—he had teeth marks on his shoulder, had he been in any doubt. Why couldn't he have tried to put it right with her, told her he loved her and had been unable to bear being so near to her without touching her, holding her...? Even to himself his attempt at apology had sounded pitiful.

'Sullivan!' The voice recalled him. 'Is that your opinion too?'

'I'll sink the damn ships myself if it comes to it,' he said with feeling, and then got to his feet. 'You will have to forgive me, my friends. I have some unfinished business to attend to.'

The ribald comments that might have greeted this remark were held back, but Adams detained Ben as he rose to leave. 'It seems Alex Hunt was not best pleased you married that wench, Ben. 'Tis said he was about to ask her himself.'

Ben raised an eyebrow. 'Much joy it would have brought him. She has the makings of a good patriot!'

'Nevertheless, watch your back. Hunt's not a man to trust in a dark alley, and he'd be glad to see you with your belly slit.'

'I'd not trust that snake on King Street in broad daylight,' Ben assured him with a wry grin. But his eyes darkened with a dangerous gleam. There would come a reckoning between himself and Captain Alex Hunt before much longer.

He emerged from the tavern and cast a glance at the sky. There was not so much as a sliver of moon behind the clouds and he reluctantly abandoned his rash impulse to ride to Eastwood immediately. It would be nothing less than suicide to attempt it tonight. Instead he turned his mind to Cedars—he had one or two things to discuss with John and could no doubt beg a bed for the night. At least if he delayed until tomorrow he could see about a gift for Emma. He had some emeralds, the fruits of a profitable deal some years ago, and, recalling the emerald pendant she owned, decided to have them set into earrings and a bracelet to match it.

Emma paused in the middle of folding the two simple green dresses for Jinny's sisters, and listened to Lucifer's sudden paroxysm of barking. Someone was coming. Her heart missed a beat. Ben had left early yesterday morning and she had hardly dared hope he would return so soon. Despite herself, her spirits rose and she left the dresses on the bed and went swiftly downstairs, expecting to hear his sharp command to the dog.

But Lucifer's barking grew more frantic, and, with a questioning look at Jinny, she threw open the door. Her heart lurched in dismay at the sight of the perfectly groomed officer soothing his nervous young horse. 'Captain Hunt!'

He did not dismount but looked speculatively at Lucifer, who was now growling menacingly, hackles raised, and then he raised his eyes to the stables where Toby was standing holding a musket across his chest. 'Your husband keeps you well guarded in his absence, I see.'

She went down the steps and dropped a hand to Lucifer's back. 'It's all right, boy. You will forgive me if I do not ask you in, Captain, but as Ben is not here...'

The captain jumped from his horse and came towards her, sweeping off his cocked hat. 'But I need to speak with you, Emma,' he said in an undertone. 'It is precisely because Sullivan is not here that I came. I saw him in town and I happen to know he is planning to stay for several days——'

'How——?'

'Emma, I have to speak to you.'

She stared at him for a moment, and then sighed. 'Very well.'

'It's not right, Miss Emma!' Jinny protested, standing in the doorway behind her. 'Mr Sullivan wouldn't like it.'

'Go and give Matthew his lunch, please, Jinny,' she ordered pointedly, and preceded the captain into the house. Toby followed them and stopped just inside the door, the musket cradled in his arms. One glance at the grim disapproval on his face persuaded Emma that it would be useless to try to order him away.

She took the captain into the parlour and firmly closed the door. 'Will you sit down?'

He shook his head. 'Why did you marry him, Emma?' he demanded, a mixture of impatience and annoyance in his voice. 'Did I not tell you I would take care of you? You had only to wait a few days. There was no need for this—this foolishness!'

She did not immediately answer. Crossing to the couch and sitting down, she arranged her skirts before looking up at him. 'You told me you would take care of me, certainly,' she agreed. 'What was I to construe from that? I heard no mention of marriage, Captain. I thought you were offering to make me your mistress——'

He looked a trifle disconcerted. 'But had you waited, and had we spoken further... It was only a matter of a few days, Emma. Could you not have waited? What possessed you to marry him? Sullivan of all people! Naturally I would have made it clear that there is no one I would rather wed.'

'Perhaps you should have said that at the time,' she retorted with more than a trace of sarcasm.

'Had I known matters were so desperate that you would have even Sullivan—— You are not...are you perhaps with child?'

With a gasp, she stood up. 'You go too far, Captain! I think you should leave.'

His eyes narrowed. 'I'm sorry. But if it is not that, then what? It cannot be for his money. I understand he has renounced any claim to the Winston money and, though I like him not, I have never known him break his word. His income from the mill is hardly substantial, and the money he makes at the card tables and from cheating the excise duties cannot be relied upon; what small fortune he has will surely not keep you in grand style. If you wanted to marry for money, Emma, you could have done better than that!'

She suppressed her rising temper but her voice trembled with anger. 'Captain, you outstay your welcome. Please leave.'

Unperturbed, he went on, 'Then you must be in love with him. If so you are a fool, for he will break your heart. Between his rebel friends, his smuggling, whoring, gambling and God knows what else besides, I doubt he'll have much time for you. He cannot make you happy, my dear; he can only make you a widow.'

She would have liked to throw at him that Ben loved her as much as she loved him, but she could not force herself to voice the lie. Instead she flared hotly, 'I married him because of Matthew! He offered a tidy solution to both my plight and his. Marriage, Captain, not the sordid arrangement you had in mind!'

He sighed heavily and shook his head. 'You should have waited. At least I could have made you happy—and I would have married you.' He shrugged. 'But I can wait. Sullivan will make you a widow before long and then—who knows?'

'Oh, you are arrogant, Captain!' she exclaimed, her voice vibrant with outrage. 'Now please go. If I have to call Master Tully I cannot be responsible for the consequences.'

He smiled faintly. 'I doubt that young man would be foolish enough to attempt to harm an officer of the British Army.'

'Do not be so certain! He is——' She broke off. Lucifer was barking again and Toby's voice failed to quieten him.

Then another voice reached them, silencing the dog and snapping out a question. Emma caught her breath, looking anxiously towards the door, as Ben's voice, unmistakably raised in anger, cut across the reasoning tones of young Toby.

Before she could do anything, Captain Hunt crossed the space between them, drew her swiftly into his arms and fastened his mouth on hers in a ravaging kiss. It happened so quickly that she was caught off balance, crushed against his chest so that she could scarcely move. Her hands found his shoulders, her fingers gripping convulsively in a vain attempt to make him stop.

When the door crashed open they were, to all intents and purposes, locked in an embrace.

Hunt released her abruptly. She sprang away, gasping for breath, and sent him a furious glare as she turned to Ben with a hasty explanation on her lips. It died at the sight of the pistol in his hand, and the cold contempt in his eyes as he looked straight past her at a man who epitomised everything he despised about the British.

His voice was dangerously soft. 'I thought even you would have had more sense than to seduce my wife in my own house, Hunt. Move away, Emma.'

He raised the pistol. Appalled, she sprang between them, imploring eyes turned on her husband. 'No! Don't be stupid, Ben! It's not——'

'Yes, Sullivan,' Hunt cut in smoothly, a sardonic gleam in his eyes. 'Go on, kill me. It will be all they need to hang you.'

The words hung in the silence that followed. Emma looked from Ben's implacable features to Toby, standing in the doorway behind him and silently beseeched his help.

'He's right, sir. Not here, not in your own house. 'Twould be folly.'

Ben's gaze never wavered from the captain's, but after a moment a little of the tension eased imperceptibly from the grim lines of his face. 'Get out, Hunt,' he hissed through clenched teeth. 'Get out before I throw caution to the devil. But be sure—there'll be another time.'

Captain Hunt's eyes gleamed. 'Oh, undoubtedly there will be another time,' he murmured. And then, with an elaborate bow towards Emma, he walked out, a faint smile on his lips. Tobias followed him, and ushering Jinny and Matthew away, closed the parlour door.

'Ben, I'm sorry!' Emma looked imploringly at him. 'I cannot think what made him do such a thing! He must be mad——'

'Spare me that, Emma!' The disgust in his voice was mirrored in his eyes as he looked at her.

'But you surely do not think . . .? It was not what it seemed! He just—grabbed me. I could do nothing. You must believe that!'

His expression remained relentless as he thrust the pistol into the top of his breeches. 'If you take Firefly and hurry, you can catch up with him.'

'But I do not want to catch up with him! I——'

'You do not seem to understand.' His voice was cold as ice. 'I am telling you to go.'

She stared at him, shock reducing her voice to a faint whisper. 'What?'

'I believe I told you I would not be made a fool of.' His eyes were chilling. 'If you thought that by marrying me you could remain his mistress and yet have the security he would not give you you have been extremely stupid.'

'Ben, please!' she implored, scarcely knowing whether to be frightened or angry. 'It had nothing to do with me. He pulled me—I fell against him——'

'I am not blind, Emma!'

'Well, you are far too swift to leap to conclusions!' she flared, her eyes sparkling with angry tears. '*He* was kissing *me*!'

He raised his eyebrows. 'A fine point, since I saw no sign of resistance. Quite the contrary, in fact.'

'You mistook what you saw! It happened so quickly. I had no chance to resist. He means nothing to me, Ben, nothing. I swear it.'

'Do you expect me to believe that?' he demanded, shrugging off his coat and throwing it on to a chair. 'Or are you so free with your kisses that a man does not have to mean anything to you. Is that what you are, Emma? A whore?'

She gasped and flew at him, her hand lashing out. But he caught her wrist easily, his fingers closing viciously around it until she cried out in pain. 'Have a care,' he murmured. 'I have never yet struck a woman but there is always a first time. I advise you to leave now, quickly, while you may still catch Hunt and enjoy his escort to town.' He released her wrist abruptly and turned away.

She swirled round and made for the door, furious tears blinding her vision. But with her fingers closing round the handle she stopped, and looked back at him, brushing the tears away. 'Why are you being so cruel? Why do you refuse to believe me?'

For a moment he met her pleading eyes; a muscle moved along his jaw. Then he walked across to the table with the brandy bottle upon it and with his back to her slowly poured himself a drink. When he spoke, the hard edge had gone from his voice, only to be replaced by a thread of bitterness. 'I have never told any woman that I love her, Emma. But twice I have come back to tell you and both times I found you in Hunt's arms.' He turned and looked at her, the pain evident in his eyes. 'Well, I have learnt my lesson. I will not again be so reckless with my emotions.'

Scarcely daring to accept what she had heard, she searched his face. 'Did you say——?' She stopped and swallowed hard, her own emotions curdling and her throat dry. 'Do you love me?' she whispered finally.

He did not answer, his expression unreadable. Swallowing again, she moistened her lips. She could not let this go unanswered. Everything hung on it and there could be no more misunderstandings. Drawing a breath and lifting her chin, she said steadily, 'Do you love me? Or—or do you wish me to leave?'

With a sound of disgust, he drained the contents of his glass and turned to pour another. Instead, he leaned heavily on the table for a moment, then swung round abruptly. 'Both!' he exploded harshly. 'Damn you, Emma, I love you, but I'll not be tormented by the thought of Hunt in your bed every time I am away!'

All the despair, doubt and misery drained away. Everything was all right. She crossed the room to him and put a tentative hand on his arm, looking up at him with an uncertain smile. 'Then what must I say to make you believe you do not have to worry?' she asked softly. 'It is not him I want. I never have. It's you I love.'

He searched her face, his eyes dark and unfathomable. 'What was he doing here?'

'He wanted to know why I had married you,' she said
simply. 'He offered to take care of me himself that day
on the Common. Although,' she added with a rueful
little smile, 'I do not think he had marriage in mind!
But today he said he would have married me, had he
known that I was so desperate I would wed even you.'

His eyes bored into her. 'And is that what it was,
desperation?'

'Partly,' she admitted, and, at the little frown that
creased his brow, hastened to reassure him. 'It was the
only way I could be with you. I thought—I thought it
would break my heart, to love you so much and know
you only married me because of Matthew. But I could
not bear the thought of living without you. I thought—
I hoped you might come to think less harshly of me in
time.'

'Oh, Emma.' His arms went round her waist almost
of their own accord. But he did not draw her towards
him, some lingering doubt still making him hesitant.
'That day on the Common,' he went on, his voice oddly
taut. 'I came back to tell you I knew about the *Emma
Louise*, about Kit, that I was sorry for what I had said.
When I got to Tremont Street and realised what had been
happening in my absence, I could only think of you going
through all that while I was indulging in self-pity. I knew
then I could not let you go and I came looking for you,
knowing I loved you, knowing I had to do something
about Matthew and thinking to ask you to marry me.
And then when I found you, you were in Hunt's arms
and I thought——'

She put her fingers to his lips. 'I was so miserable. So
much had happened, so many awful things, all of it my
fault. And then Ann said I had to go and I couldn't bear
to think of leaving Matthew at Cedars. I did not know
what to do or where to go. I loved you so much and all
I could think of was that you hated me. I did not know
if I would ever see you again—or if I did, whether you

would ever forgive me. But I was so wretched it could have been anyone that day. I needed so badly to be held...'

'And all I did was make things worse for you!' Self-disgust laced his voice as his hands tightened on her waist. 'Can you ever forgive me?'

For answer she reached up and pulled his head down to hers, moving her lips coaxingly over his until, with a little groan, he pulled her roughly against him, and took her mouth hungrily. His hands moved up, caressing across her back, her bare shoulders, her neck, entwining his fingers in her hair, her arching body and eager mouth telling him far more than mere words how much she loved him.

Her legs turned to jelly as her fingers dug into the hard muscles of his arms, and little shivers of desire snaked all through her, arousing unsuspected sensations that set her trembling. Pressing her hips even closer, she felt the lean hard length of his body moulding to hers, all thought flown and all her yearning in the fierceness of her lips and tongue melting with his.

Then he dragged his mouth away, drawing a breath between his teeth, and groaned, burying his head in the hair that had tumbled from its ribbons around her shoulders.

She pulled back slightly and looked into his face, troubled and uncertain. Brushing a stray curl from her cheek, he smiled. 'Don't look like that,' he murmured. 'If we do not stop now, I cannot answer for how we shall spend the afternoon!'

Her face cleared and the slightest blush coloured her cheeks. 'Do you think,' she began tentatively, 'that Toby and Jinny would be shocked if we asked them to take Matthew and visit their mother for the afternoon?'

His lips twitched, the blue eyes dancing. 'I do not imagine Toby would be at all surprised at anything I do! But Jinny would certainly be scandalised!'

'She would get over it,' she insisted, a little surprised at her own brazen persistence.

'Wanton!' he accused softly, and kissed the tip of her nose. 'But tonight will be better.'

Disappointment cast a shadow across her face. Did he not want her as desperately as he had implied? As she wanted him?

The crestfallen look went to his heart. 'Oh, Emma!' Drawing her towards him, he linked his hands at the back of her neck. 'It is not that I would not take you here and now,' he said gently. 'But allow me my—greater experience.' He gave her a teasing half-smile. 'You will feel less inhibited with the darkness to conceal your blushes! Besides,' he added his steady gaze deepening, 'I have amends to make and do not intend to be hurried. I'd as soon have the whole night!'

Much later, sitting before her dressing-table, un-pinning her hair, she wondered at the flutter of nerves in her stomach. Why she would feel nervous now she did not know. After all, had he not stopped when he did this afternoon, she would never have been able to prevent herself giving in totally to the needs and passions surging in her blood. He could have taken her there, on the parlour floor, for all she cared. So why should she feel so uncertain now?

They had spent a wonderful afternoon, walking in the woods, fishing in the stream with Matthew, laughing and talking, exchanging explanations and reasons, the air cleared of misunderstandings and doubt. The whole at-mosphere of the house had lifted, Jinny going around singing with a knowing look in her eyes, and even Matthew seeming to sense that something had changed. And when finally they were alone they had sat for a long while before the fire, he in the armchair and she curled at his feet, warm and close.

The room was in near-darkness, a single candle throwing uncertain patches of light into the shadows,

and as she struggled with the fastenings at the back of
her dress she suddenly knew what it was, that doubt
trembling in the pit of her stomach. It was the memory
of his last assault on her body. She had tried to forget
it, to pretend it had not happened, and it was the one
thing they had not discussed, the one thing that still lay
between them.

'Shall I help you with that?'

She twisted round. How he had opened the door
without her even noticing she could not imagine. He had
removed his shirt and boots and stood there naked from
the waist up, handsome and powerful in the candlelight,
and a shiver of anticipation slid down her spine. 'Yes,
please,' she whispered shakily, and rose as he came into
the room towards her.

His fingers were adept and her dress slipped to the
floor in no time. Equally swiftly, it seemed, he contrived
to divest her of the rest of her clothes, while she stood
unresisting, trembling very slightly, never taking her eyes
from his. Only when she was naked did he allow himself
to take a step back, holding her at arm's length and
letting his gaze take in her smooth, slender body. She
did not flinch from the leisurely scrutiny, but somewhere at the back of her mind was grateful for the near
darkness.

'You are beautiful,' he murmured, his gaze returning
to hers. 'Come here.' Drawing her to him, he kissed her
with gentle seduction, his tongue teasing and persuading
while his hands caressed her back, slid down over her
buttocks and hips, arousing an almost unbearable ache
in her loins. She trembled and immediately he was still,
raising his head. 'You are cold.'

Before she could deny it, he lifted her into his arms
and carried her to the bed. Shedding his breeches, he
lay down beside her and propped himself up on his
elbow. Drawing a long curl over her shoulder, he let it

trail through his fingers and traced a line down to her breast.

'I am sorry about last time.' His voice was ragged with suppressed emotion and he did not look at her; but gently stroked her breast, idly teasing the nipple until it hardened to a peak beneath his caress. 'It should not have been like that... You have no idea how hard it was, keeping away from you. And that day, you were so lovely, so unknowingly provocative. I could not bear the thought of passing your door yet again, fighting the temptation to kick it down and spending another cold lonely night. I thought to drink myself into a stupor and sleep safely downstairs... I'll never forgive myself for hurting you like that.'

'I have forgiven you,' she whispered.

He shook his head slightly. 'The first time should be—gentle. Not—rape.'

'Then show me,' she murmured huskily.

With a soft exclamation, he began to explore her body with gentle expertise, stroking and caressing until the last shred of her nervousness dissolved and she gave herself up completely to the sensuous shivers of pleasure his touch aroused. And when he shifted his weight on top of her, her thighs parted of their own accord, inviting and eager. As he eased himself into her, she tensed momentarily, unable to banish completely the memory of his last painful entry. But this time he was careful and gentle, whispering reassuringly, until she moulded her body to his, accepting him. Then, with slow, rhythmic movements, he brought her to a shuddering climax, wave after wave of exquisite pleasure sweeping through her, his final deep thrust arching her back and wringing from her a little animal-like cry of ecstasy.

Satisfied, he relaxed against her, nuzzling her neck, his lips moving in the merest of kisses over her neck and shoulder, burying his face in the soft cloud of her hair. When he rolled away from her, he drew her into his arms, delighting in the soft glow in her eyes as she looked at him for a moment before nestling contentedly against him.

But now he had gained her trust he had no intention of allowing her to sleep for long. His own appetite whetted, he intended to show her all the delights and delicious pleasures her newly awakened body was capable both of giving and receiving. And the whole night was ahead of them.

She awoke with a warm contentment and stretched sleepily. Her body felt wonderfully languorous and with a little dreamy sigh she turned on her side and reached out for Ben. When her hand found only emptiness, she opened her eyes and looked at the crumpled pillow with a sinking disappointment.

A moment later, however, he appeared in the doorway in his boots and breeches and with a towel draped over his shoulder. A slow smile creased his features. 'Good morning!'

She sat up, drawing up her knees and pulling the covers modestly to her chin. 'Good morning.'

'Jinny came in earlier,' he informed her, advancing into the room and picking up her discarded clothing. 'I rather think she left somewhat hastily—no doubt a little disconcerted at the sight of our naked bodies all tangled up in the bedclothes!'

'What?' She stared at him aghast, an expression which drew only a chuckle from him as he dropped her clothes on to the bed and threw her robe at her.

'Get up and we'll go riding, and give her time to prepare a vast lunch. I am excessively hungry, for some reason!'

'Lunch?' Her eyes widened. 'Whatever time is it?'

'Eleven, or thereabouts.'

'My God!' She leapt out of bed, ignoring his roar of laughter at her horrified face, and would have made a

·

grab for her clothes except that he caught her to him, appreciatively sliding his hands down her body. 'Let me go,' she protested half-heartedly.

He looked down at her, his eyes soft with a mixture of pride and speculation. 'Whatever did I unleash last night, witch?' he murmured. 'I never suspected you of nurturing such wanton passions!'

'Neither did I,' she admitted, and suddenly had the unnerving thought that if her aunt could have seen her last night she would have had a seizure. A man's carnal desires were something a lady had to submit to, certainly not enjoy and never actively participate in—such behaviour being reserved for whores and heathens. Growing up with four older brothers and unashamedly eavesdropping on their conversations, it had been impossible for her to grow up innocent of what happened between a man and a woman beneath the sheets. But she had been left with the belief that it was a woman's lot to give pleasure and a man's to take it. Ben had shredded all such myths last night. Her only doubt now was whether he had found as much pleasure in her body as she had in his. Shyly she ventured to ask. 'Did I...? I mean, was it...?' She floundered, and then rushed on, 'You have known so many women——'

'Not as many as rumour would have you believe,' he told her with a faint smile. 'Does that trouble you? It should not, my love. It suits my purpose, so I encourage it and you must not mind that. But there have been enough that I know when I have found something special.' He raised her chin and kissed her. 'You, my little wanton, were born for it.'

She lifted her eyebrows. 'Is that supposed to be a compliment?'

For answer, he moved his hands down over her breasts, tweaking her nipples, and looked at her speculatively. 'Well,' he mused, 'I don't suppose you would object if

I suggested...' His voice trailed away as his gaze followed the caressing movements of his fingers.

With a strangled gasp she twisted away, scooping up her robe. 'Oh, no, you don't! I could not suffer Jinny's knowing looks if we do not appear till midway through the afternoon!'

He laughed and turned to go. 'Ten minutes, then!' he threw over his shoulder. 'But you shall not escape so lightly tonight!'

That promise carried her through the day in a state of euphoria. Yet she scarcely dared trust the feelings bubbling through her veins, and every time her thoughts touched upon Kit she felt a pang of guilt. But Ben had only to look at her in that particular way, and take her in his arms, and she knew it could not be wrong. She had given herself to him, body and soul, and her heart soared with happiness.

Helping Jinny chop vegetables for the soup, she found herself wishing things could always stay like this: Ben and Toby working side by side to mend one of the carriage wheels in the stable, she and Jinny preparing dinner together—the servant-master relationship dissolving and reforming as the situation demanded. And Matthew's happy laughter drowned by Lucifer's excited barking as the boy threw sticks for him.

It was getting dark. 'I'll light the candles,' she said, tipping the chopped turnips into the pot, and then went outside to call Matthew in. As she did so, a rider came hurtling into the clearing, skidding to a halt in front of her.

He sprang to the ground, cast a swift glance over her and gave a brief nod of greeting. 'You'll be Ben's wife,' he said breathlessly, and held out his hand. 'I'm Tom Ellis. Is he here?'

'Yes, he——'

Ben himself emerged from the stable and came towards them, greeting the young man with easy familiarity.

'Tom! You've ridden hard, by the looks of your horse!
Come inside and have a drink.' The sharp perception in
his eyes belied the casual tone, and Emma felt a prickle
of unease.

Tom shook his head. 'Thanks, but I only came to tell
you...' Drawing a dozen handbills from inside his jerkin,
he thrust them into Ben's hand. 'I'm away back to town.'
He turned to remount, but Ben, scanning the bills, stayed
him.

'What is it?' Emma demanded, misliking the
expression on her husband's face. 'What has happened?'

'One of the tea ships has arrived,' he told her, his eyes
gleaming with anticipation as he passed her one of the
notices. It called the citizens of Boston to an emergency
meeting in Faneuil Hall the following morning.

''Tis the *Dartmouth*,' Tom supplied. 'She's anchored
off Castle William and the whole town's a-buzz.'

'I can imagine,' Ben said drily. 'Give me a few minutes
and I'll ride with you.'

'Ben!' Emma's involuntary cry of dismay drew the
eyes of both men. But one glance at Ben's expression
and she knew she must be cautious. However great his
love for her, he had another passion and she would not—
dared not—have him choose between them. So she thrust
aside her dismay and tried to look suitably exasperated.
'You are both mad! That horse will not carry you another
dozen yards, Tom Ellis, and even if you left it and bor-
rowed one of ours it will soon be too dark to go anywhere, let alone all the way to town! And if there is going
to be a meeting tomorrow, nothing is likely to happen
tonight, surely? So have dinner with us, Tom, stay the
night and you can both leave at first light and miss
nothing but a lot of tavern talk and speculation.'

Jinny made a timely appearance in the doorway as
Tom started to protest that there was nothing wrong with
tavern talk. The observation died on his lips and he visibly wavered as the girl smiled at him. Ben's expression

as he met Emma's gaze was harder to read. But finally
he gave a sigh of capitulation, shot a wry half-smile at
Tom and said, 'She is right, of course. And I should
hate to miss my dinner!'

Later, Emma left the two men discussing the implications of the Dartmouth's arrival and the possible
courses of action open to them. All of which seemed
likely to provoke a confrontation with the authorities
that sent a shiver of apprehension over her. So she left
them and went upstairs.

'Jinny, will you pack a few things for yourself and
Matthew before you retire?' she said as the girl un-
hooked the back of her gown. 'We will go with them
tomorrow.'

'Yes, Miss Emma!' Jinny's heightened colour and
sparkling eyes were more than enough to confirm how
things stood between her and Tom Ellis.

'You had better make a start, then. I can manage by
myself now and I don't suppose Ben and Tom will be
long, as they mean to leave early in the morning.'

The comment was not lost on Jinny as she bobbed a
hasty curtsy and hurried away, leaving Emma to smile
over the thought that her maid would be unlikely to
spend the night alone!

When Ben came up, she was ready for bed and packing
a trunk. He stood in the doorway and frowned at her.
'Emma? What are you doing?'

'I'm coming with you,' she said simply, carefully
folding a gown over its layer of tissue, and then
straightening up to look squarely at him.

'No, you are not! You will stay here.'

'I will not!' Two days ago, she would not have argued
however hurt she had felt by such a curt dismissal. Now,
however, she refused to be set aside so easily.

'There is no way of knowing what will happen
tomorrow,' he told her brusquely. 'Things could turn

nasty and I would rather know you were well away from harm.'

'You did say I could make a few purchases for the house,' she pointed out blithely. 'And if you are going to town it is a perfect opportunity for me to attend to them. Or you could help me after the meeting if you prefer.'

'I may not return immediately from the meeting, my love. There may well be things to do—I may even have to go out of town if whatever decision is reached requires the support of our friends in the outlying areas. You know Sam Adams relies on me and others like me to keep the remoter farmers informed. Tell me what it is you want for the house and I will see to it.'

She looked at him, searching his face. Perhaps there was another reason he did not want her with him. Had she been a complete fool?

'Whatever you are thinking, stop it at once!' he commanded, crossing the room in a few strides and giving her a little shake. 'However many women I may have known in the past, Emma, there is not one of them holds any attraction for me now. You are the only woman in my life, and you must believe that. There is only one reason I am going into town and that is the meeting.' He looked down at her, seeking confirmation that she did not doubt him. Satisfied with her silent nod, he injected a lighter note into his voice. 'Besides, if you came with me you would expect me to join you for dinner, and send messages of my whereabouts and fret if I did not come home until late——'

'I should not!' she interrupted indignantly, pulling away from him. 'I know better. But marooned out here with no news at all I shall worry myself into a decline! And I want to be *involved*, Ben. I want to know what is happening. I won't be excluded from this part of your life. It affects me too.'

He was silent for a moment, then, 'I suppose if I forbade you to come you would find some way to trick poor Toby and follow me,' he said, with such annoyance in his voice that she caught her breath. But there was a glimmer of humour in his eyes and, encouraged by it, she shrugged.

'I suppose it is possible.'

For a long moment he regarded her with a mixture of pride, love and exasperation on his face. 'Do you give me your word that you will not attempt to go to the meeting?' he demanded finally. 'The place will be over-full and feelings run high——'

'Oh, but if I were with you——'

'No.' He said it with such flat finality that she dared not argue lest he forbade her to go with him at all. 'Your word, Emma.'

'I promise,' she said meekly.

He gave a brief nod. 'Very well, then. Now, have you finished that?' indicating the trunk. 'For I've a notion to remind you who is master here.' And he pulled her roughly towards him, claiming her mouth in a kiss both hungry and impatient that told her the remark was not entirely flippant!

CHAPTER ELEVEN

THE wind gusted spasmodically across the Common as Emma stood watching Matthew throw Ellen's bread to the seagulls.

They had been in town for over a fortnight and she grew daily more glad that she had insisted on coming, for it was doubtful whether Ben would have got back to Eastwood at all in that time. As it was she saw very little of him during the day and frequently he did not come home until very late at night. But then he was hers, unreservedly, totally hers, and their lovemaking seemed all the more intense and passionate for the time they spent apart.

Only once had he not come home until dawn. She knew from his attire and his curt advice not to wait up for him where he was going, but he did not volunteer the information and she did not question him. But she had lain awake worrying, hurt beyond measure that still he did not trust her with knowledge of his smuggling activities, still had not forgiven her. But in the morning, as though guessing her unhappiness, he had taken her in his arms and said gently, 'I do not want you involved in this, Emma. I do not want Hunt to be able to use you to get to me. If you are questioned it is better you do not have to lie.' And with that she had to be content.

The endless meetings that claimed so much of his time had achieved very little, and the row over the tea ships grew increasingly more bitter. The initial meeting that had brought them to town had resolved that the arriving tea must not be landed, nor pay duty, but should be returned to England untouched and undamaged, in the same vessels. That now seemed impossible; and with the *Dartmouth* and the *Eleanor* docked at Griffins' Wharf, the *William* run aground off Cape Cod and the *Beaver* quarantined with smallpox, Governor Hutchinson had ordered the harbour exits blocked with warships to prevent them leaving without clearance. Matters now appeared to be at something of an impasse and Emma very much feared that any chance of an amicable solution was lost. She had grown used to sharing Ben with his Cause—indeed, she was now as caught up in the conflict as he, anxious every day until he came home, when she could sit at his feet by the fire to hear the news.

A mass meeting was called for the morrow, delegates being summoned from five neighbouring towns. But Ben, under the guise of mill business as a precaution against his being stopped, had left early to alert supporters in the remoter outlying areas. As many Americans as possible were being summoned to a huge show of strength and opinion.

As Emma stared over Matthew's head, preoccupied with troubled thoughts about how it would all come out, a man on horseback rode across her field of vision. There was something vaguely familiar about him... As her attention snapped back into focus, and the man drew closer, a cold hand clutched at her stomach. Drawing a sharp breath, she turned swiftly away, ducking her head further into her hood. He passed by on the other side of the carriage, and, although he was some yards away before she dared to look, there was no mistaking the man. William Carlisle!

Immediately she drew Matthew away, and hastened to the carriage. 'Jack, take us home!' she commanded, unable to prevent her voice from trembling.

She was still shaking when they arrived back at the house and she left Matthew to help Jack with the horse while she retreated to the refurbished drawing-room to steady her nerves with a tiny splash of brandy. She shuddered with distaste, but it served its purpose, and the panic racing through her veins finally began to subside.

If William Carlisle had come to Boston it was for only one reason—to take her back. And he could not do that, of course, for she was safely wed to Ben. Yet the thought gave her only small comfort, for Ben was not here and not likely to be back for hours, and she did not relish the prospect of facing Carlisle alone.

It would not take him long, she reasoned, to discover where she was, and she spent the next two hours alert for every sound, convinced that he would come pounding on the door at any moment. When it grew near dusk and still there was no sign of him, she wondered if he might have gone to Eastwood. But Ben was so well known in the town, and this past fortnight had been so involved in the meetings and general furore, that it seemed unlikely anyone would have directed Carlisle there. And the possibility that having discovered she was married he had meekly accepted defeat and decided to leave her alone was so remote that she was finally forced to wonder if she might not have been mistaken. Perhaps, after all, it had not been him and all her panic was for nothing.

By the time Ben came home, exhausted yet satisfied, she had almost convinced herself of it. And so much of her anxiety melted away merely at the sight of him that she thrust Carlisle to the back of her mind. After all, what could he do to her with the formidable Ben Sullivan to protect her?

'I've to go out again, my love,' he told her apologetically as he changed for dinner. 'I am sorry, but we need to discuss what to do if tomorrow's meeting goes against us. We have to *try* official means to get clearance for the ships to leave, but it is very unlikely we will succeed. This deadlock must be broken somehow though, and we have to do something soon.'

It was not until much later, when she had given up waiting for him and had got ready for bed, that she suddenly remembered Carlisle, and so preoccupied was she with her thoughts that she did not hear Ben come in. 'Whatever is the matter?' he said from the doorway. 'You were not worried about me?'

She raised her head from her knees and smiled at him. 'Of course! But I was thinking of something else. I saw Carlisle this afternoon.'

His face registered surprise. 'Carlisle? The man you were supposed to marry? Are you sure?' He came across to the bed and sat on the edge, frowning. 'It seems unlikely.'

'Why? Whatever else he may be, he is not stupid. It would not take a genius to guess where I went.'

'No. But he did not come into Boston Harbour, that much is certain! And anyway, only a fool would cross the Atlantic in November on the slender chance that he would find you here.'

He was right, of course. Yet a nagging unease remained. Perhaps it was just that she had been so happy these past two weeks that she could not believe it would last, and she was just waiting for something—anything—to spoil it.

He regarded her for a moment, missing nothing of her disquiet, and, drawing her into his arms, he said gently, 'You were probably mistaken, my love. Otherwise he surely would have come here by now. But in the unlikely event that it was him you saw, what does it matter? You are married to me and there is not much he can do about that. And if he is fool enough to come here making trouble he will have me to deal with.' He put a hand under her chin so that she had to meet his gaze. 'Is that not reassuring enough for you?' he teased coaxingly.

She sighed, dismissing her lingering anxiety, and smiled at him. 'Yes.'

'And...I will ask around the inns and taverns tomorrow. If there is a stranger in town asking questions about you, I shall hear about it.' He smiled and planted a kiss on the tip of her nose. 'Now, can we get on with more important things?'

For answer, she wound her arm around his neck and lay back on the pillows, pulling him down with her, and in the minutes that followed had little thought for William Carlisle.

Blade bucked and danced skittishly, as though he sensed the impending gallop across the Common, but Ben handled him easily enough, holding him to a barely restrained walk as they turned into the street.

They had scarcely gone a dozen yards when a youth stepped out suddenly in front of them, and grabbed at Blade's bridle. The horse tossed and reared, failing to loosen the youth's grip, and for a moment Ben was fully occupied bringing him under control. 'What the devil do you think you're doing?' He glared down angrily at the young ruffian.

Unshaven and poorly clad, the boy seemed unperturbed. 'You Sullivan?'

'Yes. What of it?'

'The name William Carlisle mean anything to you?'

A muscle tensed along Ben's jaw, and he sent the boy a withering look. 'Get out of my way. I am in a hurry.'

'He wants to talk to you. Now. About yer wife.'

Ben's grip tightened on the reins. 'I suggest you tell Carlisle,' he said stonily, 'that where my wife is concerned there is nothing to discuss.' He dug his heels into Blade's flanks.

'If you don't talk to 'im,' the lout shouted after him, 'you'll be sorry!'

His breath hissing between his teeth, Ben wheeled the horse violently, his eyes blazing furiously as he came back. 'Are you threatening me?' he demanded, his voice dangerously controlled.

'Not I!' He threw up his hands, and took a step back as the big horse advanced slowly. 'Can't answer for Carlisle, o' course. I'd say 'e's a nasty piece o' work when he don't get 'is way.' He shrugged. 'Don't much matter to me—I been paid to deliver a message and that I done.'

For a moment Ben looked down at the sneering, insolent face and would have taken a sadistic pleasure in putting his boot to it. But Emma had been fearful and it might be as well to see Carlisle and persuade him it would be better for his health if he were to keep out of their way until he could take the next ship home.

'Where is he?'

'Ship an' Compass.'

'Very well!' he snapped. 'You in front. And run! I'm sure you do not want to feel these hoofs crushing your spine.'

It was mid-morning, and there were few signs of real activity at the Ship and Compass, a tavern that did most of its trade late into the night. 'I'll take the horse,' the youth said as Ben dismounted. 'Mr Carlisle's upstairs. Second door.'

Reluctant to abandon his beloved Blade to the care of such vermin, he nevertheless felt happier leaving the boy thus occupied than having to worry about his being at his back. He went up the dingy stairway, instinctively drawing the slender knife from its hiding place in his boot—a habit assumed much earlier in his hazardous career—and paused outside the second door. 'Carlisle!'

A silk-smooth voice from within answered at once. 'Come on in, Sullivan.'

Ben turned the handle and pushed the door wide with his boot. Reassuringly, it swung right back on its hinges. Across the room a man sat in a shabby armchair, indolently stretched out before a blazing fire, with a glass in one hand and a bottle in the other. Ben's swift, appraising scrutiny missed nothing. A man in his mid-forties, beginning to run to fat, his eyes too close together, his lips too loose, leering unpleasantly when he attempted to smile. No wonder Emma had fled.

'Come in, Sullivan. We cannot talk if you continue to stand out there.' His voice had the silken pleasantness which Ben immediately distrusted. He was reminded of a coiled snake. 'I apologise for the seediness of my surroundings,' Carlisle went on, curling his lip in obvious distaste. 'But I shall not keep you long.'

Keeping one ear alert for sounds of footfalls on the stairs, Ben thrust his knife into his belt and crossed the threshold, knowing he could fell Carlisle with a single blow if necessary.

Some instinct, some slight movement of the air behind him, warned him of danger, gave him a fraction of a second to flinch away. But too late. The blow that crashed into the back of his head was enough to send him sprawling to the floor, his head exploding with pain, and a swirling blackness, threatening to sink him into oblivion.

'Miss Emma...' Jinny stood uncertainly in the nursery doorway.

Emma looked up. 'Yes, Jinny, what is it?'

'It's Captain Hunt. He's downstairs and he says he needs to see you urgently. I showed him into the drawing-room.'

'Captain Hunt?' she echoed in dismay. 'Whatever does he want?' Standing up with a sigh, she straightened her skirts, 'All right, I will go down and see him.'

'Shall I bring anything?' Jinny asked doubtfully.

'No. I cannot think what he wants and I have no intention of encouraging him to linger!' She tucked a stray curl into place and went downstairs.

'Captain Hunt.' She greeted him coolly. 'I am aston-
ished to see you here. I did not think you would be so
foolish.'

The brief shadow of a smile had no warmth in it. 'I
had to come, Emma——'

'You take a great risk. Fortunately Ben is not here—
I assume you know there is a meeting in the South
Church?'

'Yes, but——'

'Captain, I have nothing to say to you. Except perhaps
thank you. That little incident at Eastwood set things
right between Ben and I. He loves me, Alex, as I love
him, and I am very, very happy. Now, please go.'

The Captain's face contorted. 'You make this impossible, Emma! I do not know how to tell you——'

She looked at him, suddenly still. 'Tell me what?'

He hesitated, seeming to search for words. Finally he
said, 'Did you know William Carlisle is here?'

She tensed and said warily, 'I saw him yesterday, on
the Common. But—do you know him?'

'I—made his acquaintance.' He sighed heavily, looking
uncomfortable. 'I am sorry, Emma. Would it were
anyone but I with such news. First your brother,
now——'

'Now what?' A cold misgiving clutched at her
stomach. 'What has happened?'

'It's Ben. Emma, he's dead. Carlisle killed him. He
sent a message that he wanted to talk to him about you.
He really must be in love with you, else he would never
have walked into such a transparent trap. He did not
stand a chance.' She could only stare at him and he
moved swiftly forward to grip her shoulders. 'It happened not half an hour since and Carlisle is on his way
here. You must come with me—I shall take you to Castle
William. You will be safe there and I can get help to
deal with him.'

'I don't believe you,' she whispered hoarsely. 'You are lying. How could you know all this? How——?'

'Emma, I was there.' He drew Ben's knife from his belt and held it out to her. She recognised it immediately and uttered a strangled little gasp, looking up at him with a sudden flare of accusation burning in her eyes. 'No,' he protested. 'It was not I. There was no love lost between us and I cannot pretend to any grief at his death, but I wanted to see him hang for his crimes. I am no backstreet murderer. Carlisle killed him. With you a widow he intends to take you back to England and marry you. He is on his way here now and he has a ship waiting up the coast.'

A cold horror had begun to seep through her. Carlisle, she was sure, was capable of anything, and a chilling numbness settled on her. He gave her a little shake. 'If you want to avoid him, you must come with me now. You have no choice.'

Dully she shook her head. 'Where is he, Captain? Where is Ben? I have to see him. I have to be sure——'

'Don't be a fool!' he interrupted harshly. 'Do you want Carlisle to take you to England? He has half a dozen men with him. I cannot protect you here, Emma. You will have to come with me. Do you understand?' He took her arm. 'Come,' he added more gently. 'You will be safe at Castle William.'

She went unresistingly, but her heart gave a sickening lurch when she saw that it was Blade he was riding. Seeing the look on her face, the Captain squeezed her arm. 'I'm sorry. But he's faster than the one I have at present.'

The last remnant of hope dissolved. Something inside her seemed to collapse, and she made no protest when he lifted her into the saddle and sprang up behind her. She did not even demur when he pulled off his red coat to wrap around her. She simply clung on, unthinking, unfeeling, as he dug in his heels and set them away from the house at an urgent gallop.

Ben lay quite still on the floor of the little room above the Ship and Compass, fighting off the swirling mists of oblivion.

Indistinct voices spoke above him, but as a booted foot turned him over and removed the knife from his belt one of them was all-too familiar. Instinct and experience restrained him from reacting violently to it. He was no match for Alex Hunt at the moment.

But when he had gone he stirred and groaned, and made a credible show of agony as he dragged himself into a sitting position and slumped back against the wall. His neck behind his left ear felt warm and sticky but he resisted the temptation to put a hand to the wound. It throbbed excruciatingly, every movement sent darts of pain through his head, but the mists were clearing and he seemed in no immediate danger of passing out. Still, he had to find out what was going on and it would do no harm for Carlisle to think him in a worse state than he really was. With another groan, he raised his head, winced visibly and half opened his eyes. 'What do you want, Carlisle?' he muttered groggily.

Carlisle played a coil of rope through his fingers and regarded Ben with a supercilious look of triumph. 'I have no idea how much you know, Sullivan, but I made an agreement with Miss Wyatt and her brother that in return for a certain—not insignificant—sum of money to save their wretched little shipping business, Emma would become my wife. Rather foolishly she broke that agreement. And I intend to take her back to fulfil her obligations.'

'The devil you do!' Ben exploded through his teeth. 'She is—my wife!'

'Yes.' Carlisle's smile was very nearly a sneer. 'I know, dear boy. When some addle-witted fool mistakenly directed me to Cedars upon my arrival, the lady of the house was more than happy to inform me of the fate of my fiancée. But it is merely a temporary set-back, I assure you. Captain Hunt will return shortly to deal with you. It was part of our arrangement.'

'What arrangement?' Ben's voice rasped harshly. 'How did that—devil's spawn get mixed up in this?'

'You have your brother's wife to thank for that,' Carlisle gloated. 'Uncommon woman, that one. She seemed to feel he would have an interest in assisting me to—shall I say, restore Emma to her rightful place? That is where he has gone now, to bring her to me. And when we have left to meet my ship he will have the pleasure of killing you—thus leaving Emma a widow, and free to become my wife.'

'Why you——!' Ben made a violent movement to get up, and then fell back with an involuntary cry as a shaft of pain shot through his head, setting the room spinning. There was nothing feigned about that, and he realised that he would have to catch the other man off his guard to be certain of incapacitating him at the first attempt. 'You are a fool to—trust Hunt,' he ground out. 'He wants Emma for himself.'

'He wants your death more!' Carlisle declared with malicious satisfaction. 'But you are right! I do not trust him. Young Daniels will be following him to ensure he brings Emma to me and does not get any foolish ideas.' He sat feeding the rope through his fingers, a faint smile almost grotesque on the loose, moist lips as he silently congratulated himself that he had thought of everything.

Ben allowed a groan to escape him, and half closed his eyes. But his mind was working. It sounded so unlike Hunt that he was very much afraid Emma was his prey—after all, if it was his death he wanted, he could have arranged that in an alley on many a dark night. No, Hunt wanted the glory of bringing him to the gallows and a public hanging.

Carlisle seemed in no hurry to tie him up, so he would have to goad him. He had no great faith in his own ability at the moment to merely overpower the man. Finally, he said, 'We have been married some weeks, Carlisle. Suppose there is a child? Are you willing to accept another man's child?'

Carlisle's reaction was more than he had hoped for. The thought was obviously abhorrent, for the man's face suffused with angry colour and he leapt to his feet with an ugly expression contorting his features. 'Oh, no, Sullivan!' he spat. 'There will be no child. I will see to it! There—will be—no—child!'

His meaning was unmistakable, and the thought of Emma at the mercy of such an animal made him feel sick. As Carlisle bent down to tie up his feet, he suddenly kicked upwards with a force that sent the man crashing across the room into the fireplace. He lay still, a small trickle of blood oozing from the back of his head. Gingerly, Ben got up, his own head throbbing sickeningly. A brief examination was sufficient to reveal that Carlisle was merely unconscious, the blood coming from a nasty cut where he had hit the fireplace. He set about tying him up securely, and, that done, left him on the floor, locked the door from the outside and pocketed the key. He could deal with him later.

The suspicion that Hunt was after Emma was reinforced when he went to retrieve Blade. 'They wouldn't let me touch 'im, sir,' the ostler told him, eyeing the blood trickling down his neck. 'The cap'n called for 'im an' the boy took 'im out front.'

'Damn!' Ben swore harshly. 'I need another. Quickly!'

'Sorry, sir. We don't keep but one 'orse 'ere. An' 'e's off to the blacksmith. Be back in about an hour.'

Ben cursed violently, and swung on his heel, striding away. The ostler stared thoughtfully after him for a moment, and then set down the bucket he was holding and went into the tavern to see what had become of the

Englishman who'd been so generous with his money and who might be persuaded to part with more.

Ben crossed the narrow street and cut down an alley. Daylight scarcely reached down past the roof-tops and in the dark shadows he almost fell over the body sprawled in the debris. Daniels. He stared down at the corpse, suspicion crystallising into conviction and a cold fear. He had to get to Emma...

Emma paid no attention to the route they were taking as Blade carried them swiftly away from Tremont Street. A dull pain throbbed in her chest and her vision was blurred by tears that would not fall.

It was not until Hunt pulled sharply on the reins, nearly pitching her over the horse's head, that she was brought rudely back to reality. He swore violently at the boy who had run out in front of them, and then spurred Blade on again. But Emma had taken stock of her surroundings and realised that they were not going to Castle William.

'This is not the way,' she protested. 'Where are we going?'

'Somewhere safe.' He was looking straight ahead, concentrating on steering them through the town at reckless speed. 'Castle William may not be a very hospitable place for Ben Sullivan's widow at this particular moment.'

'Then—then take me to Cedars,' she suggested, shakily. But they were already heading out of town. The captain shook his head, deftly taking both reins in one hand and curling his free arm tightly about her waist. An alarm bell rang somewhere in her mind and she suddenly felt as though someone had thrown cold water in her face.

'My God!' she gasped. What a fool she had been! 'Is this some sort of sick game you are playing? Carlisle was not coming for me at all, was he? And—and Ben?

What has happened to him?' Her voice rose as she twisted round. 'Is he really dead? Tell me, for God's sake!'

'I suggest, my dear Emma,' he said imperviously, 'that you save your questions and concentrate on staying on this horse. Should you fall—or be foolish enough to attempt to jump—you will almost certainly be killed, or at the very least suffer horrible injury.'

A second's thought was enough to banish any such idea from her head. The ground was disappearing beneath them at an alarming pace and she felt precarious to say the least. So she bit her lip, squeezed her eyes shut against the tears welling up in them, and clung on desperately.

The horse was lathering badly when Hunt finally slowed the pace and slackened his hold on her. It did not help her, however, for they were several miles from town and he would have little difficulty catching her again even if she did succeed in freeing herself. They had not passed a dwelling of any description for some time. They turned into a narrower lane, then along a track, and finally picked their way across sparsely wooded country until they came to a small lake. They followed the water's edge round to a cabin, and there, finally, they stopped.

Another horse was tethered outside and as the captain sprang to the ground and turned to help her down a young soldier emerged from the cabin. 'I brought the provisions, sir,' he said, his insolent gaze lingering over Emma with undisguised admiration. 'Your musket's inside, too.'

'All right, Drummond,' Hunt snapped. 'Attend to my horse and then go up the track and keep watch.'

'Sir.'

'I want to know what is going on,' Emma insisted, with only a slight tremor in her voice. 'Where is Ben?

What have you done to him? And Carlisle—where is he? What do you *want*?'

For answer he took her arm and propelled her into the cabin. It felt damp and smelled of mildew and the gloomy light from the small window revealed a room which looked as though it had not been used for years. A door at one end, leading to a smaller room, hung precariously on one hinge; a layer of dust lay over everything and cobwebs clung thickly in the corners. If anything, it felt colder inside than out and she shivered.

'Sit down,' Hunt ordered, delving into a bundle on the floor. 'I'll light a fire.' She glanced involuntarily towards the door and he added sharply, 'Don't be foolish!' and, picking up the musket, he laid it across his knees as he bent down before the fire.

Controlling her voice with difficulty, she stared at his back. 'Is Ben dead?'

'I sincerely hope not,' he answered mildly.

The sudden flood of relief made her legs weak, and, groping for the nearest chair, she sat down heavily. The captain finally coaxed a flame out of the logs, prodded it into life and straightened up. 'Unless Carlisle has finished him off,' he added, and turned to look at her. 'Unfortunately your husband has the instincts of a cat and contrived to dodge a carefully aimed blow intended merely to stun him for a few moments. The result being that he was rendered virtually senseless.'

He bent down and rummaged in the sack again, bringing out a muslin bundle which he set on a low stool and proceeded to unwrap, revealing bread and cheese. 'However,' he went on, 'when I removed his knife he did not appear totally lifeless, and I have every confidence that Carlisle is sufficiently incompetent to permit him to escape. Especially as I dealt with the oaf he hired to do his dirty work. Then, my dear Emma, your husband will no doubt go home, discover you gone and set off in pursuit. I imagine he will have little difficulty following us. Are you hungry?'

She stared at the food and felt sick. As if she could eat! She looked up at him, thrusting away her doubts. She must believe, as he did, that Ben had escaped Carlisle. 'He is not a fool, Captain! He will know it is a trap and he will not come alone.'

'On the contrary, my dear. I am sure he will not suspect anything. I rather think his feelings for you are such that he will rush headlong to the rescue without a thought. Drummond will give me warning of his approach and it will not be difficult to overpower him.' He pulled a canteen from the sack and held it out to her. 'Water? Or would you prefer brandy?' His mouth curled in a mocking smile. 'Drummond has thoughtfully provided both.'

Acknowledging her thirst, she took the canteen, gulping several mouthfuls before handing it back. 'And Carlisle? What is his part in this?'

'His lust for you, and his determination to get you away from Sullivan gave me the opportunity I needed.' He shrugged dismissively. 'He has been useful, and I have no doubt Sullivan will deal with him satisfactorily.'

He was so confident, so sure. 'And what is all this supposed to achieve?' she demanded. 'If you wished to kill him, why did you not do so when you had the chance?'

'But that would be too easy.' He smiled faintly. 'And there would be no satisfaction in it. I want to see him hang. I want the town to see him for what he really is— not some sort of hero, but a thief and a traitor.'

'To hang him for such crimes you must have proof,' she pointed out fervently. 'And if you had it you would have used it, so...'

'Proof,' he agreed, 'or a confession.' He replaced the brandy bottle in the sack and then stood looking down at her. 'At every opportunity he has eluded me, made a fool of me, and ended up with the winning hand. Now I have something he values more than anything else. You.' He moved forward and drew her to her feet. Instinctively she drew back, but his fingers dug into her arms belying the soft caress of his voice as his eyes lingered over the curve of her breasts. 'How do you think he will react to watching while I avail myself of the pleasures of your body? Do you think he will agree to give himself up? Confess, if I promise to stop? It would give me the greatest pleasure to hear him blurting out the names of his smuggling friends and the places he hides his contraband—to say nothing of the treasonous plots he is hatching with that pack of rebels he spends so much time with, and perhaps even Carlisle's murder.'

Emma had listened with a growing disbelief. Now she wrenched herself free and stared at him in horror. 'You are mad!' she cried, backing away. Yet he was not insane—unless it was insanity bred of jealousy and hatred, fuelled into an obsession with revenge. There was a glitter in his eyes that sent a shiver of fear down her spine. A cold, calculating confidence that could not contemplate defeat. 'He will never betray his friends!' she spat contemptuously. 'Never!'

'You think not?' She had backed herself against a wall and now she was trapped as he stood in front of her. 'I wonder how much of this he will be able to stand?' He cupped her breasts, moving his hands over them, feeling the nipples beneath the fabric of her dress. 'Can you imagine what it will do to him? Watching you, the woman he loves, being abused by the one man in all Boston he despises?' Furiously, she struck his hands away and lashed out at his face, a sick disgust curdling her stomach. But he grabbed her wrist, his fingers paralysing her arm. 'I have always admired your spirit, my dear Emma,' he murmured with deadly control. 'And, although I do not expect you to believe this, I regret what must happen here. I fear it will not be pleasant for you and I could have wished things to be different——'

'Liar!' she spat, struggling to free her arm. 'You do not have to do this—you are enjoying yourself, you sadistic monster!'

'I will see Sullivan squirm,' he said softly, his eyes gleaming. 'I will have him beg on his knees. I will hear him tell me everything I want to know.'

'He will kill you!' she whispered harshly.

'He will not have the chance to try.' He released her wrist abruptly. 'It is time for this battle of wits between us to end. And I am going to win.' Turning away, he picked up the musket and went to sit near the door with it, leaving her shaken, fear and horror pounding in her chest.

She forced herself to be calm, to think. This must not happen. Ben must not walk into this trap. Desperately she scanned the room for some means of escape, and her eyes alighted on the knife that still lay between the bread and the cheese on the stool. A ray of hope gave her courage.

Picking up his coat from the floor, she huddled into it and crept towards the fire. Crouching in front of the meagre flames, obscuring his view of the stool, she waited until his attention was held by the task of cleaning and reloading the musket. 'At least—at least could we have some light?' she whispered pleadingly. 'It's so—so horribly gloomy in here.'

He glanced at her. It was still early in the afternoon, but the cabin boasted only one window and that was so caked with grime that little light penetrated through it. He shrugged. 'If you wish.' Standing the musket against the wall, he got up and went to the table where several candles lay amongst the debris.

The moment his back was turned, Emma snatched up the little knife and hid it in the folds of her skirt. He came to the fire and bent down to coax two dusty and reluctant wicks into life. Now! she told herself. Now is your chance! But to her horror she was frozen. She was quite incapable of plunging the knife into him, quite unable to make her legs move, to make a dash for the door even. She was mesmerised by his back, her fingers clenched impotently around the handle of the knife.

One of the candles flared into life, and then the second. With a grunt of satisfaction he straightened up and turned around. He looked directly at her and said calmly, 'Give me the knife, Emma.'

Her breath caught in her throat and, belatedly, she leapt up, brandishing the knife at him. 'Don't come near me, Captain, or I'll——'

'What?' He raised his eyebrows. 'Kill me? I think not.' Not taking his eyes from her, he moved slowly to the table and carefully set the candles down. Then he came back towards her. 'Give me the knife, Emma,' he repeated.

She shook her head, backed away, edging towards the door. But with a swift movement forward he curled one arm around her waist and with his other hand deftly twisted the knife from her fingers. Holding her hard against him, he kissed her savagely. She struggled, but he merely gave a throaty chuckle. 'Oh, Emma!' he murmured, his mouth against hers. 'I've a mind not to wait for Sullivan, but to take you now . . .' She could feel the urgency in him as he moved his body against hers.

The pounding of a horse's hoofs saved her. He released her reluctantly as Drummond threw the door open and stopped, reddening. 'Sorry, sir. Someone's coming. But it's not Sullivan.'

'What?' Hunt's voice cracked with impatience. 'What do you mean it's not Sullivan?'

'This man's shorter, stockier. He doesn't sit a horse like Sullivan. I've seen *him* often enough from a distance and it's not him, sir.'

'Damn!' Hunt swore violently and flung away from Emma.

'Carlisle...' The name died on her lips. If he was here, instead of Ben, it could only mean...

Suddenly the captain swung back, swooping down to pull a coil of rope from the canvas bag and the cloth from beneath the bread. 'I will not give you up to him,' he ground out forcefully, and before she could do anything he caught her arm and pulled her across the room, throwing an order over his shoulder. 'Get the horses round the back.'

'What are you going to do?' she gasped as he dragged her into the other room and pushed her against the wall.

'Shut up!' He wrenched her arms back and tied her wrists, then bent and did the same to her ankles. With rising panic she watched him twist the piece of cloth into a gag.

'Oh, no, don't do that!' she cried. 'I promise I'll not——' But her words were cut off as he tied it around her mouth and pushed her roughly to the floor.

At the sound of another horse, he spun round and strode out, dragging the unhinged door back into place and casting her into semi-darkness. A moment later she heard the outside door crash back on its hinges.

'Where is she, Hunt?' Carlisle's voice sent a shudder through her. She could imagine his face, purple with rage. She felt as though a tight band were crushing her chest. Had he killed Ben?

'Put that thing down, Carlisle,' Hunt's voice was harsh with impatience. 'Before you blow yourself up. Drummond!'

The explosion of a gunshot shook the cabin walls, and a convulsion of fear shuddered through her. She squeezed her eyes shut and realised with horror that it did not much matter who killed whom, for the fate in store for her was equally chilling. Scuffles and indistinct grunts told her that the two men were fighting. Chairs scraped

and fell over, and then a resounding crash as something—the table probably—overturned. Then another
shot rent the air.

For a few moments there was utter silence. Emma held
her breath, straining to hear, her heart pounding painfully. A strange light flickered around the propped-up
door and as she stared at it in bewildered puzzlement
she became aware of a dull sound, like—— Her fear
turned to horror. Fire! Dear God, the place was on fire!

She tried to scream, but she could not get rid of the
gag in her mouth and only strangled cries came out as
she tried frantically to stand up, pushing her back against
the wall. But her legs refused to support her and she
stared with horrified fixation at the door and the light
glowing around it. There was no sound from the other
room save the crackle and roar of eager flames. Irrel-
evantly the thought came to her that something that felt
and smelled so damp had no right to burn so fiercely.

She made as much noise as she could, banging her
feet on the floor, her elbows on the wall behind her,
forcing her voice through the gag. But no one came.
God in heaven, were they all dead? Smoke began to fill
the little room and a funny little sound choked in her
throat at the paralysing realisation. She was going to die
unless she could get out quickly. She let herself slide
sideways to the floor and began to roll towards the door,
smoke stinging her eyes and filling her lungs.

Then, miraculously, the door was dragged open and
Captain Hunt came staggering towards her, his face
streaked with blood from a gash on his temple. She
almost cried with relief as he picked her up and threw
her over his shoulder, carrying her through the smoke
and almost stumbling over Carlisle's body.

Outside, the young soldier, Drummond, lay sprawled
on the ground. He groaned, half turned and put out a
hand. But Hunt ignored him and carried her round to
where the horses were tethered. Pausing only to cut the

rope round her ankles, he lifted her into Blade's saddle, vaulted up behind her and spurred the horse away, leaving the unfortunate Drummond to fall back unconscious.

CHAPTER TWELVE

BEN arrived, his face and coat splattered with blood, at the front steps of the house on Tremont Street, and almost fell against the door as he pounded his fist against it.

'Where's Emma?' he demanded harshly as soon as Jinny opened it.

'Oh, sir!' Her face crumpled and fresh tears spilled from already reddened eyes as she stepped back to allow him in. 'Thank goodness it's you!' she sobbed. 'We thought—oh, look at your p-poor head——'

'Never mind that!' he snapped impatiently. 'Where is Emma?'

'Gone, sir!' The girl gulped and hastily brushed her apron over her eyes. 'She—went off with that—that Captain Hunt without a w-word and w-without even her cloak! Jack said h-he saw them riding through—through the gates as if the d-devil himself was after them. And b-both of them on your horse, sir! We-we didn't know what to think. And—and then this other man came——'

He gripped her arm. 'What other man? What did he look like?'

Tearfully, Jinny described William Carlisle. 'Oh. Sir, he was evil. M-Matthew was with me and he—he threatened to hurt him. I—I had to tell him she'd gone with the captain . . .'

Her voice dissolved into weeping and Ben cursed forcefully. Someone had obviously released Carlisle *and* provided him with a horse! 'How long ago?'

'Only a f-few minutes, sir.'

'Is Matthew all right?'

She nodded. 'Ellen's got him in the k-kitchen. What's happened, sir? Is Miss Emma in d-danger? It's my fault—I had to tell him——'

She looked so distraught that he made a supreme effort to keep his voice calm. 'It's not your fault, Jinny. She is in danger, yes. But she is not stupid, and she has more than her fair share of courage. But I have to go after them. Run and tell Jack to bring the horse——'

'I can't, sir!' She twisted her hands in her apron. 'When Miss Emma went off like that we d-didn't know what to do. We didn't know where you was so Jack's gone to—to Cedars to fetch Master John. I'm sorry, sir. We didn't know what else to do——'

He swallowed a violent oath and squeezed her arm. 'It's all right. You were not to know. And normally it would have been the right thing to do but—damn, I need a horse!' He looked down at her. 'Run next door to Canning. Tell him I need his horse urgently.'

As the girl fled, he ran up the stairs two at a time, his head feeling as though a hammer were crashing into the side of it, and the wound still seeping blood. He collected his pistol, thrusting it into the top of his breeches, and his other long-bladed dagger and went downstairs again. Ellen was coming from the kitchen. 'Get something to bind this damn wound, will you?' he threw at her, before going into the drawing-room and pouring himself a large brandy, which he took at a single swallow.

By the time Jinny returned a few minutes later to say the horse was being saddled for him, Ellen had stanched the blood and wound a makeshift bandage around his head, and the brandy had at least steadied his erratic pulse and arrested the wild anxiety that threatened to drive out any rational thought.

Fortunately, he had little difficulty ascertaining which way Hunt and Emma had gone, so conspicuous had been their headlong flight. And the thought that Carlisle was some minutes ahead of him, presumably following the trail with equal ease, spurred him on with an added urgency pounding through his veins.

He paused only when he reached the top of a low rise, and the road forked, south to Milton, west to Needham. Glancing around, a thin plume of white smoke rising above the trees caught his eye. He frowned; there was nothing down there but an oversized pond that passed as a lake and—a derelict cabin. He drew his breath with a hiss. Yet he held back, inherent caution ringing warning bells in his mind. If it was Hunt down there, it had all been too easy. He had left a trail of witnesses a babe could follow, so conspicuous had he been. He could be walking into a trap. He steadied his thoughts.

But before he could think anything the unmistakable sound of a shot some distance away settled the matter. His chest contracted painfully with a new fear, and, throwing caution to the devil, set his heels to the horse's flanks.

Another shot followed the first, and as he drew closer the thin spiral of smoke became a thick, black cloud. By the time he reached it, the cabin was ablaze. A young soldier lay sprawled in front of the door, a pool of blood spreading outwards around his head. It was not Hunt, but it was confirmation enough. 'Emma!' Ben sprang from his horse, the harsh cry catching in his throat as he ran towards the burning building.

He was beaten back from the doorway by the heat and flames, and a feeble groan from the body of the soldier caught his attention. He bent and pulled him up by the shoulders of his uniform coat. 'Is she in there?' he exploded through clenched teeth. 'Damn you, answer me! Where's my wife?'

The shot had gouged a deep furrow in the soldier's head above his ear; it was bleeding profusely and he was barely conscious, his eyes glazing over as Ben shook him. A loud roar cut across his words and part of the roof collapsed, sending up showers of sparks and billows of black smoke. He dragged the man away from the fierce blaze and half fell, half sat down beside him, staring with helpless desperation at the inferno before him.

'Gone.' It was little more than a whisper, and for a moment Ben thought he had imagined it in the noise of falling timbers and crackling flames. But the young man beside him moved his arm slightly and coughed, and he twisted round, grabbing the front of his coat.

'What? Hunt and my wife—where are they?'

'Gone,' he gasped, clearly in great pain. 'Gone.'

A flood of relief rocked Ben back on his heels. But she was not safe yet and after a moment he got up, picking up the soldier's hat and filled it with water from the lake. As he raised him up sufficiently to persuade him to drink, a spasm of pain twisted the blood-soaked face and it was a few minutes before Ben could bring him round enough to talk.

'Listen to me,' he commanded fiercely. 'If Hunt's gone, then he left you here to die. You do not owe him anything. I'll get you to a physician—but not until you've told me where they have gone.'

The young face contorted, the words forced out between gasps. 'I don't know. Went wrong. Someone else came—not you—should have been you. Captain said— hide horses...' His voice trailed off, his eyes losing focus.

'Was it Carlisle?' Ben prompted. Behind him came a splintering crash as one end of the cabin collapsed in on itself, largely smothering the worst of the fire. 'Was it Carlisle?' he repeated.

The soldier made an effort and gasped out, 'Yes. Hid the horses—not sure what—don't remember...' His eyelids drooped and Ben shook him, heedless of his grunt of pain.

'What did Hunt want with Emma—what was he going to do?'

'Use her—use her to—make you—confess.' Ben had to bend closer straining to hear the muttered words. 'Names—places—anything—I was to be—witness. But Carlisle—you were supposed—kill Carlisle...'

'What happened to him? To Carlisle? Think, man!'
But he was already unconscious and Ben let him fall
back, getting to his feet and staring at what was left of
the cabin, still burning but dying rapidly. Walking to the
collapsed end, he stood for a moment letting his gaze
sweep over the smouldering ruins. He found what he
was looking for, a blackened arm flung out from beneath the charred and smoking timbers, grisly evidence
that Carlisle, at least, had met the fate he deserved.

He turned away and stared out across the expanse of
lake. What were the chances that Carlisle had told Hunt
he had escaped? If Hunt thought himself pursued he
might yet keep Emma safe as bait, or hostage, or as an
inducement to make him 'confess' or whatever his
warped mind had planned. But he knew the chance was
slender. Carlisle would have been furious at Hunt's du-
plicity, intent only on getting Emma back, and from what
the soldier had said, and the swiftness of that second
shot after the first, there had been little discussion. If
Hunt believed him dead, he had no use for Emma except
for his pleasure—God alone knew what he might do.

Shutting the thought out, he tried to put himself in
Hunt's place. Where would he go? Where would he take
her? A swift survey of the ground around the cabin revealed one set of hoof prints leading away from the lake
towards a wooded hollow. Collecting his horse, he followed them until they veered round, doubling back
towards the track and, presumably, the road from town.
But where would he go? Not back to town, certainly.

Carlisle's ship! It came to him like a blinding flash of
light. Carlisle had planned to take Emma to a ship he
had waiting—Hunt would know that.

Ben's mouth twisted into a grim line as he swung the
horse round and rode back to the cabin. Emma probably
thought he was dead, too. How resistant would she be
to being taken back to England? And it would suit Hunt.
He would know his career in the army was finished; he
had left a trail of bodies behind him and too many people

to talk. And anyway, without his obsession with seeing Ben hang, would he care about his career? With a ship at his disposal he could presumably take Emma wherever he wished, not necessarily to England... The more Ben thought about it, the more convinced he was that Hunt's destination was Carlisle's ship.

Visions of Emma at the captain's mercy for weeks tortured him unbearably, and his thoughts were murderous as he pulled the horse to a halt beside the young soldier. He could not leave him to bleed to death—and he might be useful.

He was still unconscious, however, and, working swiftly, Ben tore a strip off his shirt and bound the wound as best he could. With some effort he heaved the man over his shoulder and all but threw him across the saddle. With a muttered apology, he mounted behind and headed back to town, one other question nagging at him: how in God's name was he to find out in time where Carlisle had arranged to meet his ship?

It seemed to take an agonisingly long time to get back to the house and as he slid to the ground Jack came running out to meet him. 'Help me get him inside, Jack,' he ordered abruptly, and turned to drag the inert body from the saddle.

'Ben! What the devil——?'

He swung round to face his brother, a dangerous fury glittering in his eyes. 'If anything has happened to Emma, I'll kill that treacherous, scheming little bitch you married!' he spat out, and, gritting his teeth against the explosive anger rising in him, turned back to the soldier. 'Help me get this man upstairs. Jack, go and get Cornwallis.'

'My God, what has happened?' John demanded, staring at him. 'What has Ann——?'

'Not now!' Ben cut across the question violently. 'And I don't trust myself not to take it out on you. Take his feet.'

Stunned, but wisely keeping silent, John helped him carry the soldier inside, as Ben issued a string of curt orders to Ellen and Jinny, and tersely brushed Matthew's questions aside.

They laid him down on what had been Maybelle's bed and John shot him an anxious look. 'Ben, what has happened? Surely——'

'I'm taking your horse. Stay here till I get back and don't let him——' a jerk of his head indicated the man on the bed '——out of your sight. And make sure Cornwallis keeps his mouth shut.'

'Now wait a minute——' John began in some annoyance, but Ben cut him off.

'No! Emma is in danger, due in no small measure to your wife's meddling, and I don't have time to discuss it. The least you can do, for her sake, is to stay here and do as I ask!' And with that he went out and ran downstairs, impatiently tearing off the bandage that had slipped over his brow.

Within minutes he was riding down School Street, an urgency pounding in his veins and dread lying like lead in the pit of his stomach. He nursed one hope: that Carlisle had arranged for some means of transport to take himself and Emma from the tavern to the ship, and someone would be able to tell him about it.

He rode into the yard of the Ship and Compass and pulled the horse up sharply, cursing under his breath. A young lieutenant was standing beside a shabby carriage talking with the ostler. He did not particularly relish a confrontation with Hunt's subordinate at the moment.

The lieutenant looked up, registered surprise and then came towards him. 'Sullivan! Impeccable timing. You have saved me the trouble of coming looking for you.'

'I've no time for small talk, Barford,' he snapped, dismounting. 'I——'

'It will only take a minute. This fellow says Captain Hunt left here earlier with a man called Daniels and your horse,' he said speculatively. 'Daniels was found with his throat cut in that alley yonder and the captain has gone missing. Now I don't suppose you would know anything about that?'

Ben kept his impatience in check. 'I fell over the body,' he said shortly. 'Hunt killed him.'

'Prove that, can you?'

'If I had time.' He brushed past him and strode across the yard to the ostler. Grabbing the man's shirt at the throat, he almost lifted him off his feet. 'Perhaps you'd care to explain how you managed to provide Mr Carlisle with a horse only minutes after you swore to me you had none?' he ground out between his teeth. 'Then you can tell me what else he paid you for. Such as how he planned to leave here tonight with my wife?'

The man's eyes darted to the lieutenant, who had come up behind Ben. But he got no support from that quarter. 'I—dunno what you're talkin' about——'

With his free hand, Ben reached for the knife in his boot and one fluid movement brought it to the man's throat. 'Try harder,' he threatened darkly.

'Paid me to find 'im a carriage,' he blurted out nervously. 'This was all I could get——'

'To take him where?' The tip of the knife dented the man's flesh.

'I—I dunno.' Ben shook his head, his eyes glinting dangerously, and finally the man admitted sullenly, 'Dead Men's Cove.' It was the nickname given to a small inlet a few miles south of Eastwood.

'When?'

''E wanted to get there afore dark. But 'e went out and ain't come back yet.' He glanced up at the sky. 'Won't make it now, any'ow.'

Ben lowered the knife and slid it back into his boot, releasing the filthy shirt abruptly. 'Carlisle's dead.' He too glanced up at the dull sky. On horseback he might get as far as Eastwood before it started to get dark, but... He whirled round to go, only to find Barford blocking his way.

'By all accounts, the captain was here with a man called Carlisle this morning,' he said, narrowing his eyes. 'If you know anything, Sullivan——'

Ben's expression was as hard as his voice, his fist clenching in an overwhelming desire to punch the man. 'Listen, Barford, one of your men is lying in my house with a shot wound that has taken a slice out of his skull. I imagine he'll be able to tell you far more than I about what happened, if he lives. I suggest you go and try to talk to him. Now, my wife is in danger and I am in a hurry.' He started past, but the other man's hand shot out, a note of urgency in his voice.

'I need to find the captain.'

'Then you'd better get to Dead Man's Cove before I do,' he spat out, wrenching his arm free, 'because he has got my wife and I shall very probably kill him! Now get out of my way——' Thrusting the lieutenant aside, he half ran to his horse.

'Wait! I'm coming with you!' Barford shouted.

'Go to the devil!' Vaulting into the saddle, he tugged the horse's head round and rode out of the yard at a furious gallop, a hard knot of dread throbbing painfully beneath his ribs.

Huddled in the lee of a ruined cottage wall, Emma wrapped her arms around her knees and shivered uncontrollably. Sharp with the tang of salt, the breeze was biting as it gusted off the sea through the fallen stone walls, and the woefully inadequate fire was barely struggling against it.

Their erratic flight from the burning cabin had been a nightmare. Hunt had pulled off the gag when her convulsive coughing threatened to choke her, but made no more concessions. With her hands still bound and Hunt's arms crushing her sides, they had torn across open country for over an hour, turning south to give the outskirts of Boston a wide berth before heading towards the coast.

When finally they stopped for a few minutes beside a stream, more from the necessity of keeping Blade on his feet than any consideration for her, she begged him to free her raw and bleeding wrists and finally demanded in a hoarse croak, 'Where are we going? What are you going to do with me?'

But his curt reply as he cut the rope had been unencouraging, 'You will see soon enough.'

They had gone on for upwards of another hour, this time at a marginally more sensible pace. He had been tense and uncommunicative, intent on the way ahead, and she, chilled to the bone, had been too numb to drag her thoughts into any sort of order.

Now, in the failing light, shivering uncontrollably, she could think only of Ben. Was he dead? Certainly the captain believed it, believed his plan had failed totally. Why else had Carlisle arrived at the cabin instead? Hunt was sitting on the ground opposite her, his back against the wall and his musket propped up beside him. And he kept casting glances up at the sky as though impatient for darkness. What were they doing here? What was he waiting for?

She made an effort to pull herself together. Whether or not Ben was dead, she must not let Hunt succeed in whatever he now planned to do. Somehow she must escape, must tell the authorities, must not allow him to get away with all this. For Ben's sake. Moistening her lips and swallowing a painful lump in her throat, she asked again, 'What are you going to do with me? I have a right to know, surely?'

He raised his head and looked at her for a long moment. 'I am going to take care of you.'

Under no illusion about what that meant and quashing an absurd desire to laugh, she sent him a pleading look. 'Let me go, Alex,' she whispered. 'Please.' But he merely shook his head and she buried her face on her knees. If she ran, where would she go? She had little idea of where she was save that it was near the coast south of the town.

Presumably if she followed the coast north she would eventually come to Eastwood, and Toby. The thought of it brought a sudden flame of warmth to her heart. But it died swiftly. In an hour it would be dark, and he had the horse—she could not hope to reach Blade before him. And at that moment she did not think she could even summon the strength to make an attempt.

She tried again. 'Where are we going? They will be looking for you—you must know that! I will have been missed within minutes and Jinny will know it was you. They will find Ben—and—and perhaps Drummond. He was not dead, was he? I heard him. If he lives, he will tell them—and they will find us eventually——'

'Carlisle had a ship waiting,' he interrupted, and glanced yet again at the darkening sky. 'It will come in close as soon as it's dark.'

'A ship!' That gave her a jolt. 'You are taking me to England?'

He shook his head, smiling a little. 'That was Carlisle's intention, certainly. Once I had killed Sullivan he was going to take you to England and marry you. England does not hold much appeal for me, however. I was thinking more of Lisbon.'

Lisbon. There would be no help for her there. She stared at him, her mind in a whirl.

'It is a long voyage.' His voice softened. 'Plenty of time for you to accept the inevitable, my dear, and come to think of me in a less unfavourable light.'

'Never!' She shook her head, her voice trembling with emotion.

'Come, now. Think, Emma. On such a long voyage there will be plenty of time for me to father a child. I think you will be glad enough of my support. It would be foolish to try to survive in a port such as Lisbon, with no money and very possibly a child on the way.'

Horror sent a shaft of anger stabbing through her and she leapt to her feet. Was there no end to his sadistic schemes? 'You vile pig!' Her eyes flashed brightly. 'You are mad! If you think——'

'Ben is dead, Emma.' His voice cut coldly across her trembling outrage. Then he shrugged. 'And you could suffer worse fates than being with me.'

'I'll kill myself before I let you touch me!' she spat. And, spinning round, she stumbled outside, her hair, long since free from its ribbons, whipped around her face by the wind, her lip trembling and hard little tears stinging her eyes. Continually raped by that devil! A shudder of horror ran through her, and she started to run.

A few stumbling, desperate, painful strides and an iron hand grabbed her arm and spun her round. His hand dealt her a stinging slap, her cry strangled as he jerked her against him, his mouth fastening on hers in a brutal assault. The turmoil of the day, all the fear, despair, anger and hatred suddenly exploded within her, and, tearing her mouth from his, she lashed out in a white rage, fists clenched, raining furious punches on his head, arms, shoulders, chest—until finally he managed to grab her wrists. Bringing her arms down slowly, his fingers digging viciously into her flesh, there was a grim pleasure glinting in his eyes.

'Come, my little hellcat,' he murmured through his teeth and began to pull her towards the ruined walls. 'We may as well start now. It might take some of the fight out of you.'

He dragged her towards the cottage, her screams of protest whipped away by the wind and her frantic struggles futile beneath his determined grip.

Once within the walls, he threw her down callously and stood over her, a faint, almost triumphant smile of anticipation curving his mouth and gleaming in his eyes. As he began to unbutton his breeches, she bit back a cry of anguish, and scrambled frantically backwards, panic pounding through her veins. Her back hit the wall, trapped in a corner.

He laughed huskily, and, bending down, grabbed her ankles and dragged her towards him so that he straddled her legs, towering above her. Her outflung hand closed around a piece of stone fallen from the wall, and as he fumbled with his breeches she brought her knee up and kicked upwards with all the force she could summon. He yelled out in pain, doubling over and clutching his groin. In an instant she was up, smashing the rock at the side of his head, and, clutching her skirts high above her knees, took to her heels and ran.

Terror lent wings to her feet. She tore across the uneven ground, gasping for breath, desperation surging through her veins. The wind in her face stung tears to her eyes, ripped at her hair, billowed in her skirts. Stumbling and sobbing, she ran blindly, not caring where she was going, only one thought in her head, to get as far away from Alex Hunt as possible.

Then, suddenly, horribly, the ground gave way. With a horrified cry, she pitched headlong, crashing to the ground and rolling over and over down a sharp rocky slope until she finally came to rest at the bottom, the breath knocked from her body.

It took her a moment to recover her wits. And as she tentatively gathered herself up, wincing in pain, she realised that the pounding in her ears had dulled beneath a different sound—the sea! Cuts and bruises were forgotten as she stared in horror at the surging white froth of the waves and the dark expanse of water beyond. Fool! She had run the wrong way! Even in the deepening gloom, a swift glance was sufficient to tell her that there was no easy escape from the little cove. Steep rocky slopes rose up on both sides and it seemed that the only way off the beach was the way she had come.

A shower of loose stones came rattling down from above her and she stifled a gasp of alarm. Caught between the devil and the sea! Frantically she looked around. Farther along the beach an outcrop of rock jutted out towards the sea, and, hitching up her skirts, she ran towards it, scrambling around to the other side and almost falling into a small boat.

'Where are you, you damned bitch?' The captain's voice, harsh with violence, was muted by the wind as he slithered down the slope. A stab of fear went to her heart and, reaching into the bottom of the boat, she carefully lifted one of the oars. She might be trapped, but she would not give up without a fight. A desperate glance round and she caught her breath. An odd arrangement of gorse bushes and rocks might yield a more secure hiding place...

'By God, I am going to enjoy taming you, you little wildcat!' he yelled, starting along the beach towards her. 'Don't think you can escape!'

Twisting round and keeping low, she half crawled towards the gorse, dragging the oar and praying harder than she had ever prayed in her life. Wriggling between the thorny branches and jagged rocks, her hair caught and her face and arms torn on the treacherous prickles, she fought her way into a space and then gasped. A narrow crevice between the rocks led sharply upwards. She couldn't see clearly but there was a chance, a slender one, that she could get up there. Blade was at the cottage, and the musket——

'Emma!'

Oh, God, he was close! Dragging her skirts up to her waist and looping them over one arm, she clenched her fingers round the oar, loath to leave her only weapon behind, and started to clamber between the boulders and gorse, her free hand grabbing anything to help her up the steep gully.

How she got to the top she never knew, but suddenly there was grass at her feet and the shadowy outline of the cottage only a short distance away. Her knees were weak, her legs trembling, but she forced herself to run. Hunt was behind her, climbing. She had to get to Blade...

She heard him curse, and risked a swift glance back. And as she did so, her foot twisted in a rabbit hole, her skirts caught between her legs and she went crashing down with a strangled cry, the oar spinning from her grasp.

A second later, the captain was upon her, wrenching her over on to her back before throwing himself down on top of her, pinning her down, Ben's knife at her throat. As his free hand tore at her bodice, she could not even scream, and her struggles were useless. He began to fumble with her skirts. Every muscle tensed, her whole body rigid as tears squeezed beneath her tightly closed eyelashes and she bit her lips together so hard that she tasted blood.

Dimly she felt, rather than heard, the thudding of horses' hoofs vibrating in the ground beneath her. Almost immediately the loud explosion of a pistol shot rent the air. Hunt jerked upright, only to be hauled off her, a fist slamming into his jaw, sending him sprawling.

Strong arms beneath her shoulders raised her up. 'Emma! Emma, my love, are you all right? Are you hurt?'

The voice was like music. She looked up into crystal blue eyes dark with emotion, the shadowy face etched with anxiety. 'Ben? Oh, God, I thought you were dead——' His arms enfolded her, crushing her to his chest, his face buried in her hair.

'Sullivan—look out!'

He spun round, thrusting her away, as Hunt lunged at him, the long blade of Ben's knife glinting in his hand. With lightening reflexes, Ben dodged the thrust, knocking Hunt's arm up and whipping out his own knife.

The soldier who had shouted the warning leapt from his horse and pulled Emma to her feet, dragging her out of the way. Horror caught in her throat as she watched the two men circle, crouching ready to pounce, like two wild animals sizing each other up, macabre figures in the gloom. Suddenly Ben's arm jerked upwards, Hunt narrowly deflected the blow, and in a moment they were stabbing at each other in a deadly battle.

Emma's heart seemed to stop. It was like watching a vicious alley brawl, hatred burning in both men, the wicked blades clashing and searing as they came together and parted. Ben ducked, feinted back, and as Hunt's arm snaked out, plunging the dagger towards his heart, Ben leapt forward, bringing up his knife with a sudden, swift movement that would have been a slower man's death. But Hunt's whole body arched back as he twisted away, deflecting the blade so that it sliced into his shoulder and drew a dark stain of blood. His breath hissed between his teeth and he staggered backwards.

The lieutenant made an involuntary move towards him, but he threw out his arm. 'He's mine, Barford!' And with an ugly twist to his mouth, he suddenly lunged at Ben, who stepped back and countered with a thrust of his own. The two knives clashed, and for a moment were locked, each man trying to force the other's down. Then Ben wrenched his weapon away and sliced it upwards under Hunt's arm. The captain's reaction was swift, but the tip of the blade ripped up his sleeve. Even Ben's horse, already nervous, began to paw the ground and dance about in agitation as the two men moved closer, locked in vicious combat.

It was more than Emma could bear to watch, and she turned her face away. The oar was lying on the ground only a few feet away. Before she knew what she was doing, she had made a grab for it. The lieutenant uttered a shout of protest, but she ignored him, and, with all the force she could summon, swung the oar through the air and smashed it into the small of the captain's back.

He pitched forward with a yell of pain, falling on to Ben's upturned knife. And as Ben thrust the blade home he uttered little more than a startled grunt. Stepping back under the sudden weight, Ben withdrew the knife and pushed him away. He fell to the ground inches from the prancing horse. It reared up with a whinny of fright and

Emma stared in frozen horror as the hoofs crashed down, smashing the side of the dead man's face.

Ben reached her in two strides, blocking her view and drawing her head down against his chest. A violent tremor ran through her, and she clung tightly to him. 'Oh, Ben, I've been so frightened! He had such awful plans!' Her voice was ragged as the words began to tumble out. 'He was going to make you watch while he—and then Carlisle came and—the cabin caught fire and——'

'Hush!' His arms tightened protectively around her. 'It's over, my brave darling. I am here and you're safe and it's all over.' He hugged her fiercely for a long moment, expressing more in that crushing, clinging embrace than he could ever put into words. Then, slowly, he eased her away and tilted her chin, the sight of her ashen face and over-bright eyes twisting his heart. 'Are you hurt?' His voice was husky with emotion. 'He didn't harm you?'

She shook her head, but her whole body was trembling, and he peeled off his coat and wrapped her in it. 'He was going to take me to Lisbon,' she whispered. 'I tried to run—but he—he caught me and—and oh, God, if you hadn't come——'

'Don't!' He caught her to him again, and held her close, kissing her hair and entwining his fingers in the thick tendrils down her back. 'Don't think about it, my love. It's over now. It's over and I am taking you home.'

Sweeping her up into his arms, he carried her across to the ruined cottage and set her down by the dying fire. 'Will you be all right here just for a minute? I have to help the lieutenant.' He paused, looking at her with a mixture of concern and anxiety. 'I'm sorry, my love, but we have to get back to town. I know Eastwood is nearer, but . . .'

She managed a faint smile, and nodded. 'I'm all right now. Really.'

Pride blazed for a moment in his eyes and he squeezed her arm. 'Good girl.'

The lieutenant had already wrapped the captain's body in his blanket, and it took them only a few minutes to haul him across the saddle of John's horse and then fashion makeshift torches from stout pieces of timber. Soon Emma found herself being lifted once more on to Blade's back, but this time cradled safely in Ben's arms, her head resting against his chest and his heart pounding reassuringly in her ears.

Somewhere above the clouds lurked a moon, for it had not gone completely dark, and with both men familiar with the road and the torches casting an eerie glow to light their way the journey to town was safely accomplished, Emma lulled almost to the edge of sleep despite her sore and aching limbs.

At the edge of town, Lieutenant Barford pulled up his horse. 'I'll leave you here, Sullivan. You take Mrs Sullivan home and see she gets some rest. I've an unpleasant night ahead of me at HQ—but I am not going to defend the captain. I have closed my eyes to a lot of things lately but all this—well, I'll tell them what I saw and what I know. And we'll send someone for Drummond.' He turned to Emma with an apologetic smile. 'I'm sorry for all the trouble you've been put through, ma'am. I feel partly responsible. I'm very much afraid you will have an unpleasant day tomorrow—but I give you my word I'll do what I can to clear everything up for you as painlessly as possible, and I'll try to see you are not disturbed tonight.'

She smiled weakly at him. 'Thank you, Lieutenant.'

Ben shook his hand, and, as they parted company, murmured in her hair, 'I did not think I would ever have cause to be grateful to a damned Redcoat!'

'You owe him your life,' she pointed out.

He nodded, keeping his anxiety to himself. His life was still in Barford's hands, and trusting a Redcoat to defend him—him of all people—against the combined

hostility of his superiors made him extremely
uncomfortable.

Emma could have wept with relief when they finally
turned through the gates of the house on Tremont Street.
Jack's lantern swung an arc of light around them as she
almost fell from the horse into Ben's arms and his voice
was full of concern. 'Shall I go for the physician, sir?'

She lifted her head. 'No, don't.' Her voice was husky
with fatigue. 'It's nothing a good, hot bath will not set
right.'

'Just take care of Blade,' Ben told him. 'He's been
sorely treated, I'm afraid.' With his arm around her
waist, he helped her inside where Ellen, with her usual
no-nonsense practicality, had already set a kettle over
the fire and was ordering Jinny upstairs to warm the
mistress's bed.

But Jinny hovered, relief, concern and excitement all
bubbling out in a stream. 'Oh, Miss Emma! Thank
goodness you're safe. We've all been in such a worry!
Just look at your poor face, all scratched—whatever has
happened to you? Oh, but you'll never guess who's
come, miss, after all we thought——'

'Jinny!' It was Ellen, unusually sharp, who cut across
this well-meaning torrent. 'Miss Emma needs a hot bath
and her bed warmed. Get along with you.'

Ben uttered an oath as Jinny reluctantly went off.
'Who is here, Ellen? Surely John could have dealt with
any callers——'

'This one is special,' Ellen assured him. 'You take the
mistress along to the parlour—there's a good fire in there,
and I'll bring some soup directly.'

'I'd as soon have a cup of tea,' Emma murmured
longingly, still shivering inside Ben's coat.

'You shall have a brandy before anything else, my girl,'
he told her firmly and steered her through to the hall.

'Thank God!' John came hurrying towards them.
'Emma, are you all right?'

'Yes, I——' She broke off on a gasp, staring beyond him to the man standing in the parlour doorway. Feeling Ben's hand tighten on her shoulder, she knew she was not dreaming. 'Kit?' Her voice came out as a strangled whisper, and, as the bearded face broke into a smile, she wriggled out of Ben's coat and crossed the space between them to throw herself into his arms. 'Oh, Kit!'

'Steady!' With a laughing protest, he set her away from him. 'I've four cracked ribs and I'd appreciate being treated gently.'

'Oh, I'm sorry!' Filled with dismay, she stepped back, clutching the torn bodice of her dress and suddenly completely at a loss. She stared at him with hot tears pricking the back of her eyes, and at once Ben was at her side, taking brisk control.

'Kit, your timing is deplorable!' he exclaimed with a wry half-smile, and swept Emma into his arms. 'Come on. Upstairs with you, my girl. Kit is not going anywhere, and you *will* need Cornwallis if you don't get a hot bath and some rest.'

As he set her down on the bed, she caught his arm. 'Do not let him go, Ben!'

'Idiot!' He left her to fetch the brandy and returned in a few minutes, waiting while she obediently swallowed the fiery liquid, and then he reluctantly relinquished her to Jinny's care.

Jinny's cheerful flow of concerned chatter seemed a long way off as her tattered, mud-stained gown was stripped off her and herbal oil poured into the steaming bath. The girl uttered dismayed exclamations at the sight of the livid array of scrapes and bruises adorning her mistress's face and limbs, and, having helped her into the tub and sponged her down, left her to soak while she went in search of salves and ointments.

As soon as she was alone, the hard lump in Emma's throat dissolved and the long-unshed tears began to stream down her face, so that when Jinny returned she had her face in her hands, weeping uncontrollably.

'Oh, Miss Emma, don't!' Jinny knelt down beside her and wiped her face tenderly with the soft linen towel. 'What horrors you've been through I don't know, but you're safe now, and the master won't let anything bad happen to you ever again, that I do know. You should have seen his face when he realised you'd gone with the captain—and that other devil after you.'

'Oh, Jinny, I thought he was dead! I thought I'd never see him again and all through my foolishness, and I love him so much I couldn't have borne it——'

'Hush, now! I should think you'd know by now that he's not so easily seen off. Lord knows, he must have more lives than a cat, that one! And Master Kit, too! What a time to turn up alive and well! Think of that. Come on, now, you get out and we'll soon have you tucked up in bed. A good night's sleep is what you need.'

But once she was dry, and her sore places soothed with ointments, her hair brushed free of its tangles and a clean nightgown slipped over her head, Emma felt considerably better. The storm of weeping, the brandy and the bath had done much to restore her spirits and she did not want to go to bed. 'I am going downstairs,' she announced firmly, pulling on her dressing robe.

'Oh, no, you're not! You just get into bed and I'll fetch some soup.'

'I will eat it downstairs, Jinny.' She looked at her maid with such a spark of defiance in her hazel eyes that the girl wisely refrained from arguing, contenting herself with a muttered,

'Well, I don't know what the master will say!'

The master was crossing the hall from the kitchen when she went down, fatigue etched in the grim lines of his face, and her heart ached at the sight of him. 'Ben?'

He looked up, his expression softening. 'You should be in bed.' But there was no real conviction in his voice and he held out his hand to her, drawing her into the circle of his arms. He hugged her close for a moment, then drew a long, steadying breath. 'Come on,' he murmured, a little unevenly. 'Come and see Kit.'

She embraced her brother rather more gingerly this time. 'I still cannot believe it!' she marvelled. 'I had given up hope. I thought you had died.'

'It takes more than a shipwreck!' He grinned, but there was a note of bravado in his voice that did not escape her. The searching look she gave him drew only a shake of his head. 'I'll tell you about it tomorrow. But what of you?' His concerned gaze swept over her. 'From what I have been hearing, you have had quite a day!'

Her gaze flicked up to her husband, standing by the fire with one mud-encrusted boot resting on the hearth. 'But I am all right now.' She smiled, holding those enigmatic blue eyes for a moment before looking back at Kit. 'But so much has happened since you left. Maybelle——'

'I know. John told me. He also told me about you two.' He looked up at Ben and grinned. 'Congratulations! I didn't think, when I asked you to look after her, that you would go that far!'

'I am afraid I haven't looked after her very well, even so,' Ben said, his voice harsh with self-reproach.

'But it was my own fault!' she exclaimed. 'I should never have believed the captain when he said Carlisle had killed you——'

Kit put his hand on her arm. 'I'm for bed. I'm certain you two would prefer to be alone!' As Ben threw him a grateful look, he smiled briefly and squeezed his sister's arm. 'We'll talk tomorrow, I promise.' And with that he bade them goodnight.

'Come here.'

The order was softly spoken and she needed no second bidding to creep into his arms. 'I'm sorry I was so— stupid,' she whispered. 'I should never have gone with him. I should never have believed him——'

He shook his head. 'And I should not have been so easily lured into Carlisle's snare. But it is done, Emma. Over.'

She looked up at him with troubled eyes. 'But it is not over, is it? Tomorrow....'

'Tomorrow might be—difficult,' he agreed carefully. 'So you really should rest.'

'Not yet. There is so much I do not know, about what happened to you—how you found me. How the captain knew Carlisle——'

A tap on the door interrupted them and Ellen brought in a tray with steaming bowls of soup and chunks of bread and, best of all, cups of tea. She wriggled away from him, suddenly realising that she was hungry. Neither of them had eaten since breakfast and they made short work of their supper, piecing together their respective stories as they ate.

'Will Drummond be all right?' she asked, pushing her plate away. 'He—the captain—knew he was alive.' She shivered. 'He just left him there.'

'I know.' He pushed his own plate aside. 'John says he will live. And I dare say he can be persuaded to attest to how warped Hunt's mind had become.'

'Has John gone home?'

A muscle twitched along Ben's jaw. 'I hope he has gone to deal with his wife! If I get my hands on her——'

She stared at him, surprised at the violence in his voice. 'Why? What has she done?'

He did not immediately answer, but got up and came to sit on the arm of her chair, taking her hand in his. 'It was she who sent Carlisle to Hunt in the first place. He asked for the Winston house and was directed to Cedars. Once Ann discovered who he was and that he wanted you back, she sent him to Hunt.'

Perhaps fatigue was making her dull-witted, but she could see no sense in that. 'But—but why? What did she hope to gain?'

'Exactly what almost did happen. That they would hatch up a plot between them to take you away from me—Carlisle or Hunt, I don't imagine she cared which—and in the process bring me to an untimely end.

'But I don't understand! I thought she—I mean, Jaycinth said you and she had...' She faltered and looked away, unwilling to probe into that.

'I only once succumbed to her charms,' he explained gently, playing with her fingers and tracing the burn scar on the back of her hand. 'It was before she and John were betrothed, and she never forgave me for not repeating the experience, especially as rumour had it I was making love to every other woman in Boston. Her pride was hurt.' Meeting her gaze, he smiled. 'She did not give up trying, even after she wed John. And then you came and she, I believe, saw what no one else did, at least to start with. That you were going to achieve what no other woman had...' His mouth twisted into a rueful half-smile. 'The capture of my heart.'

She bit her thumb thoughtfully. 'Could she—do you think she might have had something to do with the fire?' she ventured tentatively. 'I wondered, at the time, she looked so...strange.'

'It's possible. It was certainly none of my men and I have not been able to discover the culprit. But if she had a hand in that, and caused Maybelle's death...' He cut the thought off abruptly, his face set in grim lines.

'I suppose I can understand her jealousy.' She frowned. 'But I still don't understand why she would want you dead.'

He shrugged. 'Greed. I imagine it overcame any other considerations. She is so afraid that I will suddenly have a change of heart and claim my "rightful inheritance" and that she will no longer be able to indulge her extravagant nature... She saw a chance to deal with us both at a stroke.'

Emma was silent for a moment. 'What will John do?'

'What he should have done years ago! Assert himself. It seems to take a great deal to rouse him but he left here almost apopleptic and I imagine Cedars will be shaken to its foundations tonight.' There was a grim pleasure at the thought kindling the blue of his eyes and Emma leaned her head on his arm, pushing away an involuntary pang of sympathy for Ann and enjoying the caressing touch of his fingers in hers.

A seeping warmth stole through her at the feel of his muscular arm beneath her cheek and the light touch of his lips in her hair. Drowsiness crept up on her and her eyelids drooped.

'Come on,' he whispered in her hair. 'To bed with you.' Easing her head from his arm, he got up and gently pulled her to her feet. 'It has been a hellish day and we have another to get through tomorrow.'

He looked down at her, his heart melting. How young and vulnerable she looked, her face pale, her hair tumbling over her shoulders and beneath the dressing robe the top button of the demure nightgown open, revealing a tantalising triangle of soft flesh. He had a sudden desire to kiss her, just there, and an overwhelmingly desperate need to make love to her. But she had been through a terrible ordeal and she was clearly exhausted. It would be unforgivable of him. He dropped his hands. 'Go to bed, Emma.'

Puzzled by the brusqueness of his tone, she looked up, and when his lips did little more than brush her forehead she searched his face only to find his expression strangely taut. 'Go on,' he urged softly, 'I shall come up in a little while.'

She nodded, and turned away feeling inexplicably hurt. She did not want to climb the stairs alone or crawl into bed without him. But he was already turning to prod the fire and she went to bed bewildered.

She lay in the darkness waiting for him, wondering why he did not come. Tonight of all nights, having so nearly lost him, she wanted to feel his arms around her, wanted the comfort of his strong body close to hers, holding her safe. When she heard the stair creak, heard footsteps pass her door with barely a pause and the door of Jaycinth's old room open and shut, all manner of fears beset her overwrought imagination. Was it possible—could he suspect that Hunt actually had raped her and was repulsed? Of course not! She could not believe that of him. Perhaps he was just tired. Or worried about Barford and the army.... Why had he suddenly looked so—distant?

She closed her eyes, but could see only Hunt's face, leering and ugly, and the horse's hoofs smashing down on it. Throwing back the covers, she got up and went along to his room, tapping softly on the door. After a moment the door opened and he stood in the flickering light of a single candle, clad only in his breeches and boots.

'Emma!' There was a faint surprise in his voice. 'You should be asleep.'

'I thought——' she began and then stopped, suddenly bursting out, 'Oh, Ben, I can't bear to be alone tonight. Hold me? Please.'

He drew her roughly into his arms and bent his head to hers, holding her close and brushing his lips in her hair. Crushed against the roughness of his chest, the faint odours of sweat and leather and brandy—the pure masculine smell of him—quickened her blood and of their own accord her hands moved over the smooth hardness of his back and her hips pressed imperceptibly against him. He moved the hair away from her neck, and kissed her just below her ear, his mouth moving downwards and nuzzling the nightgown over her shoulder. But the buttons held it, and his fingers moved to release them.

'Can I come in, then?' she murmured. 'I'd rather you made love to me in the bed than in the doorway!'

His eyes were dark with love and desire. 'Oh, Emma! You have no idea how much I wanted you downstairs! But you've had the devil of a day and you looked exhausted, I knew if I held you then I would not be able to stop myself and it hardly seemed reasonable to expect you to——'

So that was it! She laughed softly. 'For a man with a reputation for womanising you do not know much about women!'

He linked his hands behind her neck and smiled down at her. 'Ah, but you are quite unlike any other woman I've known! Most would have been reduced to hysterics at what you have been through today, or at the very least taken to their beds with a sleeping draught, and quite incapable of seducing a man in his own bedroom!'

'I'm not in the bedroom,' she pointed out, her eyes dancing. 'And like to freeze if you keep me out here.'

'Hussy!' He drew her in and shut the door, and as he went to sit on the bed to pull off his boots her eyes were drawn to his discarded shirt on the dresser. Lying on top of it was his knife, still dull with the smear of dried blood.

'What will they do to us?' she asked in a small voice, suddenly fearful.

He looked up, following her gaze, and cursed himself for not having dealt with it. 'It depends on Barford,' he told her matter-of-factly, and, tossing his boots aside, held out his hand. As she moved into the circle of his arms he added huskily, 'If you are going to remain in that damned nightgown——'

Smiling, she began to undo the buttons. As a tantalising amount of cleavage was revealed she paused, peeking at him through her lashes. 'There *is* one thing——'

His brow furrowed with a hint of impatience. 'What?'

'I'm covered in bruises and scratches... You will be gentle with me, won't you?'

His eyes gleamed, and he pulled away her hand and let the offending garment slip to the floor. 'Certainly not! You are a witch!'

But he was gentle. Gentle and tender and unhurried, savouring the delights of her sensuous body, his expert touch expressing far more eloquently than any words he might find how deeply he loved her—and how very much afraid he had been of losing her.

As she melted into his persuasive caress, her aching weariness slipped away and she forgot everything that had happened, forgot Alex Hunt and William Carlisle, forgot the uncertainties awaiting them tomorrow, and gave herself up completely to the man she loved.

CHAPTER THIRTEEN

THE candlelight cast glowing, flickering shadows around
the parlour as Emma sat back in the big chair by the
fire and closed her eyes, savouring what seemed to be
the first quiet moment of the day. Matthew was in bed,
Kit and Ben were out, the servants were busy in the
kitchen and she finally had a moment to herself.

All in all, things had settled themselves quite satisfactorily. Most of the morning had been spent in harrowing interviews with the Army. But Drummond had
been found to be conscious and capable of speech and,
owing his life to Ben, had confessed everything he knew
of Captain Hunt's plans. Adding that to Barford's intimate knowledge of the captain's personal grudges
against Sullivan and obsession with bringing him down,
the ostler's testimony of the comings and goings at the
Ship and Compass—including the all-important fact that
young Daniels had left the tavern with Captain Hunt
while Sullivan was still upstairs with Mr Carlisle—and
all the other snippets of information they gathered from
all and sundry, and the pompous major had, somewhat
surprisingly, offered Emma an apology for her ordeal.

'I do not hold the Army responsible for Captain
Hunt's—behaviour, Major,' she had assured him, but
had to put her hand on Ben's arm to stay the fury sim-
mering just below the surface. It had irked him, having
to ingratiate himself with an officer he would rather see
in perdition, and when there was little more than a
grudging formal apology for her suffering at the hands
of a British Army officer it was an angry glitter that
hardened the crystal blue of his eyes.

But he had held his temper and the major had finally
declared that it would be as well for everyone concerned

if Hunt's death was viewed as an unfortunate accident
and the whole regrettable business forgotten as quickly
as possible. And once she had assured him that Carlisle
had no family likely to grieve over him, and had
undertaken to write to James with the news that he had
met with an accident and a request that he pass this information on, the major had given orders for Drummond
to be taken away in an army litter and they had, at last,
been left alone.

But no sooner were they done with the Army than
Jaycinth had arrived, demanding to know if it was true
that Kit was alive—and what had Ann done to them to
put John in such a foul temper? 'He told her she must
apologise to you and Ben, and when she said she would
as soon go to the devil he said she could do the next best
thing and go and stay with her sister in Philadelphia until
she felt differently! What on earth has been going on?'

Since Emma and Ben had managed to keep Ann's part
in all this from the Army it was heartening to know that
at least John had done something positive, and they were
unlikely to see her again until they could do so with some
measure of tolerance. The bare bones of the story had
been retold for Jaycinth's benefit, and Kit had finally
recounted his own narrow escape from death. Hauled
from the rocks by a couple of fishermen—with Ben's
precious letters in their oilskin package still intact—he
and half a dozen of his men had been kept hidden until
the excitement had died down, then his men had gone
with his blessing to take their chances in the taverns of
New York, perhaps to find another ship, and he had
stayed until he could see Ben's letters safely on their way
and his ribs had healed sufficiently to allow him to ride
back to Boston.

His plans, when she asked him, were vague. 'You could
stay here,' she suggested, avoiding Jaycinth's eyes. 'Good
ships' masters are surely always in demand.'

'Not ones that lose their ships.' His voice had been
laced with self-disgust and guilt and, though she urged

him not to blame himself, she understood how he must
feel. He, who had never had so much as a fatal accident
aboard one of his ships, had now lost almost his entire
crew. 'But I admit I'd like to stay,' he conceded. 'England
has little to offer me now and the sea has lost some of
its charm for the moment. And Boston...' his eyes smiled
into Jaycinth's '...has its attractions.'

Ben had undertaken to find him some honest, gainful
employment and, sitting alone in the parlour now, Emma
mused over the pleasant prospect of Jaycinth's marrying
her brother. That she loved him was not in doubt—but
whether she could adapt to the wander-fever that was in
Kit's veins was another matter. His feelings were harder
to read, but she did not think she had misinterpreted the
expression in his eyes whenever he looked at Jaycinth
and thought himself unobserved. She doubted his love
of the sea would ever be tamed, but if Jaycinth could
learn to live with that they would be a good match for
each other. John might have other ideas, of course, for
he had Charles Arnold in mind for his sister and he was
the son of a wealthy merchant. Ben was unlikely to
change his mind about interfering in family matters, but
she was certain he could be persuaded to talk to John,
if necessary.

A tap on the door interrupted her thoughts, and Jinny
hovered in the doorway. 'What should we do about
dinner, Miss Emma?'

'I imagine my brother is enjoying the hospitality of
Cedars.' She smiled. 'And as for the master...' She
chewed her lip, thrusting away the nagging anxiety
stirring in her stomach. 'Tell Ellen to go ahead, Jinny.
I will have mine as soon as it is ready.'

But as Jinny left her alone again she could not help
a pang of regret that she had urged him to go out. Now
that the house had gone quiet she felt strangely empty.

Tom had turned up soon after noon, wondering why
Ben had missed two important meetings and full of the
latest news. He told them that yesterday the *Dartmouth's*

owner had been refused clearance for his ship to leave
the harbour and this morning another meeting had persuaded him to go to Milton to attempt to procure a pass
from the governor.

'He will never agree,' Ben had declared decisively. 'I
cannot see Hutchinson backing down now.'

Tom shook his head. 'We're all waiting in the church.
There'll be trouble if Hutchinson refuses to let us send
that damn tea back where it came from. Half the town's
for firing the lot, ships and all!'

She had watched the emotions play across her husband's face and guessed what lay beneath. He knew that
if Rotch came back from Milton without his pass the
Liberty Boys might well fire the tea ships. He knew, because the same anger and frustration coursed through
his veins. All the fermenting resentment at the years of
repression and exploitation would come to a head sooner
or later and find a violent outlet.

As he stood up abruptly, some of his anger spilled
over. 'We've given them enough chances, for God's
sake!' he exploded, walking to the window. 'They can
hardly blame us if——' He had broken off with an
exasperated gesture.

'You'll come, then? Mr Adams was asking for you.'

He had swung round, a ready reply on his lips, but
as he saw her he checked himself, a flicker of indecision
in his eyes. Then he shook his head. 'Not this time, Tom.'

'But you must go!' she had protested swiftly. 'This is
important.' However much she wanted him for herself,
wholly, completely, body and soul, she knew that would
never be. She also instinctively knew that if she allowed
him to stay with her now, when a part of what he was
lay bound up with the happenings at the church, a small
part of him would resent her, however unconsciously.

He moved forward, put his hands on her shoulders,
smiling down at her. 'After yesterday, I feel little inclined to let you out of my sight,' he told her softly.

'Idiot! You have taken care of everyone who might harm me! And you cannot tell me you do not wish to go.' He searched her face, the conflict clear in his eyes. 'Go,' she said simply. 'I shall be all right with Kit here.'

Finally he had capitulated. 'But while I am gone you should start packing. Tomorrow we will go back to Eastwood.'

Eastwood! More than anything she yearned for the tranquil beauty of Eastwood. But she quashed the yearning. 'Let's wait for the outcome of the meeting,' she cautioned.

'Whatever the outcome,' he had insisted, and smiled his slow smile at her, promising.

He had been gone all afternoon. Jaycinth had finally left, persuading Kit to go with her. 'You and Ben will be leaving for Eastwood in the morning,' she had pointed out. 'Kit may as well come back with me now. Besides,' she had added with a sparkle of mischief, 'I sent my groom home and shall need an escort!'

Scheming little minx! Emma could only hope they would be sensible. John would not be best pleased to find himself faced with yet another scandal to deal with. Ben would not be happy that she had let them go, either, but she did not see how she could have stopped them.

She sighed, fingering the emerald bracelet on her wrist that he had given her early that morning, before the turmoil of the day had broken over them. Where was he? As the twinges of anxiety began to knot her stomach, she wondered whether it was because he anticipated trouble, and events taking a turn for the worse, that he had suggested their removal to Eastwood. If there was any suggestion of danger he would want her and Matthew safely out of town. Yet what of his own safety? If a mob were intent on rampaging through the streets and destroying the tea ships, she knew he would add his voice to those counselling restraint and common sense, for, whatever his own feelings, little was ever achieved by violence and wanton destruction. And it would not have gone unnoticed that the house had been crawling with Redcoats. Suppose...

The uneasy train of her thoughts was broken by the sound of Jinny's voice in the hall and, bringing a flood of relief, Ben himself answering her. A moment later he came striding in, his hair windswept, his top coat flung open and a flush of exertion colouring his cheeks. 'Emma, fetch your cloak!' he commanded, a trifle breathlessly.

'What is it?' She stood up quickly. 'What has happened?'

'I want to show you something. Hurry!'

Minutes later he was hastening her along the dark streets, walking so quickly she almost had to run to keep up with him. Twice, in the dark, fetid alleyways he seemed to know so well, they had to dodge as cries of ''Ware below!' preceded a deluge of foul slops emptied out of windows above. By the time they reached the harbour, she had a stitch in her side and felt uncomfortably hot and prickly beneath the wool cloak, despite the cold night air stinging her face and hands.

And then the strangest sight met her eyes. Griffin's Wharf was thronged with people, lit by dozens of lanterns and torches. She stood stock still at Ben's side and stared in stunned amazement at the scene before her. Bobbing about in the harbour were several small rowing-boats, and on board the tea ships' men—some of them Indians—were busy opening tea chests, slitting the canvas and emptying the contents over the side, tossing in the broken chests afterwards.

Yet it was oddly quiet. There was no cheering or shouting, no violence, no mob hysteria, no looting. An almost tangible hush hung in the air, as though the import of what was happening deserved the reverence of everyone present.

Sam Adams's solemn words, as he closed the meeting after Rotch returned without his pass, still rang in Ben's ears. 'This meeting,' he had intoned heavily, 'can do nothing more to save the country.' A moment's utter silence and the meeting was abruptly adjourned. A group of men at the church door, dressed as Indians with their faces streaked with paint, had let out loud war whoops and set off for the wharf brandishing hatchets, axes and pistols. Ben thought he had glimpsed Paul Revere and one or two of his more volatile comrades among the war paint, but their disguises were effective and from a distance he could not be sure.

'I feared they would do something stupid,' he told Emma quietly. 'As Tom said, there was some wild talk about firing the ships—and tonight there was talk of sinking them. Thank God the water is too shallow!' He smiled down at her and squeezed her hand. 'But this...' His gaze returned to the bizarre sight in the harbour. 'This is inspired, Emma. If—*if* the tea can be destroyed with no other damage done, no one hurt, nothing else disturbed or stolen—there is a chance we can achieve something this night.'

There was a blaze of passion in his eyes as he watched the methodical, almost silent scattering of East India Company tea upon the waters of Boston Harbour. And she knew he could no more be parted from all this than she could be parted from him. He loved her, and she would always come first with him, she knew that. But she must share a part of him with his commitment to freeing these colonies from the iron hand that was stifling them.

Staring at the thick treacle of tea in the harbour and realising the implications of it, she felt her stomach churn at the thought of the troubled times that might lay ahead. And yet she was conscious of a strange feeling of expectancy, a pride in the people around her, a stirring in her blood of hope and purpose. Whatever the future held, whatever battles lay ahead, their love for each other, deepening and strengthening, was inextricably bound up with it. And she found herself hoping, as he was convinced, that their children would not be British colonials, but free Americans.

His arm slipped around her waist and as she looked up at him, his expression softened with a tenderness that melted away her anxiety. Drawing her towards him, he backed into the shadows and claimed her mouth, their lips fusing in a long, lingering kiss, their bodies moulding together in a mutual need, and everything that was going on around them, for a few minutes at least, quite forgotten.

BRIGHTON MASQUERADE

Petra Nash

Charlotte Sevington was tired of turning off proposals from fortune-hunters! A sensible girl, she knew her looks were not the attraction, nor her brisk common sense.

Visiting Brighton in preparation for a London season, common sense deserted Charlotte when she asked her beautiful cousin Carlotta to act the heiress. Few of the beau monde would be there in February, they thought.

But Lord George Wickham, awaiting the imminent arrival of the Prince Regent, made his preference for Charlotte's company obvious. Charlotte couldn't decide whether this was good or bad – until the cousins realised their little deceit was leading them into intrigue and danger . . .

TWO
HISTORICAL
ROMANCES

&

TWO
FREE GIFTS!

Masquerade historical romance bring the past alive with splendour excitement and romance. We wil send you a cuddly teddy bear and a special MYSTERY GIFT. Then, i you choose, you can go on to enjoy more exciting Masquerades every two months, for just £1.99 each! Send the coupon below at once to – Reade Service, FREEPOST, PO Box 236 Croydon, Surrey CR9 9EL.

- - - - - ┤ **NO STAMP REQUIRED** ├ - - - - →

Yes! Please rush me my 2 Free Masquerade Romances and 2 Free Gifts! Please also reserve me a Reader Service Subscription. If I decide to subscribe, I can look forward to receiving 4 Masquerade Romances every two months for just £7.96, delivered direct to my door. Post and packing is free, and there's a free Newsletter. If I choose not to subscribe I shall write to you within 10 days - I can keep the books and gifts whatever I decide. I can cancel or suspend my subscription at any time. I am over 18.

Mrs/Miss/Ms/Mr _____   EP04M

Address _____

_____ Postcode _____

Signature _____

The right is reserved to refuse an application and change the terms of this offer. Offer expires December 31st 1991. Readers in Southern Africa please write to P.O. Box 2125, Randburg, South Africa. Other Overseas and Eire, send for details. You may be mailed with other offers from Mills & Boon and other reputable companies as a result of this application. If you would prefer not to share in this opportunity, please tick box. ☐